So It Won't Go Away

So It Won't Go Away

John Lent

thistledown press

Library and Archives Canada Cataloguing in Publication

Lent, John
So it won't go away / John Lent.

ISBN 1-894345-86-X

I. Title.

PS8573.E58S6 2005   C813'.54   C2005-904853-0

Cover and book design by Jackie Forrie
Printed in Canada

Thistledown Press Ltd.
633 Main Street, Saskatoon, Saskatchewan, S7H 0J8
www.thistledown.sk.ca

Thistledown Press gratefully acknowledges the financial assistance of the
Canada Council for the Arts, the Saskatchewan Arts Board, and the
Government of Canada through the Book Publishing Industry Development
Program for its publishing program.

ACKNOWLEDGEMENTS

The author would like to thank the *NeWest Review* and the *New Quarterly* for publishing earlier versions of parts of this piece. I would also like to thank The Banff Centre For The Arts and its Leighton Artists Colony, The Professional Development Committee of Okanagan University College and Okanagan University College Faculty Association, and the people at the Wallace Stegner House in Eastend, Saskatchewan, for helping me in different ways to complete this manuscript.

Each of the following people helped me in some way over the course of the slow writing of this piece and I will just mention names here but, of course, it's always more than that: Mark Bovey, Virginia Dansereau, Neil Fraser, Judith Jurica, Mary Ellen Holland, Nancy Holmes, Randy Jones, Robert Kroetsch, George Larsen, Phil Lambert, Michael Lent, Vanessa Lent, Craig McLuckie, John Murphy, Eric Nellis, Kenneth Phillips, Jay Ruzesky, Greg Simison, Don Summerhayes, Ross Tyner, Shelby Wall, Tom Wayman, Fran Wood and Sylvie Zebroff. All my creative writing students and both of my big, warm families.

What can I say to Al Forrie, Jackie Forrie and Paddy O'Rourke at Thistledown Press except that you've allowed me to pursue a certain kind of a career as a writer and I will never be able to thank each of you enough for that.

Jude Clarke, as always.

Finally, to Seán Virgo who made such an enormous difference in the completion of this manuscript, whose eye was unerring and whose vision was truly magical: my most heartfelt gratitude.

CONTENTS

For Craig McLuckie

A Better Life

Who are we, who is each one of us, if not a combinatoria of experiences, information, books we have read, things imagined? Each life is an encyclopedia, a library, an inventory of objects, a series of styles, and everything can be constantly shuffled and reordered in every way conceivable.

— Italo Calvino, "Multiplicity,"
in *Six Memos for the Next Millenium,* 1988

JANE SITS IN VERA'S CAFÉ overlooking the Royal Glenora Golf and Tennis Club. Beneath her, along The River Road, the municipal golf course stretches its green body westward. She's sitting out on the deck so she can smell the late summer night, the freshly cut grass, the willows and low river bushes receding into a burnished, bronze sun that is almost too perfect to bear, impossible in its rich, veiled leaving. Two couples sit out on the deck with her and though Jane can hear fragments of their conversations, she's not paying as much attention as she might normally. She's feasting on the landscape and the soft chitter-chattering of their voices is just another surge in a plethora of crescendos and diminuendos of soft sound. Late summer evenings in Edmonton! Just to sit and stare into the fullness of it, smell its freshness, only slightly aware of activity around her, of a field of time shifting backwards and forwards in the thick air, placing her here certainly, but also here in the sense that she may well be in the vortex of many worlds, this moment a gate into some of them.

Lately, she'd been thinking of her father a good deal. Isn't that the way of it, though? she thinks. We always understand things later on, only after, when it is often too late. It's one of God's jokes, like sex, isn't it? Jane has spent most of her life trying to understand her father, Charles, and though she has suspected at times that she'd learned to understand him too well, that was never the case. Mysteries keep unfolding, even nine years after his death, and Jane supposes they always will. The problem, of course, is that as each mystery presents itself, she wants to reach him again.

When she thinks of the two of them sometimes, her father and mother, when she imagines them getting married in Moncton in 1946, fresh from the war, without a dime, facing the future being created around them at that point, having the dreams they must have had, Jane realises how gutsy they'd been. Two kids, really, her mother from a large family of girls in Moncton — a family that had never gotten over the depression that wiped out her father's jewellery business — and her father from a huge family of Irish Catholic teachers and drinkers and musicians in the small coal town of Westville, in Pictou County in Nova Scotia. How did they do what they did? *Heavenly days!* as her mother would say, *good gracious!*

"Will you be having wine with your dinner, madame?"
"No, thanks. Do you have any carbonated water?"
"Yes."

"I'll have a bottle of whatever you have, plus a coffee with cream and sugar."

"Yes."

"Thanks."

"It's beautiful, isn't it?"

Jane doesn't expect the young woman to break through the veneer of being her waitress, so she looks up and takes her in: an attractive young brunette, short hair, university look, about twenty-two. Liv Tyler eyes and mouth. Courtney Love hair. The waitress is staring, too, smiling at the scene receding below them in the river valley. Jane grins, "Yes it sure is. How long have you worked here at Vera's?"

"Since last Christmas, actually," the girl says, then extends her hand, "my name is Yvonne," she says, "I'm sorry ... but I was *almost* in one of your classes last semester."

"Oh ... "

"But I couldn't get off the waitlist."

"Which class?"

"362, The Novel of Development ... "

"Yes, it *was* packed to the gills."

"Well, maybe this fall."

"That would be great."

The young girl walks back into the restaurant, but turns around when Jane asks her, "Where are you from?"

"Here. Edmonton."

"Southside or Northside?"

"Southside."

"What's your last name?"

"Crowley"

"Was your father Jim Crowley?"

The girl blushes and stammers, "*Yes!*"

"And your mother Bernadette Dansereau?"

"Yes!"

"She was one of my best friends a long time ago."

"That's unbelievable!"

"I know you have to go back."

"We'll talk later," the girl smiles and disappears into the restaurant.

Jane laughs out loud. Bernadette, for heaven's sake. They'd been best friends through grade eleven and had lost contact after that. Bernadette had moved away to have the baby . . . everyone did in those days . . . and by the time she'd come back, Jane was on her way to university and their paths never crossed again. Jane had talked to Bernadette on the phone two years into Jane's undergraduate degree. Bernadette had phoned to ask her to come to her wedding in Calgary just before Christmas. Jane couldn't go because of her exams and that had been the last contact between them, almost thirty years ago now. Here was this younger version of Bernadette, just as pretty as her mother had been, materialising at Vera's. Talk about time fields.

Against the inside of her palm, Jane feels the cool, sweet sweat of the wine glass the girl has filled with carbonated water. It is like a caress. She cups her hand around the surface of the glass while her eyes seek the setting sun. There seems something fundamental, elemental even, in this conscious gesture. Jane feels alert suddenly, almost alarmed, but excited. It's always like this when it happens, this wild foreshadowing in the sensuous. That's how it seems to work, though everything else about it Jane can never predict. She holds the circle of crystal water up into the air, welcoming whatever it is this time, her eyes squinting behind the circle until it and the golden disc of the sun not only align, but are one and the same size. Jane takes a deep breath at the sight of this, then laughs. For some reason she remembers that final scene in the movie they made of Thomas Mann's *Death in Venice*. Dirk Bogarde slouches in a lawn chair, dying of cholera, staring out to the sea to inhale the beauty of a young boy he sees there. The boy lifts up his hand and makes a circle of his palm around the setting sun. This happens as the sweet, eerily ambiguous notes of the slow movement in Mahler's 5th *Symphony* twist around in the background, never resolving, and while Dirk Bogarde's pathetic attempts to look young run down his pale and sickly face and onto his white suit. He's dying, of course, and Jane knows she's not dying. Instead, she smiles and toasts the evening by raising the glass again, then washes down the carbonated, cool water so that it descends like a baptism into her stomach. Let it come.

~~~

I just pulled the car up under this shelter in the parking lot. I'll sit and get the sounds of the rain to lessen a bit, have a smoke before I go up to see her. Of course, I was supposed to have given this up ages ago, and mostly have, and yet . . . it is so sweet, like any oblivion, I guess. I'm not necessarily in favour of any of them. *You know.* But there is a quiet intensity about certain kinds of sins and pleasures, a furtive, hermetic quality even, that draws you into a meditative zone. *You know.* Like you're sitting here, having your last cigarette before going up to visit your mother. Okay. And, as you inhale, there is something wide about the moment itself. The rain out on the street behind you. The darkness of Edmonton in early spring. The steady sounds of traffic. Your mother waiting. The lives of you and your brothers and sisters, the story you're working on and need a new beginning for, the cigarette, your longing that it be the last cigarette, your suspicion that it won't be, your mother and the life she's lead, your long absences from these streets, Malcolm Lowry, everything you've ever done compressing itself into this moment . . . here . . . now . . . and you're reaching for language. "You've got lots on your plate, dear," as my mother would say.

I need a bridge and I'm going to build one, one way or another. I mentioned Lowry. The truth of the matter is . . . and even I find it difficult to admit . . . I spent seven years of my life working on Malcolm Lowry's fiction. I wanted to learn as much as I could about writing a kind of narrative, a story that didn't approach the interior from too far outside itself, but clattered around instead *within* a consciousness, directly. Lowry was a great example of this. As a result, some argue that the body of his work, like Proust's, is simply an extended *bildungsroman*, a prolonged novel of development. From one angle, that's probably accurate. The same could be said of Joyce, of course. Of Margaret Laurence. But aside from so many other things that intrigue me about Lowry and his writing, his handling of characters as a *gestalt* field of mirrors of the self still baffles me. On one level, all four characters in *Under the Volcano* are Lowry himself, even Yvonne. I love the way he sets up these fields before and after *Under the Volcano*. I get the same feeling in Kundera sometimes, Ondaatje, Munro and Carver.

The reason I'm bringing this up has to do with the bridge I need. I'm from this Irish Catholic family of nine that lived in south Edmonton in the 50s and 60s. Because of things that happened, most likely our father's drinking, the seven of us children were thrown closely together. That happens sometimes. You're thrown into a communal ecstasy of optimism because you have no choice. You *need* one another, and you *need* to manufacture safety. And you *do*, and that *doing* is a great, convoluted story in itself, and it can and cannot be told because it is so big and has so many sides to it, so many layers and counter-layers, surprises and contradictions.

At one point in my writing life, I took this material and tried to capture some of it by inventing three brothers and sisters — Rick, Neil and Jane — whose stories begin to tell the bigger, impossible story. Following this family seems important to me. The big, impossible story seems important to me.

I've rented *New Waterford Girl* and my mom and I are going to watch it tonight. She's made some sandwiches, and we'll just sit back and watch the movie. I wonder if she's made a batch of nuts and bolts, too, whether she's used as much garlic as she did last time. Depending on the amounts of garlic, you can't stop eating them. It's endless.

I've seen *New Waterford Girl* twice. I rented it for my mom to watch because of the way it deals with growing up in Nova Scotia. Even though its focus is Cape Breton, it'll still remind my mom of so many things that happened to her and dad, and so many textures that pull you back and also announce . . . like a huge fucking billboard . . . why you'd have to *leave* the Maritimes, too, depending on what you wanted. This is precisely what my parents did for us, moving us all out to Edmonton in 1952. Watching these kinds of movies, or reading these kinds of novels, is always a mixed experience: the hilarity of the lives in the foreground played against the distance created by your leaving those lives and surfaces forever, and your knowledge, even, that the single *act* of leaving was the most important insurance policy of no return, never going back *into* these lives ever again. Strange, powerful stuff. Joyce. Lawrence. Munro. The whole history of this kind of novel, the novel of development. Exile. The growth of the artist. Exile as catalyst for aesthetics. The girl on the train in this movie, pulling away from her past in order to recreate it in art. All those mysteries and paradoxes. I wonder how people who grew up in farming communities in Saskatchewan or southern Alberta feel about the same things. *You know.* You wake up one evening in a high-rise in some city somewhere. You're middle-aged, in the middle of your life even. You're staring out a window at a spring night, the flickering lights of the city below like breath, as if the city was a body itself, its own big story, and you're just sitting there longing for that first landscape: the stores on the main street, the dust of the side-roads at dusk, the palpable promise of something always *just about to happen*, maybe around this corner *here*, and that deeper sense that, *no*, you either cannot return ever again or, *no*, you've never left it, it's still here.

I've rented this movie. The smoke's over. She's waiting. It'll be great.

~~~

Jane stands up from her table and walks to the washroom down a small, white hallway connecting the deck with the main part of the restaurant. There is a Chagall print of a wedding framed on the door of the washroom and the part of her brain that never shuts down can't help thinking it's so strange that one-hundred years later — always after — an artistic movement can get claimed into the ordinary like this, almost hilariously dragged into it so its images are everywhere whereas at the beginning, when these pieces were first conceived, there was hardly a wall that would accept them. And then the same part of Jane worries that this almost comical reproduction of images, their very accessibility now, might not be the instrument of the death of these images. Hard to say, but Jane is so close to the print her cheeks practically brush up against the figures in Chagall's painting as she opens the door. Halfway through this opening, Jane can feel the weight of a new air, the exhilaration of it, and she almost faints in the process of pushing against it. It's as if she has moved through the air of the deck and the hallway of the restaurant into a thicker, a slower version of that air. She can feel the new weight against the door as she pushes against it, then pulls it back behind herself. There is music in this air, too, but instead of John Coltrane's "Blue Train," which had been chugging away in the background out on the deck, this is more refined, less composed, tinny, air-filled, like a million tiny chimes ringing somewhere by the sea. What's going to happen to me, Jane wonders, accepting whatever it is in advance as part of the bigness of time, its surprises.

I am in another place. I can smell the sea. I walk straight ahead through another door that shouldn't be here and I am on an old wooden boardwalk that recedes for miles along the sea, broken by gnarled and twisted junipers and gorse that have grown eastward, humped against a wind that has blown off the sea so consistently these shrubs and trees are the visual evidence of its force. It reminds me of walking along Dallas Road in Victoria at dusk, but I know it isn't the west coast somehow. It's somewhere else, isn't it? Other people are out in this landscape, though they are wearing outfits that are dated, belong to the thirties/forties, not now. I may be back there somewhere, I think, excited. And I walk into a warm evening air, the smell of the kelp like a spice, the warm waft of the summer seawind brushing up against my cheeks. I stop and sit on a green bench overlooking the sea and begin to watch three ships pop up on the horizon and draw closer as I sit here. I can tell they are destroyers from World War II, except they look new, and are occupied by young men in dated uniforms, getting the ships ready to dock.

Two young men in green army fatigues are sitting on the bench closest to me and I can hear their voices as they pass a bottle back and forth between them. The two young men never look at one another while they are talking. They pass the bottle back and forth, take swigs from it, all the while staring out into the movement of the ships and, behind the ships, at the sun setting far away on the dark black horizon of the ocean. One of the young men is ginger-haired, the other dark-haired.

"I don't know what we'll do when I get back," the dark-haired one says as he takes a swig from the bottle, "If I get back," and he laughs for both of them.

"Aw," says the ginger-haired man," you'll just get hitched and move out west and have lots of babies in some crazy place like Calgary or Edmonton."

"Think so?"

"You bet."

"I wonder."

"Well, what does she think?"

"Oh, Colette doesn't talk about after the war much. We talk a lot about now, though, me being here in Halifax, shipping out to England, what might happen over there . . . "

"Yeah . . . "

"You know . . . it's hard to think beyond this . . . "

"Well, I can see it all perfectly," the ginger-haired man laughs, "I can see you guys in some small house, setting up camp, far away from the Maritimes, somewhere where there's money."

"I wonder."

"Bob's yer uncle!"

"It'd be nice to think that, for sure."

"Your kids having a better chance out there, farther on down the road."

"Better than this," my father says and the ginger-haired man takes a big swig from the bottle, then passes it back to my father.

"Do you see those kids growing up somewhere out west?" the ginger haired man asks.

"Yeah, I can see that. Having a few things maybe. Some security maybe. Not always running around broke, like we'll always be."

"That'd be something, eh?"

"No kidding."

"They could look after you in your old age you silly old bugger!"

"Damn right!" and my father laughs the laugh that becomes the trademark of my childhood. I cough quietly, wondering if they'll hear me, wondering how wide this visit is, how much it can take.

They both look over at me abruptly.

"Evenin' ma'am," the ginger-haired man says.

"Hi," my father says, shyly.

"Good evening," I say, then turn to stare out at the sea, my heart surging with it.

"Are you from around here?" the ginger-haired man asks.

"No, I'm not," I say, "I'm from out west actually."

"Oh," my father says, "we were just talking about out west."

"I'm from Edmonton," I say.

"Well, how'd you end up here?" the ginger-haired man asks, "so far from home?"

"It's too long a story," I say, smiling at both of them.

"That's okay," my father says, "we've both got long stories, too. Boring stories."

"You shipping out soon?" I ask.

"Tomorrow," the ginger-haired man says, "on the middle ship, right out there." His arm sweeps out to indicate which ship.

"Yes," my father says, "shipping out to Sheffield, then the continent."

"Well, along with everyone else back home here, I sure admire you guys for doing this."

"Well, thank you," my father says, "thank you. That's nice."

"Yes, it is," the ginger-haired man says.

I look into my father's eyes directly, "I will never forget you," I say.

He stares just as directly back, "Nor us, you," and he smiles a perfect smile that I cannot interpret. "It'll be a help just to remember your smiling face," my father says.

I want to tell them they'll come home safely, but hesitate, then blurt out, "We will inherit a better life," I say.

"What's that," my father asks, "what's that you said?"

"We will inherit a better life because of you. I just wanted you to know that."

"I hope so," the ginger-haired man says while my father looks at me, puzzled, half-caught, his face a question.

And just as suddenly Jane is sitting on the toilet in the bathroom at Vera's, reaching around to flush the toilet, then washing her hands in the sink. She allows her hands to come up and cover her face in warm water, and feels them trembling in this return. Jane stares back at herself, deeply into her own eyes, trying to gauge all the tricks of time and space her head has hauled into her otherwise normal life. Strange, she thinks, that one kind of redemption might only be imagined in *this* way: returning to the past to adjust it, set it straight. Wouldn't it be wonderful to be able to adjust it like that, she thinks while another part of her, of course, is laughing at the overly-rational side of her head that has already decided the scene on the boardwalk *didn't* happen, *wasn't* real.

A few years back, after her visit to Giverny during which she'd had a chance to see Monet's Garden, she'd given up trying to control these small moments, these seams in the otherwise linear fabric of her experience of time and space. She just let them happen now and valued them for the rich field of image and metaphor they provided, aside from attempting to establish their truth in any other ways. They were gifts. That's how she received them. It was hilarious in some ways for her own political sense of things was to the far left of centre, and yet she knew . . . *she knew* . . . her old, buried Catholic childhood had been powerful in its training, especially in the metaphysical. Jane saw the world — time and space included — as a more magical and wide density now than she ever had before, and when she was being honest with herself, she liked it more this way. Jane worked with highly-trained intellectuals. She worked with them every day. They knew nothing of these things. Nothing. They had been of no help at all. There you go, Jane thought. Who knows anything, really?

~~~

My mother is fierce with energy. It is one of the reasons she's lived so long. She is eighty now and has outlived everyone in her family. She had a bad fall two years ago, and had to have a hip replacement. Then she had emergency surgery to have her gall bladder removed. She jokes that she's lurching around with her walker like an old confederate soldier limping back from the war, but her determination and wiry strength are amazing. When I nudge her apartment door open, she stumps down the hallway towards me, that old grin animating her face, her lips soft against my cheek. Origins. Returns.

"Everything's ready son," she says, laughing ahead of me back down the hallway. "The sandwiches are in here on the coffee table and the TV's on."

"We're going to have a party, you and me," I say.

"We are!"

I watch everything about her as she settles into her chair, her small face lit with excitement as it always has been. I think it's her greatest achievement sometimes. No matter what was happening to her or around her, she always sustained a startling ability to turn whatever it was into a party, transform the most ordinary material into gold.

~~~

The white hallway has regained its solidity. The bold colours of the Chagall print blare like the thin shrill trumpets in Miles Davis' *Sketches from Spain* as Jane walks back down the hallway and into the white light where her chair and table await her in the evening sun.

The two couples are still talking, whispering sometimes, intimate. An elderly woman has taken a table near the railing, closer to the edge of the deck. She seems poised, self-assured. She is dressed for the occasion, a lovely light blue suit and a lop-sided black hat that conceals most of her face. She is either writing in a booklet she has brought along, or she is reading. Jane is not sure which. No, she *is* writing after all. Fascinating. Jane wishes she'd remove her hat. All this happens as Jane regains her chair, and sips the water that has stayed remarkably carbonated.

Jane stretches one hand flat out on the table and stares down into the golf course below. All by himself with his clubs, a young man is standing in the middle of the fairway that advances towards the deck Jane is sitting on. In fact, the green he's approaching is just beneath the deck, past some willow trees that partly conceal it with their pendulous, lacy weight. Yvonne has just placed Jane's avocado salad in front of her when Jane hears the boy yell something gleeful from the middle of the fairway. He looks up at Jane now, for Yvonne has already left, and he yells out something Jane cannot hear. So urgent or direct is this that Jane actually yells back, "I can't hear you!" And though the people around her pause for a second, the young man just smiles up at Jane directly and grins and waves a modest hand into the night air. Jane recognises who he is. He must have just placed his second shot either right on the green or, even, right in the cup, for an eagle. He disappears now into the depth of the willows below Jane and she looks around the deck, wondering. Only the elderly woman seems slightly amused by her behaviour. The other couples are in denial, Jane guesses, but they have been all night anyway.

She's had a strange day, and, somehow, in the goofy way these things happen sometimes, she's been reminded of her father all day long, everywhere she went, and in everything she did. In being reminded of him, she realised that his life had been an incredibly generous life even though it had been racked by addictions, especially the drinking and smoking which had done him in. She'd always known it was too superficial to allow addictions to define people. It was dangerous to do that, even silly. Jane had had some direct struggles with her dad, though, and they were never pretty. He wasn't always dignified; he wasn't always in control; he wasn't always nice. In fact, like most addicts, he could be downright mean and selfish sometimes. But there was still a gentleness in him, a decency that went back through his experiences in the war to the depression they'd lived through in Nova Scotia in the thirties. There was a tangible, unquestioned dignity and decency about him that had to do with altruism being his best gauge of any person's behaviour.

When Jane visited her mother earlier in the morning, Colette brought out some of the old albums again — she'd been doing that a lot lately — and this morning she concentrated on photos taken when they'd moved out to Edmonton from Nova Scotia in 1952, all the way from Antigonish. And there he'd been, handsome devil that he could be sometimes, grinning sheepishly back at Jane through these black and white landscapes filled with curling linoleum, primitive radios and TV sets, couches covered with hand-sewn throws because the couches were falling apart, all the great, lovely, broken battlefields of Jane's childhood, all the unknowing in it, the insecurity about money, anxieties about food, and all through it, smiling away, putting a good face on everything, both parents hauling their peppy little optimistic faces through the 50s and 60s. Somewhere in the middle of looking at those photos, a sadness overwhelmed Jane. She couldn't explain it. Her mother even asked her if she was all right and, of course, Jane brushed it off. But when she got downstairs, when she walked out the elevator and started her car and pulled out onto 106th Street and, eventually, the Whitemud Freeway, she began to cry. Hurtling down the highway that burrowed through south Edmonton, flanked on all sides, even overhead, by strange, abstract, Celtic designs and rings of concrete, with thousands of steel and plastic cars like hers braiding their ways through these rings, all of it seemed so eerie to her after the photographs, that she exited on 50th street and pulled over into a small strip mall to get herself together.

There was a vitality, a muscle, even a strange sweetness to the sadness that took her over on the highway. She imagined she'd registered the progression of her father's life more intensely than she ever had before: its dignity, its modesty, its lack of safety, and, on another level, her failure to see those things in him, so caught up as she'd been in his final struggles. It's the physical imagery of those final, wretched struggles that you remember when it's the other ones you really want to remember. That's all. And as each generation outreaches the one that creates it, that gives it life, it needs to stare back at that origin, at the landscape of those beginnings, and get down on its knees to acknowledge and respect it. Thank it instead of merely patronising its supple, fading, sometimes ungracious departure.

It was something her mother said before Jane left. She was chirping away as she always did when she showed Jane photos. She was lost in the memories they stimulated, and was going on about what she and Jane's father had been planning when they'd spent their honeymoon in a cabin out in Shediac Bay, just outside Moncton. He was coming down as best he could from everything that had happened to him, all the excitement of the war aside from its dangers, all the places he'd seen, the stimulation and the risks they presented and the friendships he'd forged in that kind of tension. She'd seen it, she said, in all his fidgeting, his restlessness, the way he dreamed at night. Meanwhile, of course, she was coming *up* from the low-key life she'd led waiting at home for him, a life of letters overseas, of dreaming of futures, children, a small house somewhere where they could create and raise a family. So there they were, the two of them, at cross-purposes in some ways, inevitable if Jane thought about it. It's just the way things were then: complicated, paradoxical, shaky. But aside from all that, no matter how different their two energies had been in that cabin, when they'd sat out on its porch late at night, him nursing a rye and her curled up next to him on the rattan love seat, his arm around her shoulders, his other long hand dangling a smoke from the armrest it positioned itself on, no matter what else might have been pulling them apart, they'd known, she said, that they had to get away from the Maritimes and their families, had to head out west where the future was, the new world he'd fought for. "We wanted you kids to have a better life," she said to Jane, "and we knew it had to be somewhere else. We knew it couldn't be 'down home.'"

Jane kept repeating the phrase 'a better life' on the long, thin ride out on the Whitemud Freeway back to her condominium, eight lanes of traffic weaving in and out of the undulations of the old farm fields it was rolling over. Jane knew she *had* that life. The two of them had been right from the start. This *was* the new world she was driving through.

~~~

The movie turns out being better for Mom than I'd expected. She keeps howling with laughter, especially at the scenes in which the whole family is hovering around the bathroom door having conversations, taking turns using the toilet. Mom slaps her knees in disbelief and throws her own anecdotes against the flickering plot of the movie. I can tell she really likes the feel of the piece. It reminds both of us of warm-hearted British films like *The Full Monty, The Snapper, Billy Elliott, Waking Ned Divine.*

It makes me feel childishly excited to see Mom having such a great time. It's not always like this. We disagree about a lot of things. I'm the son who moved away. I'm the son that's been elusive, disapproving sometimes, lucky in my job and the kind of life I've made in the Okanagan. I'm the son who feels removed from this life here, separate from it, living in some perverse or necessary exile. I'm the son who insists upon writing all these revealing stories about my own family. So to see her breaking out in real belly-laughs, and for me to be laughing right along with her, is a kind of blessing. A release. A strange kind of return even. My own emotions are jangled and fragile in the surge of this moment between us.

At the end of the movie, I feel it all coming like a great, blue freight train rolling down the tracks. All my awareness of this mythical moment, all the novels I'd read, why I'd read them. By the time the young girl is ready to board the train and escape to New York, she hesitates, of course. In her moment of leaving she has just begun to see why she might want to stay, and is just beginning to see why, if she boards the train, she will never be able to return in the same way, as the same person. She hesitates, confesses to her mother that maybe she'll stay after all. In a fierceness that is surprising in the plot, the mother takes her by the arm and pushes her on the train, forcing the moment and the permanence of its decision. And, as the young heroine sits on the train and stares back out the window at her parents, her town, beginning to recede through the glass windows, she opens a note from her mother that reveals that the mother has known all along what is really happening to her daughter. All the ruses of false pregnancies aside, the note reveals that the mother is fully aware of the immensity of what her daughter has decided to do, and approves of it. *What the heart is.* Caught up in the revolving weights of this scene in the movie, I turn to my mother's laughter and blurt out, just to help my mother register the full weight of this final scene, its meaning, "See Mom, the mother knew all along that the girl had to leave!" As I say this, I shove my right hand into a bowl of diminishing nuts and bolts, my eyes welling up.

"Oh I *knew* that, dear," my mother's voice announces. "I knew that from the beginning."

Ask me anything.

~~~

As Jane is finishing her chicken tortellini, she notices a note has been tucked under her wine glass. Her head darts up to take in the scene and the only change in it is that the elderly woman is no longer there and her table has been cleared and is ready for other customers, as if it had never been used. In a scrawl Jane recognises only too well, someone has written, "Well, it *is* a better life you know. The trick is to live it. Don't think about it *too* much."

Jane runs down the hallway to the entrance to the café, but the parking lot and the street are empty. The elderly woman has vanished into the thick night air. Jane turns around and walks back to her table and finishes her meal as the sun sets around her. While the deep blue darkness encroaches upon the intricate, layered scene Jane is the centre of, the air fills with birdsong and the rhythm of crickets rasping their brittle tunes fiercely back up into the night sky.

MILES FROM CORK

For Adrienne, my mother, and Jeanne B, another mother

COLETTE CONNELLY STOOD ON HER TIP-TOES, a burgundy and rust-coloured scarf billowing back over her shoulders, her arms scrunched up against her sides. She was shielding her camera like a little girl on a school trip. Her son, Neil, was slouching against the rented car at the back of the parking lot. He heard the shutter click and watched his mother as she checked the numbers carefully, then placed the camera back into its black vinyl carrying case. She did this with a reverence he couldn't understand. She was excited and intimidated by this 'newfangled gadget' her sisters had given her in the airport. She turned back to him, shouting over the wind, "I think I got the whole harbour, dear. The girls will love it!"

"Is it called an *estuary*, Mom? Do you know?"

"Estuary, dear? You could be right. Estuary."

His mother loved words. Estuary was more musical than harbour, and more specific, too.

"You promise to take her then?" his father had whispered to him a month before he'd died, grabbing Neil by the wrist one afternoon when they were watching a hockey game. "You'll *do* that for me?" A small strip of

~32~

soiled yellow paper had been blowing horizontally in front of the air conditioner. "I will, Dad. Sure I will."

Neil looked at her standing there, decked out in her new green corduroy suit, ever hopeful, and he felt, as always, humbled by something deep and permanent. In defence, he smiled right back into her eyes. He made a face at her and reached into the side pocket of his sportscoat for his smokes. He squinted slyly into the match, lit the smoke and took a deep drag.

"You'll have to stop that, you know," she shouted through the wind and over the sounds of the water breaking against the ancient stone walls. "It's going to kill you."

"Aw, Mom, it might. Might not, too."

"It's probably what drove her away."

"Jesus!"

"Don't swear!"

"It *didn't* drive her away, and I'll swear if I want to, Jesus, Mary and Joseph. I'm forty years old."

An old man shuffled out of the ruins of Fort Charles, led by a small girl in a red raincoat. She must have been his granddaughter or his great-granddaughter even. They were bright, mysterious figures on a metaphysical chess-board, some canvas by De Chirico. Sure. It was their slow progress across the geometric squares, two moving figures gliding silently in front of the crumbling stone walls of the fort and against the grey mist that rose from the estuary. Kinsale sat, squat and silent across the water, its tiny steeples and roofs glistening in the pale light.

Neil noticed that his mother was crying. He walked over and put his arm around her tiny shoulders. "Mom, you okay?"

"Oh yes, dear. It's nothing."

"Well, it must be *something* . . . "

"It's being so close to Cobh."

"Cobh?"

"Where we all left from, Neil. Where it all started for us."

The thick, woven dreamland that had cradled Neil as a child had been an impenetrable and dazzling emerald forest of Irish stories and voices and names and music and places. Words like *home* or *old country,* that should have meant the Nova Scotia they'd left in 1954, really referred to Ireland, the land that had claimed Neil's mother from childhood: where her heart had anchors in a mud that was thick, sweet and marbled in sighs.

After their father died, the three children had worried about her. It was natural. Though they knew their mother's essential independence, her ability to live *in* the moment, to exult in the smallest things — crowing over a bus ticket like a bird over an unexpected worm — they still worried about a loneliness they suspected she might have ignored all her life, but which Neil didn't want her bumping into now. Not at this stage. It was all right for him, not for her. She'd been too generous to have to knock up against that dark stranger now. It wouldn't have been fair.

"They're called the little people, dear, the wee folk, sometimes leprechauns. In Ireland itself, that is. Eire

SO IT WON'T GO AWAY

proper. Over here, it's different. There's no belief in them here, just people like me telling stories to boys like you!" She'd turned back to her ironing, the blue Alberta January sky framing her through the kitchen window, the house creaking in the -35° C cold. He was five years old and dreaming as he sat there looking at her. He was dreaming of Ireland and his mother's knowledge, her voice.

She'd been his navigator all the way down from Dublin. Neil knew his Dad would have howled at the two of them. She'd always driven her husband crazy with her maps and exit ramps and signs and road calculations. And though she'd allowed them to kid her about it, she still took it seriously. He'd look sideways at her and realise it was a matter of two landscapes: the one they were driving through, and another one, of words and names and instructions, that became a second version of the one they were driving through — a landscape of language and facts and details which she would store away and pull out whenever she needed it — one that was, in some ways, the most important landscape, the most real.

Killarney. The Rose of Sharon. Mount Cashel. Every time they slipped through a town he'd look over and watch her writing down the name, taking in the scenery for later, memorising it. It was incredible. She was seventy-one and voracious, not just for the excitement of the actual journey they were taking, but an anticipated excitement of re-living it later on for her sisters. That was at least half of what was going on, more than half maybe. It made him wonder. Had his mother's passage through *everything* in her life been like this? Had there always been two landscapes — one of objects and one of words? Is that why he found it so difficult to connect with her sometimes, because she seemed always ahead of him somewhere, already looking back on a present he was trapped in, a present he *wanted* to be trapped in?

He looked past her shoulders to the sea. Her face was buried in his coat while a cigarette dangled from his lips. He stared out into the grey, dark waters of the Atlantic crashing against the stones of Fort Charles, his mother leaning against him, away from the wind. Except for the old man and the girl on the bench in front of the far seawall across from them, the parking lot was empty against another kind of emptiness created by the roar of the sea over whatever else had sound — in the town, across the bay, on the highway — all sound silenced by this sea, the same sea that had carried his ancestors out of here. He could hear it pounding in on the rocks past the fort, churning before him, peppered with whitecaps, surging as real as words, but hard to take in because of the wide force of it.

"It can't be that simple!"

"It *is* that simple."

"You're being so arbitrary."

"The situation itself *is* arbitrary."

"You've been with Shelley for fifteen years!"

"I *know* that, Rick."

"Why should that have to be over just because of one, accidental, weird deal?"

"I don't know. It just is."

"That's incredible."

"Yeah. I'd have to agree. But there you go."

SO IT WON'T GO AWAY

They were sitting on Rick's deck in Vernon. Wiley was sniffing and snivelling as they talked, on the lookout for something, no matter how small. It was late. Neil was staying over. It was just the two brothers sitting in the dark beneath the Manitoba maple. Jennifer was already asleep. The soft, clear Okanagan summer night shuffled above them, deep in smells of mowed lawns, and the sounds of houses and distant traffic rustling in the trees.

"You want another drink?" Rick asked him.

"Just bring out the bottle."

"You dumb fuck."

Rick returned with a coffee for himself and the half-empty bottle of Jameson's for Neil.

Neil poured a full dram of the whiskey into his small plastic glass, raised it to his brother, winked at him, and gulped the whole thing down. "Ah, and now for a smoke," he said.

He'd left Shelley the week before. Even he'd been surprised by how quickly and surely he'd sprung into action: *him*, Neil, famous for never making decisions — Neil the undecided — had changed his life in ten hours. Or Shelley had changed it for him. Or a cliché had changed both of them irrevocably. *Cliché.* As powerful as myth sometimes.

It *was* a cliché, and he *knew* it, and he should have been able to see through it, absorb it, ignore it, understand it even, but he couldn't. Or he didn't want to. It seemed too much for Neil. It had to do with bodies, flesh, possession. Intimacy. Trust. The list was endless. And yet, and yet. Neil had been unfaithful. Not often, but it had happened. Of course, it had meant nothing to him. He'd enjoyed the excitement of it, but nothing had undermined his love for

Shelley, his attraction to her. His need of her. Why, then, would he have this reaction now? He wasn't sure. He just had it. It was the thought of Shelley sleeping with another man. Even he knew it had to be more complicated than that though it didn't feel like it. Maybe he'd known this would happen. Maybe it would be good for both of them once they got past the cliché surface of it all. He wasn't sure.

It's just that there was something exciting — another cliché — something *free* about it all for him, aside from the pain it caused him. He leaned back into the lawnchair on Rick's deck, took a long drag from his cigarette, poured another three fingers of Jameson's. Maybe this was what he'd really wanted all along, and a vague twitch of guilt rose to the surface of these pleasures to spoil them, but dove back down again, out of sight.

"Gonna take Mom to Ireland."

"How're you going to do that?"

"I've set it all up."

"That's great, Neil." Rick looked over at him and smiled. "To get away. Maybe that *is* good."

"Yeah, well."

"No. Really!"

"Mom'll love it. I promised Dad — I told you. But she'll love it. And I'll love it, too. Just to be away from it all physically, you know . . . and who knows . . . ?maybe I'll get *lucky!*"

Both of them howled.

"Some wee Irish colleen with dark hair and flashing green eyes . . . boy, I *tell* ya!" Neil shouted.

"Named Bridget?"

"Bridget Brophy! Sure! Why not?"

The old man and the girl had taken a seat overlooking the Atlantic at the west end of Fort Charles. Neil and his mother had wandered into the Fort, past all the crumbling grey walls, the sound of the waves receding into the background. She'd taken photos while Neil read some of the plaques, then they'd both returned to the parking lot. They leaned against the hood of the car. Neil was having a long, slow smoke, abstracted. His mother's eyes kept focusing on the old man and the girl, so clean and fresh in their red and blue raincoats, sitting on the bright green bench, a grey mist rising up to tickle their feet on the cobblestone, the sea itself becoming darker, more restless.

His mother rooted around in her purse and pulled out a small, sealed package. She opened it up and placed a pile of crackers and a small packet of cream cheese onto some napkins she spread on the hood of the car. She produced a small plastic knife. "Help yourself, dear."

"How do you do it, Mom?"

"Do what, dear?"

"Always be so prepared?"

"Well, that's our *motto*, isn't it?"

"Motto? Our *family's* motto?"

"Heavens no! The Girl Guide's motto. Not our family motto! Good grief!"

He'd sensed it begin to happen just before the ferry, outside Holyhead, in Wales, when they'd been caught in a construction zone that looked all too familiar to their new world eyes. Everything up to that point had been breathtaking. They *had* returned into an 'old' world, and it had delivered its texture and magic blow by blow. Neil knew it had to end eventually, though. He just wasn't sure what would cause the unravelling, or if he could protect his mother from it. He watched her, gauging her, thinking, of course, that he knew her better than she did herself.

Heathrow. *Check.* Black cab into the centre of London. *Check.* Two nights at The Tavistock near Russell Square. *Check.* Short walks to Dillon's Bookstore, The British Museum, Shaftesbury. *Check.* Seeing Maggie Smith in *Lettuce and Lovage. Check. Double check.* Harrod's. Sloan Square. *Check.* The rented car. The highway out. The countryside. Wales. Betys-y-Coed. *Check, check, check.* All the myths intact.

Then. Slowly. Just outside Holyhead when they got stalled in a construction traffic jam. The bleached landscape. The scraped countryside. The warning signs. Huge yellow construction cats lurching over the land. Thousands of fluorescent highway cones, then humans with flags. They could have been anywhere suddenly, anywhere ordinary. Neil noticed the modesty of the homes on the outskirts of Holyhead, the poverty even, the look of it, the feel of it, the smell. It was as if a small rupture had occurred and was beginning to tear along a seam in the landscape itself, taking some of their excitement with it. It *had* to happen, he knew; it's just that he'd rather it only happened to him, not her. But he could see the small signs of disappointment in her eyes.

His mother sighed and stared up into Neil's eyes playfully, teasing him so he wouldn't worry about her tears. He smiled back down at her and wrapped her up more closely in his arms, mocking himself, muttering "There, there, old thing. I've got you now. You're going to be all right for sure!"

He's trying so hard to be tough. He's done that all his life: joking and wise-cracking his way through much of it. As if it didn't matter to him, the heart. As if he didn't have one to protect. Leaning back against the car, blowing his smoke out into the air, defiant. A small child. I know him. He thinks he's doing all this for me. He thinks it's only me being comforted. And it is me, I know, but it's him, too. The weight in him, of sadness. It's always been there, since he was small. Not easy for Shelley to have someone disappear into it for so long sometimes. Not easy at all. And I don't know it's over with them. I doubt it. There's something about that elderly gentleman. Something about him. And the sea, that long, long sea stretching westward, carrying all of them away.

She had been exhausted when they'd checked into the B&B in Dublin. They'd driven all the way to the ferry, across the Irish Sea, and into Dublin. Though they'd gotten lost three times trying to find it, they'd eventually settled into two rooms in a fine, old turn-of-the-century house sitting back from the wide sidewalks of Howth Street. They decided not to brave the downtown district together, but save it for the morning, so he walked out and got them some take-out fish and chips. When they finished, she announced she was going to bed early in order to be '*up and at 'em*' first thing in the morning. She gave him a peck on the side of the cheek, then disappeared through a small door into her room. He could hear her rustling around for a time, then watched as the lamp clicked off and the thin band of light at the bottom of the door disappeared.

He'd sat for a while, reading passages in Thomas Cahill's *How The Irish Saved Civilization*. He'd promised her he'd find out who Sheela-na-gig was. His mother had spotted these odd, female figures, like gargoyles, popping up in the corners of photographs of buildings and Churches she hoped to visit when they were down in Cork. Sure enough, on page 150, there was a photograph and, beneath it, an explanation. *The idol, above left, is Sheela-na-gig, a motif found throughout Britain and Ireland, although very difficult to photograph well because the surviving examples are in extremely inaccessible nooks and have usually been damaged by weather or censorship. The sheela parts her vulva both as an invitation to sex and as a reminder of her fertility. Her face, although sometimes smiling, is moronic and brutal, and usually skeletal. She is, like Kali of India, death-in-life and life-in-death.* Great, Neil thought, smiling to himself. I'll have a good time explaining this.

He'd walked out and saw a bit of Dublin himself that night. He left the rental car back at the B&B and took a cab down to O'Connell Street.

At the hotel in London, he'd read about situations like it springing up in Edinburgh. There was a whole article on these young, professional women working as high-end hookers in legalised brothels because the money was so good. He forgave himself for the way it happened because he'd stumbled into it so innocently, sitting in a small pub by himself, getting hammered.

The pub was just off Stephen's Green, on a side-street, and it had that distinctive Irish 'feel' to it, at least through the eyes of a tourist. Of course, Neil thought of Rick as he sat there because Rick had done so much work on Joyce and Dublin. Neil felt he'd been to Dublin many times before because he'd listened to his brother talk for hours and in such detail about the city and its voices.

The women in Dublin were wondrous and he couldn't quite say why. The dark hair, the green-eyes, the gentle brogue? An omnipresent sexual undertow? He wasn't sure. It was perhaps the way they dressed, in loose sweaters over jeans or short tartan skirts and knee-socks. He'd stumbled into a pub that had a lot of late evening traffic, a bit of the university crowd. He could pick them off. He'd sat in the midst of them and let a soft sensuality sift around him.

"A hundred pounds?"

"True, it's a lot. I know. But it's worth it."

"How's that?"

"It's the kind of women they've recruited. You wouldn't believe it, son."

"What kind is that?"

"Professionals. Lawyers. Art students. Business women. You'll never see the like!"

His mother was still leaning into him. The wind had picked up and Neil wondered if the old man and the girl would stay. It was getting so cold.

I'm leaning against Neil here in Fort Charles, staring past his shoulder at the sea coming in, and I'm thinking of a summer when I was fifteen and Ireland had overtaken me, the idea of it. It's the kind of thing that happens sometimes and I don't know why. It just happens. Something big overtakes you and changes the way you see everything else that might also be happening in your life.

Sometimes it's a landscape. Sometimes a person. Or a belief. When I was little, growing up in Catholic Moncton, I was encased in all the rituals of the Church, and I had such a personal sense of God then that a voice could overtake me for months — his voice — a voice I could talk to, a comfort. It seemed as real as anything else that happened to me then. Being with Neil here in Ireland, standing in a parking lot so near to Cobh, me at my age and he at his, is also taking me over. I can feel it.

It was the summer of 1937. I was sitting out on the sand dunes in Shediac by myself, staring out into the ocean, facing Ireland, watching the ships appear lazily on the horizon, then draw up and pass me. I'd sit there for hours, wondering what might happen to me: if I'd fall in love, if I'd have children of my own. I'd sat there that summer in a trance of Ireland. I believed it had power, magic. Soon something else was going to happen to me. I knew it. Whatever it was, I wanted it to be as inlaid with magic as Ireland seemed to me then: as green and as gentle, as frightening even.

His mother broke their embrace and walked over to the railing at the southwest corner of Fort Charles and leaned forward over it, her elbows resting upon the green iron. Neil watched her. What a tough old bird she is, he thought. Nothing slows her down for long.

I am looking back across the ocean into the eyes of that girl I was then. The elderly man and the girl are whispering to one another on a bench slightly down from and a bit behind me. I can almost hear what they're saying, but the wind muffles the cadence of their voices just enough to obscure them. Those silly seagulls out there are squawking and swooping over the dark water, always looking for something. Neil's back at the car, smoking.

Since Charles died, I've thought more and more of my children, the texture of their lives. If I actually say the words — I just want you to be happy — I mean something big by them. I want each of them to have a bite of the magic that has always filled me up, made me so blessed. Their worlds are very different from mine — I know that — and whatever that magic is will be different, too. I still wish it for each of them, even in the not knowing of it. Whatever else fills them up, I want them caught in the fist of something breathless and powerful, with lips as sweet and wet as a god's.

When I look at Neil sometimes, I can telescope his future forward, past my presence in it even, and imagine him as a gentle, elderly man whose life has been full and whose peace is obvious in his smile lines. In this vision he is a man who is easy in his own skin, and the life he's led to produce this strength and calm has been full of love and movement, laughter and depth. I can see him walking cautiously down some street, a city street perhaps, heading out for his daily lunch, or the mail, something like that. It's wonderful to see him so full, so beyond the restlessness that defines him now. He'll get there; he'll arrive at himself yet. Just you wait and see.

His mother turned back to the parking lot and waved at him, shouting over the force of the wind, "Just you wait and see!"

He waved back at her, then reached inside his pocket for another smoke.

There she was, his mother, taking it all in as usual. Just minutes ago she'd been crying. Now she was laughing and waving, shouting something out to him he couldn't hear for the surge of the waves and the wind.

She'd been crying for the past, he suspected, for all the stories of how her people had been forced to leave here, board ships in Cobh, and sail out to the new world. She'd been crying for everything they'd lost in that departure, all the sadness of it they never quite overcame, and which still surfaced in conversations hundreds of years later sitting around in kitchens and livingrooms near malls and powerlines, drapes drawn against the harsh new light. The power of that departure, the arrival afterward, then the wide, thin spreading out of the blood across a landscape so vast you could put Ireland in its pocket.

She was squinting into the wind, her scarf blowing back behind her, the gulls swooping and diving overhead, crying out into the sea. He could tell she was back in Edmonton, thinking of home, the details of the life she lived there: the bus schedules, the shopping centres, Rick and Jane. She was miles from Cork now. It was unbelievable how resilient she was. As she stood there grinning into the Atlantic, she transformed. More and more these days — the older she actually got — Neil sensed her as a younger and younger person. So much was this the case that he felt sometimes, even though he'd laugh about it afterwards, that she was returning at the end of her life to the little girl she'd started out as, looking back at him with so much hope and innocence, so much good will and love. He couldn't believe it sometimes, it was so strong.

DOOR IN THE RAIN

IT'S LATE, YOU'RE LATE, AND THE RAIN'S COMING DOWN so hard you see it bouncing off the cement of the patio in front of the back door to the old house. There's not a light on inside and you didn't expect one. There is no one living here anymore. You're probably the first person to come by in ages. It's sixty years old now, just a decade older than you are. What you can't wrap your head around is that neither you nor the house is young anymore.

It's quite laughable, the cliché of it, especially *to* the young. They stand behind you — an infinity of time stretching vastly in front of them — and laugh, thinking, well, what did you *expect*? You *lived* all that time. You *did* all those things, right and wrong. You've *earned* not being able to dream of the future anymore. There isn't going to *be* much future, is there? You've consumed most of it already. And you *did* consume it, literally. So what's the big surprise? Why would you be standing here with your wet hand on the door, in this dark rain, puzzled, disoriented, feeling robbed even?

You shake your head in an effort to exorcise these young, whispering inquisitors and begin to concentrate on the field before you, this surprise that shouldn't be.

You remember laughing yourself at the clichés that would roll out of the mouths of adults. The incredulous banality of their stunned proclamations: "When did *you* grow up? You were just born last week, it seems!" Or, "My, my, it seems like only yesterday you were just a gleam in your crazy dad's eye." And you'd retreat into the old bathroom, close the white wooden door behind you and click its lock, make faces into the small mirror, rolling your eyes at the billowing conversations drifting down the hallway from the living room, the endless predictability of their voices, nattering, nattering, and even then the sound, the faint sound, almost understood in those voices, of redemption sniffing around like an old, loveable pet.

This hand now, this door. It works both ways, coming and going.

It's where you grew up, and at least it's still here. Other objects from your growing up have vanished into the dark, wet night, and cannot be found. And there is something talismanic about the concrete reality of this house. You can touch it; run your hand flat against the crumbling glass stucco to the left of the door frame. The simple act of touching the surface of this place grounds you in the storm, anchors you in time. And that's what you need more than anything: to be anchored so you are not washed away into the dark, slippery mindlessness of the night. Oh sure, you understand that in a short time, you might be washed away into it, like that, but not for now, not this minute. Relax. Turn the handle. That's right. Slowly.

You can sense linoleum beneath your feet and small stairs going up into where you remember the kitchen was. That's right. Linoleum. And you wonder, do they make it anymore? Just a brightness in your head and fragments of things you'd expect in dreams, that kind of physical landscape: completely mobile, surreal. That's when you see the white window frame first, its glass and the thick dark night still hovering beyond the glass, then this mouth working away: a gargantuan, wet, red-lipped mouth stretching and smacking its lips and snickering in all its mucus and saliva around an old, cigarette-seasoned tongue undulating at the centre of things, and directing everything it has to say at you.

"It's the ones who *expect* their privilege, their luck, who actually think somehow — in some strange perversion of self-serving but otherwise non-existent history — that they *deserve* to *have* what they have, *they're* the ones you have to watch out for. *They're* the ones, boy. Clutching their wee fucking chequebooks, the silly old bastards, as cheap as you'd ever find anywhere, always scrabbling around in the bottom of their sequinned fucking purses for that last nickel, that elusive penny. You know the ones. You see them in Safeway stores. You know who I'm talking about. *They're* the dangerous ones, and they're completely underrated, almost invisible. We let them get away with everything, the miserable old shits, *we do*! Everything! They sit there in their cheap (but what they themselves think is rather expensive) *finery* for Christ's sake, and prattle on about the dangerous times we live in, what's happened to the kids these days, how we need more law and order, and the thing is, *the fucking thing is*, they'll vote as far to the right as they can because they're so fucking cheap and they're worried someone's going to fucking come along and *relieve* them of all the fucking money they've got stashed away and that they still believe is theirs by some divine fucking *right*, the withered old bastards that they are, too, and what do we *do* about these people? We let them get away with everything. They're *old* for pity's sake. We romanticise them, these miserable old heaps of fucking bone, and we don't see the truth about them: they're *still* dominating things; *still* got their talons sinking into our flesh. You better believe it, *especially* us *losers* who might have ruined our lives with drink and smoke and pleasure — all the dirty things, of course — oh yes, especially us, they've got their fucking talons into *our* necks for sure. And we just let them have this power when (*a*) they don't deserve it and (*b*) and more important, *we* don't deserve it. Life's tough enough as it is, boy. I don't need this shit, people writing letters like that, I don't fucking *deserve* to be betrayed like that by some self-important, inflated old bag of crap! What the fuck do *you* think? Are you *with* me? *Well?*"

But you can't get your answer out, even if you had one, for the mouth and all its smacking, salivating machinery has vanished suddenly and you're in an oaken hallway, a musty passageway with dark pictures of medieval landscapes sedated, whimpering under glass and ornate frames painted gold so you think they're metal, but they're not. They're wooden and you know that, and it's one of the first times, as a kid, that you consider the difference between a thing and what is actually or precisely 'real' beneath its surface, and meanwhile, your later, older, despairing self intrudes upon this child's logic suddenly and whispers *Wittgenstein* in your ear, sounding impatient, irritated, and you shout back, *who? Who?* And you think again of that wet, bulbous mouth working away down the hall, then forget about it *and* the voice in your ear because some light has grown intense. You have found another room, another *something* in another room. And this time you find you are pressed against a pink cheek, a woman's cheek not a man's, and your ear and cheek are being held against her cheek and ear. You can't see this person directly, but you are drawn in by the touch of the skin and a voice that surfaces through the skin, vibrating, smooth, lulling.

"Well you know, dear, Mrs. Mingtag and Mrs. Boynton would both *love* to be here, to sit down on these Louis 14th Restoration chairs, dear, right here in the *foyer* of things, in the *preamble* as it were of all their luxury and exquisite taste, they'd *love* to, but *sadly* cannot attend. The legal advice they'd received, from the *executrix*, yes dear, that's the proper term, *executrix*, prevented them as it were. So, for now, it's just the two of us here in the dark, waiting, waiting for pity's sake. And I think of all the times I've told him you can't just do whatever *pleases* you all the time; there are *others* to consider first. But he won't listen to me and here I am, living in a city I never even *dreamed* I'd see, trying to do the right thing for you kiddies. The children. I worry that he does not see this. He does not *comprehend* the *enormity* of his own *constructions*. This is his family we are talking about, after all. His *family*. Surely he has *some* responsibilities that he cannot always mock or laugh at in that way. I am not expecting a *lot* for pity's sake. Heavenly day! If I *were*, I wouldn't be sitting here, would I, holding you all broken in my arms like this. All broken in the *ante-chamber*, the *foyer*, the *vestibule*, and I know, I know I cannot resist these words for they are keys into rooms, I am sure of it, if only you know the right words you will *belong*, gain entry, I can *sense* it. And it's the exact opposite with him. He can't wait to *lose* the right words, the proper words, and start swearing and undermining nice things, civil things, ordered things. He can't resist. He *has* to make fun of everything *sacred* for pity's sake, everything *normal*. It's that family he's from, they're all mavericks each and every one of them, all strange. How do you live your life in the face of such a wall of constant, merciless mockery? What am I supposed to *do* for heaven's sake? Is there anyone can tell me?"

And you're in the light again, the brightest you've seen so far, then here, outside the door in the rain, its dark wetness dripping from the cuffs of your brown jacket, and then *here*, sitting right here now, reading, adjusting your knees and feet, getting comfortable. Ah!

THE MAN WHO LOST EVERYTHING

WHAT IS IT? WHAT IS IT? Why am I like this?

Because I worry about this world we're living in, a glibness in it that has overtaken my generation, and the slow erosion of opportunities for dignity in the face of that glibness. There are moments, as irrational as they may be, when I find myself in the grip of an emotion so strong it borders on hatred. When I examine it, I realise that, right or wrong, I'm hating something pathetically insecure yet self-congratulatory about upper-middle-class conventions, the listless limitations built into them, the safety, the caution, yet the restlessness beneath those surfaces — needs that fester like open sores if you care to see through to them. I hate the unrequited ambition aching in the midst of gatherings of such people sometimes, men and women standing around trying to one-up one another. Hard to explain. I have always been suspicious of a cruelty, a condescension and a flat-out greed built into the world, a sick kind of desperate pride that's hard to define and hard to forgive; that is fuelled by the diminishment of others but betrays a longing for the opposite of that diminishment, for something thick and spiritual and humble. Spiritual anorexia. And yet I love this world I am thinking about. I am of it. These are my people. They have tenderness and dignity. Caught again —

"Lighten up!"

"Yeah, yeah, yeah . . . "

"You better. It's ridiculous."

"I know."

"I don't know if you *do*!"

"Okay, then. I don't."

"Don't do this, Rick. I mean it. Not now."

"There is *nothing* I can say!"

"I'll see you later."

"Have a nice time."

"Oh, yeah! I'll have a nice time." Jennifer pulled the door shut and gunned the engine. She looked into the rear-view mirror, adjusting her new sun-glasses on the tip of her nose, then looked back at him. Rick was standing in his old jeans and T-shirt, slumped against the side of the house in the deep shade.

She looked dazzling to him in her new, pale-green, two-piece beach outfit. When he thought of how carefully she'd packed a picnic lunch for them in the wicker basket which sat in the back seat of the car now, the cover of a plastic, red-checked table-cloth poking out of the basket, staring him down, he felt nausea for how badly he was treating her. But he also knew if he got in the car and went with her, he'd be mad all afternoon. He didn't want to be mad all afternoon. He was as tired of being mad as she was tired of him. He shrugged. "I'm sorry," he said, staring at the black, dark asphalt of the driveway, "I'm as tired of me as you are." He looked up at her. "It's the not-smoking. I can't explain it. I'm just irritated by everything, everybody. I'm sorry."

"Fuck, I don't care anymore," she said, "I know you're sorry. Take it easy. It's all right. I'll be home later."

Rick stared after the car as it sped up the hill behind the house. He'd done the one thing he couldn't afford to do, and it made him so tired he could barely walk back to the deck. When he did collapse into the ragged blue lawnchair, Wiley was all over him, panting, drooling, biting his boots. He shooed her away and the pup curled up at the end of the deck, staring back at him, her big, wet, brown eyes another reproach.

Rick threw his head back and gazed up into the cobalt, mid-day Okanagan summer sky. He was going to be as miserable here as he knew he would have been out at the club. You take yourself with you wherever you go.

~~~

Strasbourg was more beautiful than Rick had remembered it. He'd worried, naturally, that he'd romanticised the place. He hadn't trusted his memory and had been prepared for the worst when he arrived. Instead, quel surprise!, he'd walked past the front desk at The Hotel Gutenberg early in the morning and over to his favourite old café, The Glace Place. Two of the waiters who'd worked there in 1988 were still working there, and one of them, the older, dark-haired one, recognised him after all these years.

He took a seat at an outside table so he could stare up at the Cathedral and watch everyone walk to work down the rue des Hallesbardes. He retrieved his notebook from his backpack and ordered a café grande. In time, the pre-work pedestrians began to stuff the streets, many of them stopping at the café for a coffee. The sun shone gold off the freshly-hosed cobblestone and Rick sat, hypnotised. He looked up at

the Western Rose window in the façade of the Cathedral and
it amassed a quiet presence as he sat there, rooted to the
ground by his metal chair. He was tempted to write
something in his notebook, but he'd trained himself not to do
that anymore. It was over. Consummatum est. Instead, he
sat, revelling in the people, in the cigarette he fondled in his
left hand now: how it felt to draw its newness up to his lips
over the smell of the dark, bitter coffee, and light it, inhaling
it in the sweet-smelling wet spring air. Rick felt such
goodwill suddenly he thought his heart might break under
the weight of it. His eyes welled up in emotions he couldn't
name. He took a deep second drag off his Rothman's Blue,
blinking into the sun.

~~~

The Okanagan Country Club was established in the late
thirties by a small group of Vernon couples, many of them
British, who had purchased some land on Kalamalka
Lake, constructed a small clubhouse, cleared a beach and
built some tennis courts. It was a modest little club still,
but because they limited its membership, it was tricky to
become a member. Rick and Jennifer had waited seven
years and had just been admitted in the spring. As a result,
they'd taken up tennis again, a sport they'd played
together when they'd first met. And Jennifer's two sisters
were members of the club, too, so Rick and Jennifer could
spend time with their nieces and nephews in a great, up-
beat, easy-to-pull-off setting.

The club was innocent, unpretentious, but there was
something about it that made Rick edgy at times,
belligerent, wary. He wasn't always sure he wanted to be
there. On one level — even though he knew he was being

ridiculous for he had pushed for their joining the club —
he felt he didn't belong; it wasn't his world.

What Jennifer wanted was simple, innocent. She
wanted them to spend the morning and afternoon with
some friends out at the club. How could he spoil it so
easily? It didn't seem possible. And it bothered him, too,
that he felt exhausted, tired of the endless circle of self-
accusation he still found himself spinning in years later
when he should have gotten past it. He was still peering
out of his old child's eyes like one of Raphael's cherubs,
his head in both cupped hands, staring down whimsically
at a cobblestone street in a little village, watching all the
commotion from afar, removed and bemused.

Wiley needed a treat. She was nipping at his boots.
Rick opened his eyes and smiled. "Wiley need a num-
num?" He scratched Wiley's temple and ears. "Let's go get
a fuckin' num-num for Wiley."

They walked into the kitchen where Rick took a green
Milkbone out of the package he kept at the back of the
bottom drawer, across from the stove. "Here you go!" he
said, "a green one!" Wiley's eyes were alert, excited,
watering. "My personal favourite!" Rick made Wiley sit,
then watched as she snapped it out of his hand and
bounced back through the door to the deck, green
Milkbone sticking up out of her mouth on a ludicrously
triumphant angle. He followed her and sat back down
again, closed his eyes.

A couple of times lately Rick sensed he was right on
the edge of understanding why he was so angry beneath
everything he also seemed to be. He'd laugh about it even.
He loved people. He loved making people feel at home,
making people laugh. He believed in good things. He

loved Jennifer. He loved the life they'd built in Vernon: the house, the car, the dog, the safety. He wasn't embarrassed by any of these things. It was just that beneath such safety, he felt a strange, chronic uncomfortableness.

This restlessness was the tip of an iceberg, and the iceberg was a political anger in him that was deep, old, passionate and had to do with privilege, opportunity, judgement, fairness. He'd always considered himself a microcosm for his times. If he could see what was wrong in him, he might understand what was wrong on a larger scale. It made sense. He'd seen it work before, especially when he'd quit drinking.

Not wanting to go with Jennifer to the club was not a new feeling, and it disarmed him to realise he could remember the same unease going as far back as being with his first girlfriend, Naomi, in Edmonton when he was eighteen.

In Edmonton, in the fifties, class lines had been clearly announced. He and Jane and Neil had no illusions about where they stood from that point of view, but the anarchic pride of their parents allowed them to ignore class lines completely. It wasn't an innocent pride, either. Throughout his boyhood, like a horizon line in a painting, Rick's father's voice had encircled him, limited him, anchored him: his father's voice railing against pretensions, the cruelties in any kind of class structures, the cheapness that you could never forgive in upper-middle-class life. His father had been especially convincing when he'd been drinking which, as he got older, was all the time.

Rick's restlessness was something he came by honestly. There was always an essential truth beneath whatever else might have been wrong in his father's attitude; it was a political window through which Rick had been trained to see, and he never really regretted it. Even when it caused him misery, he felt he owed his dear-old-dad for that kind of seeing. And he judged himself from the point of view of that sight, too. The big problem with the club and other things in Rick's life was that it was the nineties, a particularly smug world. A whole generation — his generation — was turning fifty, talking about RRSPs, early retirement packages, condos on golf courses. A generation that had once distinguished itself for its idealism was actively ignoring the welfare of other generations, looking down on them, even, measuring everything by cold, hard cash. It was hard to believe.

"I'd rather be smoking."

Rick knew how convoluted all the logic of such unhappiness and depression was, and how easy it would be to get trapped in it forever and not find your way out. He didn't want that to happen. He wanted to lose everything that held him back and move forward into the world with a new kind of tempered love. "Yeah, right," he whispered out loud. Wiley was at his feet again. It was time to go in and do something.

~~~

Neil had shown up late two nights ago, bombed, depressed, flailing. Rick had known Neil and Shelley were going through a tough time. Shelley had gone away for a month to visit her mother in Victoria. Neil was organising a trip with their own mother to Ireland, but his emotions were all over the place. It was eerie for Rick to sit with his brother, out on that deck in the hot summer night, and watch as he drank and smoked his brains into oblivion.

Rick had quit drinking ten years back. His sister, Jane, five. Rick had just quit smoking, four months now. He looked at Neil and couldn't help thinking of their communal need to stuff things in, inhale everything, lose consciousness to the physical. It was the whole, crazed wheel of addictions and it was going to spin around him forever it seemed, never let him go. It didn't matter, all the theories about addictions and families. Rick was well-informed. What mattered was what was right in front of him and that night it had been his brother. Rick had had to sit there in the dark — as Neil had become more relaxed, more funny, more full — knowing all this was going to have to be undone, that Neil was on an edge full of consequence. But Rick knew, too, that he couldn't say much. What could he say? Neil knew him. He knew what Rick had gone through. All Rick could do was sit and listen.

There were moments when Rick wanted to drop everything earnest in his life, re-embrace his own drinking and smoking, start laughing that abandoned laugh again. He could hear the delicious chaos of it in Neil's voice. Rick had become so serious that sometimes he wanted to scream. He resented paying that price on top of the others. It seemed too steep. But something else in him knew that that kind of laughter didn't acknowledge the world he'd been delivered into as a straight, lean consciousness: the magic there, the awful wonder of it, another kind of irresistible laughter at the heart of it. He wouldn't give up his new world even if living in it made everything else so fucking stupid sometimes.

He looked at his brother as Neil got more and more loaded and laughed at the hilarity of genetic patterns: by day, a mild-mannered college instructor; by night, a lurching, foul beast slouching towards righteousness to have a crap. It was true. They stood out for their kindness, their empathy. He loved trying to provide for other people what he could never receive himself. And in time, he realised there was a wounded self in him that was mad. When he still drank, it would come out late at night in a flood of sarcasm and criticism that was hilarious and deadly. After he'd quit drinking, he was surprised to find the anger still there. And when he decided to quit smoking, the anger surfaced with a vengeance. It wasn't beneath the surface any longer. It was brazen, illogical, and directed at almost everything, but especially easy targets like the club.

~~~

It was late in the evening. Rick was sitting at a sidewalk table in the square called Maison des Tanneurs. He'd been sitting there for an hour and a half. He'd sipped one bottle of cold Alsatian Riesling and had just ordered a second. He'd eaten an exquisite meal of tarte flambé, a speciality he'd come to love over these past six months. He'd ordered a small espresso as a breather before starting the second bottle of wine, and it had just arrived in its tiny porcelain cup and saucer, white against the blue of the tablecloth. He lit up a Rothman's, raised the espresso to the sky in the west, to the thick, gnarled-red hues of the sunset there, and took a deep drag off the cigarette. "Salut," he whispered to the fracturing sun; "salut!" to the deep, lengthy charcoal shadows the medieval towers cast onto the cobblestone at his feet. Rick sighed. A boatload of tourists floated by on the canal like a silent, slow image out of a Fellini movie. He could hear indistinct

human voices, excited, whispering, but soft in the late dusk.
Three lovely women walked by his table, arm in arm. One of
them, the most striking one with deep auburn hair, looked
back at him and winked shamelessly. Rick returned her smile
and watched as the women took seats at a table one
restaurant away. The auburn-haired girl kept glancing over
at him, smiling. His wine arrived. Cold beads of water
slipped down the dark green glass of the bottle as he poured
his first glass. Somewhere in the crumbling, stone distance,
the old iron bells of the cathedral began to toll a rich, human
note back up into the diminishing light.

~~~

He was flicking through the channels while Wiley feasted
on another Milkbone. When she was finished, she flipped
herself over onto the new Gabeh rug and rubbed her spine
into the thick, textured wool, pedalling her four tiny paws
up into the air, a grin stretching across her snout. Look
how happy she is, he thought, how natural. She's not
examining it. She's not weighing the gravity of each of her
decisions. *Shall I part my hair behind? Do I dare to eat a*
peach?

Outside, in. You examined things from the outside. Or,
on the other hand, you examined things from the inside.
From the outside, the iceberg seemed political. From the
inside, what seemed political began to appear less and less
exalted and, in fact, masked something that was embarrass-
ingly personal and physical: the body; desire; a need to be
filled up, stuffed, sated. Wiley was on her back on the rug,
her paws pedalling the soft summer air in the half-light
coming through the bamboo blinds. *Do I dare to eat a*
peach?

Drinking, smoking, sex: a man's hands twittering, eyes bugged out in a desperate longing to be held, fondled, stuffed, stroked. Guzzling and inhaling things in a big grab against death. There was this awful version of that grab. We usually didn't see that vision. What we saw was a more graceful, tarted-up and easier-to-take image, conducted behind a façade of reason, propriety, grace. No matter. In the end, nothing other than this grab really mattered. It was waiting at the end of all revolutions, no matter how we tried to exalt them in other ways. Inside, out.

Could this grab, though, have its own mystery, its own dignity, its own love? Was there another way of seeing it so you could fall into it, embrace it, be inhaled by it in some annihilating metaphysics? Gobbled up by an equally voracious God? Consumed by love in the end, some twisted, divine addiction that accounted for all the lesser ones? It'd be nice to think that, Rick thought. It'd help. *I shall wear white flannel trousers and walk upon the beach.* All I want is to smoke, Rick sighed. I wouldn't be angry or restless if I could smoke. I could handle anything as long as I could smoke my way through it. I could handle The Country Club. Rick laughed for he saw himself from a distance suddenly, this naked man, a bottle and a cigarette in one hand, his erect penis in the other, working away, and his eyes bulging in a physical satisfaction that was total. Some metaphysics. *I have heard the mermaids singing, each to each.* So why don't we just stuff ourselves, he wondered. Why not? *Because it wouldn't be enough,* some voice whispered through the breeze shuffling through the half-opened windows in front of the bamboo blinds. *It would never be enough.* Rick knew it was true.

There was something bigger, something that filled or stuffed better than the physical, but it was difficult to get at, like the far, impossible ends of jazz. *I do not think that they will sing to me.* Don't count on it, Rick whispered to himself, they will sing in the end. We will all sing. We're singing right now.

In the stillness of their living room, he sat with his hands on his knees, his heart steady, thumping away. Sometimes, though he knew how ridiculously conceited this line of thinking was, he felt in his own difficulties all the shuffling, evolving, slowly conceiving awareness of his own continent. When he'd lived in Strasbourg, he'd come to understand how superior the French felt towards North America. He'd never imagined so much resentment towards where he was from, especially for America: its power, its wealth, its overweening, self-congratulatory tackiness. These attitudes surprised him, and because he was Canadian, he found them refreshing because, like the Scots and the Irish, Canadians had had to live next to a powerful, imperial force that had its own annoying myopia. And yet, and yet. He'd found himself defending North America, too, and he suspected he knew something about it the French didn't know, or if they did, knew only as a vague abstraction. What he knew was that, faltering and imperfect a culture as it might be, North America had been conducting a human experiment for the past three-hundred years that was unprecedented. If there was a new design for humans, that design would most likely surface out of it. No other culture had been involved in such a risky undertaking. Sitting on his couch in the middle of a hot summer day in the Okanagan, imagining a naked figure sitting next to him getting stuffed in every orifice until it collapsed in a complete surrender to the physical, longing for something else, Rick could see vaguely that these things were a collective image of what he sensed was being born. Some infinitely gentle, infinitely suffering thing, or some rough beast, its time come round at last was hard to say, up for grabs. Hybrid. Mutant.

The phone rang down the hallway.

"Hello?"

"Hi, Uncle Rick?"

"Yes?"

"It's Miranda!"

"Well I *thought* it was you!"

"It *is!*"

"Well, *good!*"

"Uncle Rick?"

"Yes?"

"My mom says Auntie Jennifer is out at the Club."

"Yes she is. She was hoping you'd be out there, too."

"Well, I'm going to be."

"Good. So she doesn't have to worry."

"No."

"Good."

"Uncle Rick?"

"Yes Miranda?"

"My mom says that if I asked you, maybe you and me could drive out to the Club on our bikes!"

"Oh."

"What do you think of *that*?"

"Well, it sounds pretty good, but . . . "

"Uncle Rick?"

"Yes Miranda?"

"We would have a lot of fun!"

"That's *true*."

"We would surprise Auntie Jennifer."

"That's true, too."

"Uncle Rick?"

"Yes Miranda?"

"When do you want to go?"

"Can you be here in half an hour?"

"Yes I can."

"Then we'll start out then."

"Uncle Rick?"

"Yes Miranda?"

"Don't forget your helmet."

"Oh, right."

"I sometimes forget and my mom gets mad."

"Well, I don't want your mom mad at *me*. That's for sure."

"No."

"Miranda?"

"Yes, Uncle Rick?"

"This will be a lot of fun."

"I know."

"Bye."

"Bye."

~~~

Rick stared down into the chipped white grail of the toilet bowl in the darkness of his apartment in Petite France in Strasbourg. Large chunks of last night's tarte flambé circled before him in the water and the sight of them made him heave one last time while his right hand reached up for the handle and flushed. I didn't realise how much wine I was drinking, he thought. It snuck up on me. I'll have to be more careful.

Rick washed his hands and face in the sink, stared at himself in the mirror and adjusted the waistband of the sweats he wore as pyjamas. He walked through the dark into the kitchen, past the bedroom. He could see her auburn hair on the pillow through the half-opened door, and, quietly, he pulled the door closed until he heard it click. *She'll sleep for a bit,* he thought, *then she'll go.* Fractured images of her porcelain breasts hovering above his lips faded to the shaky imbalance of his hangover. He moved precariously through the kitchen, suffering a mammoth spell of vertigo near the toaster, then put on some coffee. While it poured itself through, he leaned forward resting both hands on the cupboard counter around the sink, staring vacantly into its stainless steel bottom. It was getting stained around the drain basket. When the coffee was through, he poured himself a cup and took his ashtray and smokes with him into the living room where he placed himself at the big window in the plush chair. He set the cup and ashtray down on the wide white windowsill that ran just above the electric heater panel, and pulled the drapes so he could look out into the darkness of Strasbourg's early dawn. He lit up a smoke, sipped his coffee, and leaned back into the soft chair.

He often woke up early in the morning in Strasbourg, especially if he'd been drinking. There was something about his sleeping patterns that left him wide awake and hungover in the dark. The scene below him, two storeys down into the square, was a hodgepodge of fourteenth century buildings that had been continually restored over the centuries. Cobblestone streets and lanes ran erratically through it. There wasn't a right angle anywhere. It was eerie. He felt as *if he'd retreated into the past, into a labyrinth of history, a place where he could fall back into his ancestors and be conscious of nothing but its impossible reality, its strange comfort. When he'd closed down all his connections to Vernon, he'd promised himself that he'd dedicate the last years of his life to pleasure and that, for his money at least, Strasbourg had been the most pleasurable and sensual landscape he'd ever experienced. It was perfect. He'd lost everything to get here. Rick sighed and leaned forward to butt out his cigarette. He took another sip of the black, bitter coffee. He took a cigarette out of the package and leaned back into the chair, lighting up the smoke as he did so. He exhaled the smoke, and in so doing could sense the weight of his own presence in the room, his body twittering in its confusion, the movement of his blood correcting his metabolism and driving the hangover away. He would feel fine before she got up. He'd feel great then.*

But he didn't feel fine now. He was free-falling through a medieval gate, down into a chaos he didn't want to think about. He stared into the city and could see the single spire of the cathedral thrusting up into the air. All the small café owners and butchers and bakers would be spilling out into the streets soon, he'd hear them opening up the city as they had every morning for thousands of years. And as he sat in the heart of this history, sated physically, staring into the pre-dawn darkness, trying to see anything specific in the thick, charcoal light, he sighed and reached for the coffee cup. He heard her stir suddenly, then silence. He hoped she was dreaming. He didn't want her in here right now to see him like this. He wanted to be by himself. He'd feel great later on. He'd be perfect.

Maybe she was dreaming of a new world full of light somewhere past this thick history. Maybe she was dreaming of that.

~~~

They'd passed the Shell station on the left and Polson Park Mall on the right as they'd turned onto the highway that led to the beach and the country club. He kept her helmet in sight. They were travelling so closely they could shout to one another. He laughed at the spectacle of her tiny legs pumping away, excited, and he thought of Wiley again, taking such natural pleasure on the rug. Miranda was ecstatic, her eight-year-old body working furiously, pushing itself beyond itself, her emotions high, thinking of what a big girl she'd turned out being in terms of all her audiences, but especially Auntie Jennifer who didn't have a clue she could do this, who'd be surprised like crazy.

Irly Bird Lumber. Polson Park Bowling Lanes. The Super-Value Food Emporium. Vintage Books. The Vernon Bakery. Napa Auto Parts. BC Hydro Offices. Sun Valley Sports. BC Gas Offices. Prymer Construction with its piles of dirt baking in the raw sunlight. The veterinarian's office. Vernon Golf and Country Club on the right, a soft green breeze wafting up from its humidity and lushness; foursomes everywhere, swinging clubs, steel shafts arcing in bolts of lightning under the sun. Rick and Miranda were pedalling into all the tacky, wonderful contradictions, the wild energy they represented. The cars whisked past them both ways. He was following Miranda out to the lake, her body a blur of glee.

Rick felt a rush. Miranda seemed older than him suddenly. He was a child and he could sense himself looking down on himself, and whatever it was that surfaced up through him forgave some of the anger that was also there, and he grinned sheepishly into the sun, Miranda guiding him on.

It was great for a second. He forgot who he was. But even when it all came back and he was right there, back in his body, still struggling, he still felt great. The rush wasn't over. It was different, not over. He was following Miranda into another world, driving into North America.

MODESTY

How often had I felt I was working for the wrong people?
— William McIlvanney, *Strange Loyalties*

THERE IS A LOOK ON PEOPLE'S FACES SOMETIMES that will present itself at the strangest moments, ambushing me, for I've become wary about days that leave me open to it. Some of the time it has nothing to do with money; other times it might only have to do with money.

The look is born, usually, in a moment of self-consciousness caused by specific circumstances: entering a room of strangers, wearing a new item of clothing, hoping to meet someone in a mall, trying to buy fresh tomatoes in Safeway, hoping you can look as respectable as the others you've pulled up to chat with at a wedding reception, the hope that your picnic will be perfect — the table will be perfect, the wasps will go away, everyone will be decent, even happy — the look on a child's face when a car door slams and a parent is expected. It's a fragile, human stare filled with expectations that things will be all right, and that things won't be all right, that kind of vulnerability, puzzling, something never resolved in the moment itself, the moment of the look I mean: a kind of perpetual motion machine. The guts it takes to wear that look out into the world.

~~~

There were times when the highway — at night, like this, after his evening class — would acquire a dark, floating depth that matched how he was feeling, so that driving down the soft asphalt whispering through Winfield, past Wood Lake and up the soft, stubbled hills to Vernon, was like breathing, thinking, living in his body twice.

Neil had just had one of those days again and was feeling his usual blues. He knew it would take a couple of days to get out of them. That's just the way it worked sometimes.

A coyote lurched out onto the highway in front of him and disappeared as quickly into the pitch darkness near a rest stop on Wood Lake. The water of the lake flickered in Neil's peripheral vision. He rolled down the window and listened to the early spring air buffet the car, the tall ponderosa pines arch and crack in it. The lake seemed a sound in itself though Neil knew he couldn't hear anything above the sound of the air on the car.

There was something wrong between him and Shelley. He wasn't sure what it was, though. Whatever it was, it was different from anything that had happened to distance them in the past. Whatever it was, was new. He had the feeling — though he couldn't figure out why — that whatever was new, was another man.

Just the thought of Shelley with another guy devastated him — like dropping through a hole in the earth — and, in an odd way, excited him, too. The unnerving part was that it was, for once, beyond his control and he didn't know what to do. When it came to sex, he was always guessing.

~~~

Hieronymous Bosch days. The darker side of that look I was talking about, the grotesque side. That's what I think of them as being. And even though I might be smiling about them now, looking back on them, they're not easy to survive. Who was that German painter? George Grosz? Same concept.

It's just that you walk out so innocently into the world one morning and, for no apparent reason, *bam!* , it begins to transform before your eyes. The human landscape mutates as you enter it. All the need and greed and loathing and frustration and longing become incarnate in the flesh you're walking into, so the prettiest face, the most dignified face, regardless, begins to metamorphose. Noses get stretched out, bigger, nostril hair announcing itself. You can suddenly see the pattern of the make-up that was supposed to be concealed; knuckles appear huge and ugly; freckles and warts acquire immediate significance; faces twist, ears enlarge, hair looks feeble and spikey and rat-infested, blue-rinsed; bodies bulge out or become gaunt and wracked with sinew and stretching and tension; shit and urine and menstrual blood and snot begin to appear in any orifice; eyes bug out with desire and a desperate ugliness that can almost not be borne. And people want things, are grunting for it, want to be stuffed and stuffed and all semblance of class disappears and we are all equal suddenly, but who wants this democracy? And as you wonder about this, your whole world collapses into a big, wet, sensuous whine of gluttony. And this was just the first ten minutes in your favourite coffee shop! Where you *know* everyone! Imagine what waits for you out on the street?

The good thing about that kind of day is it humbles you — in case you thought the world a refined, stylish place — and grants you a kind of power: if the human landscape *is* this desperate, you don't have to measure yourself so cruelly by it. The bad thing about these kinds of days is that you don't exactly recover from them. You *do*, of course, but it's not easy.

~~~

It wasn't just Shelley, though that was the predominant thing. His students were beginning to bother him, too, and he knew that was a bad sign. You couldn't allow them to get to you. You couldn't become a martyr.

Neil had always loved teaching, and the key to his particular style was that he floated his classes out into a hilarious, surreal focus by maintaining a wide horizon of respect. If he could keep that horizon clear, there were great results sometimes. If he got tired and allowed it to shrink, the whole skyline would collapse and everything turn to shit. He couldn't afford to get tired. And the first sign of getting tired was a martyrish, wheedling annoyance with the very students he likely wanted to help most.

"Did you get a chance to read it yet, Neil?"

"I just *got* it! This afternoon!"

"Yeah, sorry. But I just thought maybe you'd have had a chance to go over it you know? Edit it for me? While you were having supper or something?"

"You're supposed to edit it yourself."

"Well, yeah, you know *me* though. It's much better when *you* do it."

"What are you going to do when you're not in a class like this?"

"Get a grammar and spelling program in my computer?"

"Christ!"

Some of Neil's students wouldn't have any idea until later how they could push and annoy him, and that was small comfort in the thick of it.

"I just can't read anybody else's stuff, Neil."

"You mean the other students, or everybody's?"

"Everybody's, I guess."

"Why is that?"

"I don't know. I'm sorry, I don't want anybody else's stuff, or writing, to *interfere*, you know? Like, with my own creativity you know? I don't want to be, like, *influenced*?"

"You've *got* to read other writers' work, Wendy."

"Why?"

Neil had another month to go and the semester would be over and he'd recover and get his strength back for the fall. But he still had to be careful. Sometimes, he knew, he worried too much and he needed to put the brakes on that. But worrying was built into him; it came easily, like breath.

The world he'd grown up in, back on the Southside of Edmonton, had been so humble, so free. There hadn't been automatic expectations in that world; there were modest expectations, but nothing outlandish, nothing too greedy. In the end, if he looked back on it all, Neil knew how lucky he'd been though he also knew he'd worked hard. But luck, luck. He'd been lucky. Lucky to get where he'd ended up, through all the worrying that comes like breath when you don't expect things, when nothing is offered to you on a silver platter, on any platter, and you have to figure out all the moves, in and around things, on your own. That kind of worrying.

He was two miles out of Oyama, ascending the hills over the west side of Kalamalka Lake, when the lights of Vernon popped up in the distance, twelve miles away down the dark, still water. It always seemed strange to him to see these lights so early at night, whereas during the day you couldn't see Vernon until you drove over the last hill near the dump and actually turned a corner at the old Lookout to descend right down into it. Perspective. Distance. Sight. It was different at night.

He drew a cigarette out of the package lying flat on the passenger seat. His hands knew exactly where the package was, exactly how to extract one and light it in the darkness. He passed a Dodge half-ton while he lit the smoke. How does the body know how to *do* all these things?

Lucky. He'd stumbled into university almost accidentally, then just stayed there, for nine years as a student, almost another twenty as a teacher. He'd loved the world of the university and he'd been lucky in it. He knew that in his bones. And living in this world the way he had lived removed him slowly but irrevocably from the world he had grown up in as a child. In that world, he'd become an authority figure who couldn't be trusted completely now. He'd acquired expectations. He'd grown into fancy-schmancy tastes. He'd crossed over. He was safe.

He worried like breathing. He was never safe.

~~~

Maybe the Hieronymous Bosch days surface to balance something out about that other look I was thinking about. I don't know. They sure put the brakes on some things — like unforgivable innocence or protected privilege, the walls of confidence and surety the first look faced. A good thing, all in all, that they come up. They keep me honest, wary.

When we were living in Edinburgh in 1995 and were quite lonely, we circumvented that loneliness and the kind of work we were both lost too much in sometimes, by going on long, wonderful hikes, or, as they call them in Scotland, hill walks. A friend of ours had loaned us a book that contained pull-out hikes in Great Britain and there were loads of them in the section on Scotland. So we'd make a small lunch and head out in the Volvo, once a week usually, taking on a good two-hour walk near a small town or village we could explore afterwards.

One Saturday morning we decided to drive south of Peebles to a walk along the Tweed near an old Scottish landmark known as Traquair House. If you started out at Traquair House, you could follow the river south to another town called Galashiels, then take a bus back to the car. The walk along the river was incredibly quiet. It was late November, but the weather, though misty and damp, was not cold. So we walked along the dirt path, the river mumbling always at the back of things, and we yacked away like the old friends we'd become, talking about everybody back home in the Okanagan, easing our feeling that we were likely too isolated, and needed more company. As we neared the small village, the path turned east and we approached an old stone bridge that crossed the river and led into the town. We could see houses suddenly and random noises that indicated human business and activity, maybe a lumber company or a stone quarry being worked.

Standing in the middle of the bridge was a big man in his late sixties walking towards us from the village. He was wearing dark blue overalls over a white T-shirt and had that rough, red, burly look some Scottish men have, full of health and sinew, shyness and humour. Suddenly, when he spied her, he stretched his arms out wide so they practically reached both sides of the bridge he was standing on, and his face broke out in an incredibly mischievous grin. "Come on up here lassie and give me a great big kiss!" he shouted, as if he were a long-lost relative. She was walking just ahead of me and, amazingly, kept walking right into that big embrace and gave him the kiss he needed. "Aw, yer an amazing wee thing," the man whispered gently to her, then turned to me extending his large hand. "And where are you from, sir?" he asked.

When he heard we were from Canada his eyes welled up as he told us of his many relatives who had emigrated there, to Manitoba years back, especially a sister he was very proud of. I could tell, of course, that he was quite loaded, must have just come from the pub, and that he was lost, in some ways, in a movie only he could see. But that was okay with us. It was wonderful to be in an exchange, to be talking with somebody. In the end, before he finally gave us directions to the pub he'd been sitting in all morning, he had us promising to come down and visit him sometime, meet his wife and see his small farm. He was more shy near the end, less confident than he'd been at the first, but as he disappeared down the path he suddenly turned around to face us as we watched him go, and shouted, once again in full humour, "When you get in the pub be sure to meet Jimmy! He'll have some great stories to tell ya that you can write about later in yer poncy notebook!" What we must have seemed to him then, what privileged world of writers and artists and sabbaticals we must have turned into later on in the re-telling. We watched him go, then turned towards the village where Jimmy waited.

~~~

Neil was ascending the last, long hill into Vernon. He was only ten minutes out. The air was thick with the shifting of winter into spring.

Shelley was out at the pool again, swimming tonight. Her early spring ritual. It got her ready for gardening, made her feel in shape again. That lean black Speedo. Her long legs. Her hair tied back and tucked away into the shiny black cap. Those breasts. Her eyes. And months of Neil ignoring her in a way, taking her for granted.

What if, after all these years, she had become interested in another man? A crush? An infatuation? The simple need for attention, to be reminded of something that marriage removes from people's lives sometimes? Sex? Neil couldn't really be disturbed by any of these things. He'd felt them all himself. He knew what they meant in the larger scheme of things. He knew what they meant in terms of his love for Shelley. So, why couldn't he accept the same logic when it was her feeling those things and not him?

Why did he feel the drop in his gut, the excitement?

Private property. Intimacy.

Safety.

He'd put such energy into protecting the life he'd grown into so unexpectedly, that he couldn't take much chaos. He'd lived through enough chaos as a kid. Dear Old Dad, the prince of chaos. Why was he afraid then? What was she up to? Who was she seeing?

Could Shelley undress herself in the dark with another man? Could she wrap herself around him in that darkness for pure pleasure? A pleasure that required chaos, couldn't be got at in any other way?

Of course she could.

Abruptly, west to east, Vernon spread its lights across the window of the car. All the twinkling lights of the houses on Mission Hill appeared close up, and, in the distance, the shimmering bowl of lights that lay in the geographical cradle that had become Vernon was like a bucket of lights swinging itself between three lakes. Above the distance the lights announced so clearly, was the quiet dark hum of the low, black mountains. It was a scene Neil had never gotten used to or taken for granted. He was from the prairies. He'd grown up with the long view: spotting a town twenty miles down the highway — Innisfail from Red Deer — recognising its lights in the winter darkness. When a long view popped up in the mountains, it was incredible, and he was always grateful for he felt sometimes he could get lost forever in the muscled corridors and sinews of these tight, twisting little valleys. It was another kind of beauty, another kind of perspective. You often couldn't *get* a long view here; you were too closed in. He drove down into the lights. He reminded himself to clean the window in the morning. There was too much smoke from the cigarettes that compounded the glare of the lights at night, and made it difficult to see.

~~~

The pub in Galashiels was packed with late-lunch patrons and, when we walked in, the whole place fell into a hush as we took a small table with three chairs near a window that looked out on the street. The hush relaxed after we ordered a couple of sandwiches and a beer for her, though it was clear that everyone in the pub had registered the fact that I hadn't ordered a beer for myself. Some of the men were a bit edgy about that. It was an eerie feeling for me in England and Scotland sometimes, to sit in pubs not drinking. It was such a ritual in the everyday lives of the men especially, that to be brazen about breaking it, to be making such a spectacle of myself when I could just as easily have avoided the pub and gone to a restaurant where I could have nursed my ruin privately, seemed an act of daring that was not always appreciated, and I knew it. But I loved the pubs. I couldn't resist them. The people in them were, unbeknownst to them of course, my people, and all their great arcing modesty and pride and vulnerability was where I felt most at home, even when I seemed to breaking all the laws of that arc. It was tricky sometimes, and I knew I had to be careful.

"Aw the great fuckin world's a terrible pile of shite!"

We both looked up from our lunches, swivelling our heads to find the voice's source, as did most of the customers seated around us, and there he was suddenly,

JOHN LENT

this man trying to stand up from a table in the far corner of the place. I could see the waitress roll her eyes up to the man standing behind the bar, winking at him.

"Yes, it's a fuckin festerin cesspool at times . . . you get the people and they doan know fer shite what yer up to fer sure ya know . . . I doan know . . . and I doan know . . . but of course I *do* know . . . and all the fuckin' yuppie tourists in the world with their fancy hiking shoes and wee jackets . . . what do *they* know, eh? . . . how *could* they . . . but anyway . . . "

All the while this man in his early sixties with a thick thatch of dark hair thrusting up everywhere around his face, stumbled to his feet and across the bar towards us. He was so drunk he could hardly see, but, as is sometimes the case with seasoned drinkers, just when you thought he'd fall, he'd find his balance and continue. Finally, he was smiling right down at her as she held a sandwich in her hand innocently.

"Aw look at ya, then," he whispered gently, the lines in his face creasing in the smiles he obviously wore most of time, "just look at ya!" And he bent down to kiss her hand, but in the end lost his balance and ended up, face-first, in her lap, laughing and crying simultaneously. I had broken his fall and had jumped up to hold him and get him settled in the empty chair at our table, while she just laughed and then helped him sit down, too. Out of the corner of my eye I could see the barman reach for the phone and dial a number.

"You must be Jimmy," I said, knowing that somehow, in all the twisted wonder of how things work sometimes, I had come up with exactly the right thing to say. The

~82~

people in the pub actually clapped above their laughter. Everything settled.

"How the hell'd you know that?" he asked, trying to look into my eyes, laughing helplessly.

~~~

He was driving down the main route, down the Hospital Hill, when he saw a figure emerge out of the dark of the street: a young man, running, jay-walking across the highway from the grocery store at 16th Avenue, just south of the hospital. The young man was right in front of the car but dressed so darkly, in a long blue winter jacket, that Neil had not seen him.

When Neil came to a complete stop — noting automatically that there was no one behind him, he was safe from that angle — the young man fell forward onto the hood of Neil's car, then backwards as he regained his balance. A plastic bag containing a carton of milk, some jumbo bags of chips, a two-litre bottle of Pepsi, and some brightly wrapped present, opened itself up on the windshield in front of Neil, then closed again and slid, whole, back into the young man's hands which were waiting, extended as in prayer, at the front of the car. The young man stared at Neil through the windshield. Neil stared back. The young man smiled a conspiratorial half-smile at Neil, mostly apologetic, then lurched quickly onto the sidewalk, throwing Neil a grateful wave. Neil gave him thumbs up and proceeded, descending the hill into town. The encounter might have taken seven seconds.

Neil had seen his whole world in the look on the guy's face, an incarnation sent just for him and just on this night. There was a strength in those young eyes, a wariness that humbled everything Neil had been worried about and thinking about as he'd driven into town. It seemed the young man had been able to purchase something for somebody — probably by cashing a cheque that would bounce tomorrow. Even in the guarded look in the young man's eyes Neil had divined some unexpected triumph — this guy was going to show up somewhere with a surprise; he was running home to people who'd be thrilled by his pulling off something unexpected, whatever it was. Neil couldn't account for this narrative appearing suddenly in his mind, and in so much detail. He couldn't account for it, but it was delivered anyway, and especially in one of its corners, a corner that caught Neil off-guard: there had been, built into this young man's look, a modesty, a vulnerability that Neil wanted to protect, nurture, and love forever. It was hard to see that look up close, though, and he revelled in it as the man disappeared into his rear-view mirror in the dark.

~~~

"Up ya go now, Jimmy. That's right. We're goin home now."

Some man from the village, either a cab driver or a friend, had shown up to collect Jimmy and helped him out the door, whispering to him gently, urging him forward. Jimmy was compliant, even cheerful. At the door he turned around and blew her a kiss which she blew back.

As soon as he was gone, three or four customers came to our table and began to tell us about Jimmy. He was famous in Scotland, they said. He was the most famous of all the people in their town and they obviously loved him and were proud of him. He was the best stone mason in all of Scotland, famous for his stone dykes. Before the drink had got hold of him, he'd been summoned up and down the length and breadth of the country to complete the most intricate work in stone. He had the best eye in Scotland for a straight line. Even still, they said, he'd sober up once in a while to take on a difficult job which he'd complete and which would allow him to stay drunk for months. It was sad, they said, what had happened to Jimmy after his parents had died and it was understandable why the drink would take him over in time. They spoke about him with a reverence that was easy to see and feel. "He's an artist," one middle-aged woman whispered to me as she handed the waitress a ten pound note and her bill, "an artist, surely."

~~~

Neil knew his own worries were legitimate and intricate. It wasn't that they weren't real. But as he pulled up to the traffic light at the bottom of the hill and stared across at Earl's Restaurant sitting squat in the Fruit Union Plaza Mall near the government Liquor Store, he understood a scale to things. There was a scale. Money ran the scale. Money created opportunity, privilege, safety.

Of all his worrying, Neil didn't worry about money. He hadn't worried about money for three years, but hadn't realised it until tonight. It was an enormous thing. Maybe it was one of the biggest things in his life for a long time, but he hadn't seen it. He didn't actually *have* any money; he was always broke, waiting to be paid no matter how high he'd ascended on the union scale, but he didn't really have to worry about money. What a huge thing that is, he thought. His father had never experienced it.

The young man's face had carried that worry about money as a natural part of its expression, and it was mixed in with what was also in that look: loss, tenderness, joy, relief and anxiety. Worrying about money was a big part of how all these other things existed, too. A big part.

And it wasn't fair.

Neil pulled into the parking lot in front of Earl's. He couldn't drive. He was shaking in the darkness.

No one should have to live *that* worried, *all* the time. Neil had never forgotten what that worry was like, nor the long perspective you had to cultivate in order to survive it. It had nothing to do with brains, talent, work.

He opened the car door and threw up into the night noises he could hear now in front of Earl's. He thought of an interview he'd read with Studs Terkel in the back of one of Shelley's fashion magazines. When asked what he'd like to come back as, Terkel said he'd like to return as a doorman at a ritzy hotel in Chicago where he could harangue rich people and remind them of their responsibilities.

Neil could hear a group of high-school students leaving Earl's. They were discussing renting a stretch-limo for their grad later in the spring.

"They come right to your house and pick you up later, too."

"Cool."

"And it's only $500 for the night."

"Awesome."

Neil closed the door and stared out the window as the group of students faded behind him and got into a Nissan Pathfinder.

~·~·~

Before Jimmy had been escorted out of the pub he'd regaled her with bright, outrageous stories of his life, his loves. He paced them with questions about where we were from and what we did, fascinated especially by her painting, wary of my writing. I mostly listened. But near the end, for whatever strange reason, Jimmy began to stare into my eyes, looking for something, wanting some kind of comfort, I thought. Eventually he seized both my hands and sang me a Scottish lament in Gaelic. He began sobbing deeply at the end of his singing, still holding my hands fiercely. Finally, he opened his eyes and through his tears said to me, "I know you're fucked up boy . . . livin in yer head as much as you do with all that fuckin sorrow . . . but listen to me . . . *no*, listen now . . . " And he leaned so close to me, still clutching my hands, that our faces were practically touching, "You're goan ta be all right . . . just trust me . . . I know all about these things."

~·~·~

Neil walked around to the trunk of the car and used an old T-shirt to wipe off his face and clean himself up. Shelley would be back from her swimming by now. The house would be warm and soft in the late evening, full of their talking and jokes. Maybe he'd convince her to go for a walk. Maybe they'd put on some favourite old music, he'd pour them a drink, and they'd make love.

"Do you need some help? You all right man?

Startled, Neil looked up from the T-shirt.

The young man he'd hit just five minutes ago was still holding the bag of stuff from the store, though he was also holding a six-pack of Kokanee he must have just bought in the Liquor Store.

"God, I sure hope you weren't hurt up there," Neil said.

"Christ no, man. Shit, don't worry about it. It was my fault for fuck's sake . . . running across the street from the store like that. Shit!"

"I should have seen you," Neil said, "I'm sorry."

"You *couldn't* have seen me in that dark, man. Look at me! I'm just fine. It's *you* we should be worrying about."

BRIDGE

IT WAS TWO IN THE MORNING and the house was as quiet as it got in the middle of the night: the fridge clicking on from time to time, the almost inaudible whir of Rick's computer in the office off the living room, the flick of the spoon he was using to stir his last cup of coffee before he, too, went to bed. Then he heard it above these noises: a soft, whimpering sigh from the bedroom where she was sleeping. She was lying there, turning over on her side maybe, pulling the flannel up closer, tucking it under her chin with her hand, lost in a dream, frightened. He stood still, staring out into the charcoal heat of the late summer night, laying his spoon down on the arborite, taking a strip of Scott Towel off the dispenser and wiping the area around his coffee cup from side to side, seeing his own reflection staring back at him through the glass in the window, and he thought his heart would break.

She was in the fourth month of a serious flare. She was taking so many pills she had to keep them regimented in a small, plastic pill dispenser that divided each day up into four compartments. The high doses of prednisone had worn her down. Her face had bloated out into a face she couldn't recognise, and she'd put on so much weight she had to wear different clothes. The pills had manipulated her emotions, too, causing an initial, two-month euphoria that collapsed, in time, into an equally artificial but real depression, a low that dragged her down into herself and all the defeats she sensed the lupus created for her. The prednisone caused tremors, weakening of muscles, and, in time, a tiredness that could scarcely be borne, no matter how tough she was. This was the fifth serious lupus flare she'd had in twenty-four years, and they'd just discovered it had been caused accidentally. This knowledge was just another thing in a long list of things they were dealing with. Rick couldn't believe it sometimes, how much was being asked of her in this. He couldn't believe it, but it was true. And though he knew as well as she did that the prednisone was saving her kidneys, he also knew that its side-effects took her away for a time, removed her, no matter how much they tried to kid and tease one another. Hearing her sigh surface in the middle of the night was this distance between them, and he felt sometimes that he couldn't breach it.

Hearing it carried him far into a larger longing that did him in anyway, and was as difficult as sitting somewhere above the earth, high above it, and staring out at the hard-surfaced world itself and accepting every damn thing in it.

How could there be such aches in our lives, such childlike fears of hurt coming down howling like an Old Testament wind?

The lawyers had been out in full force the morning before, looking for redemption, and finding it in the shiny, chrome, bulbous surfaces of cars, boats, toasters, all the stuff from the early fifties they'd first seen as children and had rejected in their teens only to come back and bow down before them now in their early fifties, thirty years later.

Yes, the lawyers, accountants, the managers, the super-
intendents, all the guys he'd known as a kid who'd been so
obviously ambitious, were now softening at the edges,
seeking redemption in their mid-lives, trying to find more
gentle versions of themselves sitting in small cafes, or in
intimate jazz clubs late at night, or seated demurely in
front of subtle chamber orchestras playing to small rooms
of classical *afficionados*, or even, often a last resort, at
poetry readings in art gallery basements. They were trying
to make up for all the dominance that had fed them for so
long, but didn't fill them up anymore, and they were
seeking it in the last refuge: art, the real heroin of culture.
Having avoided the depth of it all their lives, they were
now snuggling up to it, suckling on its horny, hairy tit in
their mature years, eyes bugging out in a need so obvious
it hurt to look at them. The fact of the matter was they
were good people, hard-working people — even innocent
in their own ways — and Rick knew they longed for
something that had been given as a gift to him. He'd been
the lucky one. He couldn't afford to feel superior or angry
though he was still tempted sometimes. He knew they'd
missed out on something vast. They wanted to uncover
the secrets that had been concealed from them by the way
they'd lived their lives. It was a spectacle, and no laughing
matter. "I've always thought about writing something
myself," some of these people would confess to him, eyes
welling up in gradations of sensitivity, "how do you go
about finding a publisher anyway?"

Rick leaned forward over the sink, splaying his fingers
on the blue arborite to the left and right of the tarnished
stainless steel. He could see what was behind him in the
kitchen reflected in the glass. The fridge clicked on again.

He'd have to have it checked soon. They'd bought it new when they'd moved into their first house, but that had been fifteen years ago. He'd always thought of it as a brand new appliance. It was the same with the dryer. He'd been so innocent from that point of view, and Jennifer was just as bad. They didn't buy a lot of things, and when they did it was a big deal. They had relatives who bought things all the time and who looked at the two of them, shaking their heads in disbelief. "You guys need a microwave!" Or, "Why don't you just break down and get a dishwasher for Christ's sake! It's the twenty-first century now. You've got a good job!"

Rick smiled to himself and could see it reflected in the dark glass. A car drove down the lane, heading for 26th Street. The fridge clicked off into silence. He could hear Jennifer sigh again, louder this time. He went in and stood beside her, then knelt down on the floor, one hand gripping the pine railing at the side of the bed, the other brushing her forehead. "Hi" he whispered to her, "everything's fine."

"Am I asleep?" she smiled at him through the heavy slits of her eyes.

"Yeah," he said.

"Are you coming to bed?"

"In a while," he said. He brushed her forehead again. "Just sleep."

When he was eighteen, in 1966, he'd visited his mother in the General Hospital in Edmonton. She'd gotten seriously ill with a ruptured appendix and, while she was in for that, the doctors had decided to remove her teeth. She was only forty-four when this happened, Rick realised, six years younger than he was now. She'd had too many children, the doctors said, and a serious calcium deficiency was beginning to break her system down. He'd sat there in his eighteen-year-old body, thinking his eighteen-year-old thoughts, and had stared at his mother, her dropped jaw, the vacuum suddenly in her toothless face that had always seemed so beautiful to him. She was still coming out of the anaesthetic, and he held her hand as he sat there, something he would never have done if she'd been awake, something they were both too shy to do.

"Hi dear," she'd whispered to him eventually, without opening her eyes. The fingers of her hand re-gripped and squeezed his hand. "Are you there, sitting beside me?"

"Yes I am," he said, squeezing her fingers back, wondering who it was she thought she was talking to.

He had his father, Charles, pinned on the linoleum floor of the kitchen. Rick's hands were spread out, left to right, so he could hold his father's wrists beneath him. Rick's knees and the weight of his torso on his father's chest were enough to insure nothing more could happen. His father was laughing up into his face, twisting his torso beneath Rick's. "You'll thank me for this some day, boy!" Rick was fifteen. He couldn't stand it when, in the middle of one of these fights about his father's drinking, his father would laugh at him like this. So superior, all-knowing. "Maybe so," was all Rick could whisper back through his clenched teeth. "I don't care about that."

In the periphery of his vision he could sense his brother and sister behind him somewhere, and his mother's voice. "Come on now, you two! Really, for pity's sake!" He could hear his younger brother, Neil, begin to cry, frightened.

They had begun their fight on the second-floor landing, and had slipped and rolled down all the stairs, then landed in a heap on the kitchen floor. Finally, Rick had flipped his father off and thrown him down, flat on the floor. Quickly, he'd leapt up, then onto his father, pinning him so his father was looking directly up into his eyes. As he'd flipped his father over, he'd heard him sigh when one of Rick's knees had caught a rib in his chest. "Oh!" his father had whimpered to himself, his eyes closing briefly.

Rick walked into the living room, put on a small, low light against the bookshelves, and leaned back into the couch, stretching his legs. He heard her voice call out something in a dream, then go completely quiet. Having her sick like this seemed so unfair to him that he carried his anger at it out and over into everything else in his life. He always knew when they were at this point in a flare because he could hear his own voice grinding away, whining, so cynical and sarcastic, and saw how he'd allowed a big train of dark, accusatory thoughts to rumble down into his consciousness and collect there, like a yard of freight sitting waiting for engines to haul it away. And even though he knew this anger was simple substitution, he was still capable of wallowing in it. It could feel good, make him laugh even. Petty, he knew, but in its own way, satisfying.

Dignity. Safety. It was hard to have one without the other. That's why he'd get so mad at the safe ones, people his age who not only expected safety, but wouldn't know what it was like not to feel it. They annoyed him when he felt like this. Their breezy lack of gratitude betrayed an indifference towards people who didn't feel safety, who were always *at the mercy*, and the way the safe ones judged this second group was appalling. They didn't have a clue. These people were often running things, too, especially in these smaller cities. Or, on the other hand, in the bigger places, people like them, the go-getters on a mission, might even imagine themselves rising up, as in some medieval painting of a florid ascension into heaven! Yes, they might even imagine themselves getting elected and running the country! Sometimes, they actually *were* elected for short periods of time until they got a chance to reveal their own limitations — some sheep discovered in a back closet, some minor but twisted indiscretion. And, if that weren't bad enough, when any of these safe ones actually looked inward and sensed something unfulfilled, they'd try for the quick fix — the McDonald's approach, anything money could buy — fitness clubs, symphony societies, book clubs, art gallery boards, jazz clubs, maybe a creative writing class one night a week. Not having taken any risks themselves in order to have the very safety that had turned them into these kinds of people, they now wanted to short-cut the risks by purchasing the illusion of them in their early fifties so they could feel, in the long run, that they had everything. And sometimes they did. "Man!" Rick whispered to himself, "it's getting bad out there for me. I can't *think* like this. I can't *be* this mad."

As an antidote, he'd find himself laughing helplessly with his students, and he'd think automatically of his father, how funny he'd been, how his sense of humour would carry them through any crisis, big or small. It was the other side of things with his father. "Those bastards!" his father would yell, indicating a very large group of nameless "thems" who ran everything, who possessed all the power to get at safety of any kind. "Those bastards are *pathetic!* They actually think *we've* got it rough. If they only knew!" And he'd throw his head back, cackling through no teeth because he'd never put them in, laughing in a superior, hermetic knowledge it had taken Rick most of his life to find. "Those bastards!" Even now, in the dark quiet of the living room, in the middle of Jennifer's flare, in the middle of the night, Rick had to smile, then laugh. "Don't tell your mother," his father would often add dramatically when he was especially loaded. Rick was never sure what it was he was supposed to protect his mother from: his father's drunkenness or his father's knowledge.

Rick was standing in the arrivals section of The Vancouver International Airport. He was watching the arrival stairs carefully, looking for Jennifer. He'd even bought a new shirt and a new pair of jeans for the occasion. Finally, he spotted her gliding down the escalator behind a rotund, sedate businessman in his early fifties. She was wearing a long, thin cotton dress that was open-necked and open-sleeved, and had a tiny burgundy flower pattern set against a solid but soft cream. The dress was suspended, seemingly weightless, hanging from two thin threads from her tanned brown shoulders. Her hair was a riot of auburn lustre pulled back from her forehead and descending down her back in a French braid. When she saw him, her eyes lit up in a broad smile and he could see her blush a deep crimson. The man waiting next to him whispered, "Who's that in that white dress? She looks like a movie star or something!" Jennifer had flown down from Nelson to stay with him for the weekend. It was 1975, their first time apart and the first reunion in a strange, new place. She was blushing because she knew what they'd be doing all weekend. His hands trembled as he reached out to hold her, lift her up off the shiny, tiled floor. He could feel her small breasts through the fabric of his shirt and her dress. He could smell the richness of her hair. It smelled of the sweetness of earth and time, the smell of now. How could two people be so lucky, he wondered, so safe?

"Bastards!"

She sat on the bed sobbing, trying, every now and then, to put it into words. All he could do was hold her, listen quietly to her heaving sighs and sobs, and keep holding her, telling her it was going to be okay, staring at his shoes on the floor, not really believing his own words, feeling afraid, just as afraid as she was probably. They'd been together for ten years, and she was in her second lupus flare. She'd spent the last two months struggling with the possibility of having a baby. They were staying overnight in a small room in the Sylvia Hotel in Vancouver. He could hear the night traffic through the partly opened window. He could hear people walking and laughing down below on the sidewalks and lawns of English Bay in the soft summer dusk. Rick and Jennifer had just returned from seeing her kidney specialist about it, and he'd confirmed what they'd both suspected. Rick had known what the answer would be: a pregnancy was too risky; there were too many complications, too much danger. Finally, he could sense her tiring and he laid her down into the sheets and pulled them up over her body. He turned the small lamp out on the side of the bed and sat next to her, holding her hand until he knew she was asleep and wouldn't wake up startled, remembering everything.

He walked over to the window, lit up a smoke, and stared down into the city. There were people moving around down there, still honking horns, going places. He looked northwest to the tall dark trees hovering over the deep greens of Stanley Park, and up into the mountains he could see rising above them on the North Shore. She sighed once and he turned his face back into the room, alert. But she was asleep again, so he looked up into the sky, its thick, navy blue spotted with winking stars and constellations.

Rick and Jennifer left their flat in Edinburgh and drove the car north, across The Firth, away from all the dark stone and red and blue enamelled chaos of downtown Edinburgh, up the smooth, four-lane grey highway past Perth, to the small village of Crieff. They explored the town, the higgledy-piggledy shops and restaurants on its main street, then ascended the long walk, up through the scrub grass and heather, above the snowline and the pines, to the crest of The Knock of Crieff.

If they looked south, the lowlands receded into thin mists miles away, mists spotted by flourishes of trees and buildings which they knew were towns and cities. This vista stretching south was covered in a sheen of bright green only broken by villages and factories. If they looked north, the hills not only lost the sheen, but began to rise and tower in variations of brown and, in time, to the blinding bright whites of full snow. Jennifer and Rick were standing on the cusp of Scotland on The Knock of Crieff.

It was the spot where the Lowlands and the Highlands met one another. They'd read enough Scottish history to feel the weight of that chafing, the blood of it.

They sat on a green steel bench in the snow and ate the cheese sandwiches they'd made back in their flat in Edinburgh. The mid-afternoon silences were broken only by birds and the wind whistling high through the tops of the trees below them. They felt lucky, sitting there, holding hands, thinking of time and place and blood. It was as if they were sitting at the top of the world, overseeing it.

They heard the sighing everywhere, the wonder, the laughter.

The sun was just catching the top of the far blue hills that rose above the Bella Vista orchards across the pastel downtown buildings on the other side of the valley. Rick realised he'd been sitting on the couch all this time, mulling things over, staying up all night accidentally. It was so elemental, he laughed, to be rescued by the sun like this. Man!

In a few minutes he'd put on a pot of coffee. Then, in half an hour, he could get CBC radio from Kelowna. He heard a voice, a sigh, and started up from the couch until he realised it was himself he'd heard, a groan, his own soft sigh. He had to smile. You just had to dive in head-first. Or walk across these contradictions, some New Testament hero.

THE MOST OBVIOUS THINGS

Passions of rain, or moods in falling snow,
Grievings in loneliness, or unsubdued
Elations when the forest blooms; gusty
Emotions on wet roads on autumn nights;
                    — Wallace Stevens, *"Sunday Morning"*

"YOU AGONISE ENDLESSLY OVER THE MOST OBVIOUS THINGS. It's incredible! The rest of us already *know* all this. It's not new. What can you be thinking of? It's a waste of time."

"Whatever you say, Shelley."

"Don't."

"Don't what?"

"Get the last fucking sarcastic word in is *what.*"

"I won't."

"Why?"

"Because *you* will."

"No!"

"As usual."

"I hate this."

"I know."

"You know everything."

"I wish."

"You're sick!"

He let her have it. He shut up.

~~~

Everything about the room was pre-packaged, efficient. Cold, but safe. The hotel sat right smack dab in the middle of the main street of Penticton, cut off, sealed up, but home, too. North America. What an eerie landscape.

He was there for two days to attend a short provincial conference. Because Neil worked in Kelowna, he'd done the organising, all the usual but endlessly trivial things that needed to be set up in advance.

It was midnight on the Friday night. Everyone attending had arrived safely in the late afternoon by car or plane and had settled into the hotel. Most of them had gone out for supper at Theo's, and had decided to go to bed early to survive the all-day meeting on Saturday in the hotel's boardroom. Neil's retiring early was caused only in part by these considerations. Normally, he was one of the rambunctious ones, but this year he couldn't rise above what was happening at home. He didn't know what was going on anymore, and that kind of endlessly improvised chaos prevented him from having any fun. He sat on the edge of the queen-sized bed and flicked on the VCR. The tape he'd rented was sitting on the fake oak desk to the right of the TV. He eyed it and flushed with a ludicrous sense of embarrassment. *Dangerous Debutantes, Number 42.*

~~~

"You're just so drawn into yourself." Shelley turned away and he could see her profile against the picture window in the living room. She was indistinct, as if abstracted, once

removed because of the brightness of the light through
the window behind her, but her voice was a razor against
his skin: refined, tempered, dangerous.

On the street in front of the hedge a young family
strolled by in slow motion. A two-year old girl doddled
behind her father, their hands joined, while the mother
pushed a small, blue stroller in which the youngest child
sat trussed up in linens and lace, a white bonnet glistening
against the grey of the asphalt and the emerald green of
the lawn. "I know," Neil said, "I can't help it. It's just me.
It's what happens to me."

"But don't you see?" she said, still facing the street, still
in profile, "you ruin so many things. You can't have fun.
You actually have to *think* about having fun. You have to
figure it out."

"Does it seem that way to you?"

"How can you even ask the *question*?"

"Well, I'm asking it anyway."

"Of *course*, it seems that way to me. That's what I'm
trying to *say!*"

He inhaled her beauty, so curled in on itself, a body
that was tensed against him, at least against what he'd
become to her. She was floating in the perfect green
pastoral of the window — the young family flickering out
of eyesight now, past the bright daffodils in front of the
hedge, beyond the forsythia which was an even brighter
yellow against the sky, past Shelley herself, blooming right
in front of him — and he felt a sweet sadness overtake
him, so much so he wasn't sure which part to savour: the
obvious pain caused by his knowledge that something was
over between them for good this time, or the concealed

pleasure of simply savouring her in the present, breathing her in, feeling her closeness in his life, her love, her body.

Her body signalled something to him beneath these thoughts, something frightened of itself, that blanched, paused, then disappeared, not wanting to be brought out into the open just yet. Her body. Christ! "Anyway, I don't know why it's *me* we're belabouring here," Neil said suddenly, "all *my* fuck-ups, when it's *you* that's caused this to come apart."

"You can't be serious?" she said, turning her face to him, a dark oval against the sun.

~~~

"It has to do with story," Neil said finally, "the weight of how they want to entertain themselves, what they want to *say* about their lives."

Frank leaned back in his chair and brushed a hand through his thick, black hair. "But how do you tackle the issue of the difference between the markets for those stories, how we, like it or not, brush up against that issue all the time?" Frank asked him.

"I've tried lots of things," Neil said, grinning. "I know it's a matter of audience, but I myself am such a poor judge of that. I'm the last one to know."

"Why's that?" Sheila asked. "You've done well."

"Oh, I know," Neil said. "And I'm pleased by that. *Really.* The small presses allow someone like me to do what I want to do, write what I want to write. But when anyone asks me about blockbuster bestsellers I bog down in what seems obvious to me. And it's the same in music, painting, architecture, films, you name it . . . "

"What's so obvious?" Frank asked.

JOHN LENT

"Well, I'm afraid to say it now," Neil said, suddenly wary. "I'm worried not only that it's *not* obvious, after all, but that I'm really out to lunch. But I'll say it anyway. The *real* audience, and the *real* bucks even, I suspect, are *not* in what we see as that commercial sector anyway. That's not where the money is, even, *or* the buzz for that matter. That market, the commercial market, is too fast. The *real* market, the *real* money even, the real *buzz* is exactly where we're pushing these students, young or old: depth, quality, complexity. I believe that. I *still* believe it. I'd believe it if I was teaching music. I'd believe it if I was teaching painting."

~~~

A young couple walked nervously through the doorway of a generic hotel room somewhere in North America. All the trimwork was oak veneer and there was a pastel neutrality to the setting: a pale blue bedspread, a slightly abstract painting of red and pink flowers above it, and a plum-coloured easy-chair placed next to the bed on the mauve, wall-to-wall standard rug. It was so like the room Neil himself was sitting in that he almost laughed out loud.

A camera followed the couple as the young woman positioned herself self-consciously on the edge of the bed and the young man sat in the plum chair behind her. They faced the camera, and both faces were open, nervous, and, you could sense, excited. One of the young woman's hands fingered the fabric of the blue bedspread while the young man adjusted the cuffs of his jeans over his brown shoes. They were in their early twenties.

The soft voice of the narrator and director talked to them from somewhere behind the camera and, in a few minutes, the couple began to relax.

What kind of couple would *do* this? Neil wondered, but couldn't take his eyes off them.

"Melissa, tell the folks out there why you and Dave came here. Let's start there, now that we're relaxed and having fun."

Melissa grinned nervously into the camera and flicked her eyes back to Dave's, opening hers widely in an exaggerated question, wondering, Neil guessed, what to say. Dave just nodded at her and adjusted his cuffs again.

"Well, Mr. Smith . . . "

Oh, for God's sake! You're gonna see a lot more of me later on, my friend. You gotta call me Ted. Ted, Ted, Ted! *Everybody* calls me Ted."

"Well, Ted . . . "

"*There ya go*! Doesn't that feel better? Ted, Ted, Ted!"

"Ted, Ted, Ted," and she laughed a genuine laugh and then a smile stretched across her face.

Melissa was pretty in a cute, girl-next-door way. She wore a dark blue, tweed sportscoat over a white cotton blouse with its collar turned up. The blouse was tucked into fresh blue jeans and small black loafers, and her whole look was crisp, fresh, 'preppie.' She had long, slim legs that kept shifting as she talked. Her hair was black, cut in a page-boy bob that, along with the stylish grannie-glasses perched on her small, turned-up nose, enhanced her perkiness.

"You haven't answered my question yet," Ted whined, exaggerating a teasing quality in his voice. "You gotta talk

to old Ted. That's how the folks out there get to know
you!"

"Well, Ted," Melissa said, staring straight into the
camera now, shy but smiling, "we're not exactly sure."

"Not exactly *sure*? *Did you hear that folks*? Not exactly
sure!"

"Well," Melissa smiled, "we saw your ad and we'd
watched some of your videos, and, I don't
know . . . *David!*" She laughed and slapped David on his
knees, looking at him hopefully, her eyebrows raised, "*you
tell him!*"

"You're doing fine," David said. "just keep going."

"You're doing great, darling," Ted said.

"Well, I don't know. Coming here sounded exciting
and we sent you some photos and a letter and you phoned
us back and *here we are!*"

"And you've never done this before?"

"What do you mean, *this*?" Melissa asked.

"Well, you've never had sex on camera before?"

Melissa blurted, blushing, "*No!*"

"Have you two ever swung?"

This time David answered, "No. Never." Melissa looked
over at him, smiling.

"So, you two innocents have just come here out of the
blue to do all this?"

"All *what?*" Melissa asked.

"Well, we'll see later folks," Ted laughed, "*we'll see.*"

"What do you mean?" Melissa asked.

"Are you two going to have sex in front of the camera?"
Ted asked.

"Yes," Melissa answered.

"Okay. Good. That's a start. Now, Melissa, have you ever had sex with more than one guy at the same time?"

"No."

"Do you want to?"

"I don't know. Maybe. It depends."

"Depends on what?"

"I don't know."

"Okay, okay, okay. Don't worry about it. Have you slept with other guys since you married David?"

"No."

"No?"

"*Of course*, no!"

"So how's he gonna feel if my weird friend Jack starts fucking you, right here, on camera?"

"I don't know."

"Does it excite you?"

"A bit."

"I'm not gonna mind," David said. "I'm okay with it."

"All right. Let's talk to *you* then. You're okay with this?"

"Yes."

"Why?"

"I don't know. It's exciting, I guess." David looked over at Melissa and she smiled back. "I don't know. She's so beautiful. I'm so proud of her. It'd turn me on in a weird way."

"But you're not sure."

"In the sense that I don't know 'cause it's never happened?"

"Yeah."

"No, I'm not sure. But I think I'm okay."

"Okay, you two. Let's get started!"

~~~

The three of them were sitting in the lounge of The Delta Inn. The room was calculated in its hushed elegance, its soft lighting, the dull brass and mahogany fixtures, and forest-green, plush chairs. The floor-to-ceiling windows overlooked Okanagan Lake so no matter where you were seated you could catch the twinkling of house lights and marinas along the north shore, to Naramata on the east side, and Summerland on the west. He had suggested they come here after their all-day meeting and they were into it now, the conference over. He knew he was getting loaded, and it felt good. Frank and Sheila were, too. He was with two good old friends and it felt right. He protected himself by sticking to beer and avoiding scotch.

"You keep harping about the wrong audience, Neil. You sound so pissed off when you bring it up. What's *that* all about?" Frank asked him.

"Yeah, Neil," Sheila whispered in a parody of some west-coast new-age therapist with crystals, "share it with us; let it all out; *embrace* your pain!"

Neil looked at them ruefully, a parody himself now he knew, and laughed. "I know how mad I sound sometimes, but it's such an obvious class thing in me that I can't see it myself. It's so obvious, it's invisible. If I make it visible, it'll be embarrassing. I promise you."

"We can handle it," Frank said.

"Yes. Come on now," Sheila said, "let it out."

"I *do* think about it now and then. I see it up close because Kelowna's so small, you know? Sometimes it's brutal. The wrong audience, all my life. *You* know . . . who's going to pay attention to the stuff I write or teach? Sometimes — and I know in advance how unfair and small this is going to sound — *I warned you* — but sometimes I know it's simply a large group of bored, listless yuppies looking for culture in their late forties, early fifties after having made various fortunes, big or small."

"But why are you *mad* about that?" Frank asked.

"I know what it sounds like," Neil said, "why all this bitterness . . . envy even?" He sighed, self-mockingly. "To be honest, it isn't bitterness *or* envy. It's something else. I've never felt hard-done-by. And I certainly don't want their lives or, especially, their possessions. I just get mad at *them*."

"'Us' and 'Them', eh?" Sheila asked him, ordering another glass of white wine for herself. "You?"

"All around," Neil motioned to the waitress. "This one's on me."

"Hey!" Frank said.

"No problem," Neil waved all objections away and winked beneath the low lights of the soft, charcoal room. He felt separate for a second, watching himself. It was that old Connelly thing happening, an inheritance. He shook his head to clear it as their drinks arrived. "I know, Sheila," he said, "I know what you mean. *Us and Them.* And to be honest, I wish I didn't feel so small about it."

"Well," she said, "you know . . . you don't want it to be *too* simplistic."

"I know," Neil said, "but sometimes I fear we allow the opposite too much and don't say anything about these things because we grant them too much complexity when, in fact, they might *be* so fucking simple we can't even see them."

"Fair enough."

"I just get mad at them. And though my anger is directed at the immediate, trivial spectacle of their good fortune — their endless self-congratulation, exercising, running of marathons, jogging down west coast fucking trails . . . whatever . . . competing with one another in their shiny, wee lycra outfits — I know it's embedded much farther back in my own life. Back in Edmonton when I was a kid. It's probably *that* simple and pathetic. Back when I realised, at ten or twelve, that I would always be at the mercy of *and* patronised by this useless group of privileged souls who were innocent, gullible, cautious, greedy, but whose innocence, gullibility, caution and greed depended upon people like *me* to do their dirty work for them for the rest of our lives on the planet. And whose innocence, gullibility, caution and greed were no longer *forgivable*."

"It's just so general," Sheila said.

"Yeah, I know. I know. And beneath it all — don't you see — is this sense of worthlessness in *me* that causes all this suspicion and anger. I know it's there."

"That's just plain *stupid*!" Frank said.

"It doesn't matter! It doesn't *matter* that it's stupid. It's still *there*. There's no satisfaction in any of this," Neil said, looking at each of them. "I'm not proud of this anger. It's just that sometimes I feel I'm stuck in it, that's all. It's hard to get out of. And you can get mad about that sometimes. It explains me a bit, even to *myself*. You know?"

~~~

"I just don't know if I have what it *takes* to get through all this with you." Shelley was staring not at him but at the green afternoon through the window, the blue of the sky, the abundance of texture wrapping their house up in a real world that had never seemed so far away to Neil as it did right then. And though there was a cagey side to him that could continue this conversation — where he knew with certainty it was going to go — a side so flip, sardonic, and cunning that could survive all this in certain ways, there was another self that was beyond panic, stunned, in complete disbelief, and which registered itself physically in his chest, in the beating of his heart. He'd have to be careful.

He pretended to stifle a yawn, then said back to her, "Do whatever you want, Shelley. Or don't do it. *Whatever.* You decide. I'm tired of it all in advance, too. You're not the only one."

"Is that all you have to say?"

"I could ask the same of *you* for Christ's sake! In fact, I will. *Is that all you have to say?*"

"What do you mean?"

"What do you *think* I mean?"

"But we're talking about *you* here, not *me!*"

"*Hello?*"

"What are you trying to *do* Neil?"

"Not let you off the hook for starters . . . "

"Fuck!"

" . . . which would be easy for me to do considering . . . "

"Fuck!"

" . . . that's what I've been doing all my fucking life . . . "

"What? *What* have you been doing all your fucking life, Neil?"

" . . . "

"*Tell me Neil!* You might as well say it. Put it into words. *You're good with words.*"

"*Making it fucking easy for everybody but me* is what. And you *knew* that about me. You *knew* precisely how fucked up I am in that department, and *why* even, and you *still* did what you did, didn't you?"

"I don't know what you're talking about now."

"Oh, come *off* it. You know *exactly* what I'm talking about. Don't even *try* to pretend."

"I'm not pretending."

"You slept with Colin knowing full well how abandoned I'd feel about it, and how hard I'd try to make it easy for you to just go on like before like I was some kind of infinitely generous, ridiculously empathetic, long-suffering fucking martyr of a shit-stuffed Catholic fucking *priest* is *what*!"

"It's all about you, isn't it?"

"Well, of *course* it is, stupid! I'm all I have and I feel like I just disappeared. Of *course* it is!"

"Don't call me stupid, asshole!"

"Oh . . . now we're going to argue about *that*! Everyone else can get mad in this world except me, apparently. You can call me whatever you want. I can't call you anything."

"That's not what I meant!"

"Yes, it *is* what you meant! It's *exactly* what you meant! And it's *true*, too. And I don't know *why* it's true. But I can't express my anger. Nobody will listen. I'm written off. And everybody says — *you* say it all the time for God's sake — *Neil, you should just blow up sometimes, like everybody else. You shouldn't pretend to be so nice, so understanding all the time. You should let some of that anger out.* Yeah, sure. And whenever I *do*, like now, this morning, I end up by myself. Everyone runs away. Everyone thinks I'm crazy. King Lear on the fucking heath. Somehow *I've* screwed up, I've crossed some magic fucking line I'm not supposed to cross, and when I *get* there, wherever this anger leads me, I always end up standing there alone, feeling badly, feeling guilty and ashamed. Everyone else gets to blow it out their fucking arseholes and lick their lips afterwards, satisfied, exorcised. Fuck!"

"What are we going to *do* then?"

"See?"

"See *what?*"

"You've already gone!"

"What are you *talking* about?"

"I can tell from your tone. You've already gone. You're just being polite now."

"Aw, for *fuck's* sake Neil! How complicated do you want everything to *be?*"

"Just as fucking complicated as it actually *is*, is all."

~~~

The camera zoomed in on Melissa's face. Neil could see how nervous she was. She wasn't acting. And yet, obviously, she wanted to be there. But *why* would she want to be there? he wondered. He kept looking at her eyes as they looked earnestly back into the camera, blinking.

"What do you want me to do now?" she asked the camera.

"Why don't you let us see this body your husband keeps raving about?"

Melissa looked sideways, finding her husband's eyes off camera now, following them to another spot in the room.

It was going to be her show now. She sighed, smiled, and as the camera pulled back, stood up beside the bed. Neil could see she'd made her decision. "Well, all right," she said as she stood, her hands on her hips, "here goes."

Neil sat, transfixed, and watched as this lovely young woman began to remove her clothing, item by item. Why would she *do* this, he kept wondering, mesmerised.

She pulled her white blouse out of her blue jeans and began unbuttoning it from top to bottom. When she was finished with the last button, she shrugged and the blouse eased itself off her arms. She hesitated, staring into the camera, confused, just long enough for Ted's voice to announce, softly, no joking, "You can stop whenever you like you know . . . "

"I know."

"You don't have to do anything you don't want to do . . . "

"I know," she said, and smiled shyly back at the camera. She unbuttoned the clasp on her jeans, drew the zipper down, and removed her jeans. When she faced the camera again she was naked except for her matching bra and tiny, thong-like panties. Again she paused and smiled at the camera, then drew her arms out behind herself, leaned forward slightly, and began to remove her bra, letting it drop onto the floor.

"God, look at those breasts!" Ted said behind the camera and zoomed in on them. A hand emerged in front of the camera, extended, grotesque, "Do you mind if I touch one of them?"

Melissa looked away, found her husband's eyes, then said, "Sure."

The extended hand touched her left breast, tweaking its nipple gently, then withdrew. "We've got a live one here, folks," Ted's voice announced, "you've got beautiful breasts!"

"Thank you!" Melissa whispered modestly, trying to be playful, too.

The camera pulled back to catch all of her standing there and she leaned forward toward the camera suddenly and removed her panties, shook them off of the last ankle, then stood erect again, her hands on her hips, her smile directed right at Ted.

"Mercy!" Ted announced.

~~~

"Well, for example," Neil said, into it now, half-loaded and loving it, "did either of you see that Italian flick, *Bread and Tulips?*"

"Yeah, I did," said Frank.

"*Me too, me too!*" said Sheila.

"Okay. Well that's something then. We're all on the same page. Right?"

"You betcha!"

"Yes, *sir!*" Sheila vamped her eyes at Neil playfully, a parody of seduction.

"*Well, there ya go, lads and lassies!*" Neil announced in his best Scottish brogue, "*I'll be restin' ma case then!*"

"And how's that?" Frank asked.

"Yeah?" Sheila said.

"I don't know . . . " Neil said, then grinned at both of them, laughing hysterically at the prospect of him suddenly not knowing why he'd just said what he'd said.

Then he remembered. "Oh, *I* know," he announced dramatically, "*I* remember now, lads."

"Thanks," Sheila said, dryly.

"Present company 'xcepted, Ma'am," Neil replied. Now he was John Wayne.

"Go *on* for Christ's sake!" Sheila yelled at him.

"Well it was so fuckin' *beau-ti-ful!*" said Neil.

"It was," said Frank.

"Very sweet," said Sheila.

"No, it was so fuckin' *beau-ti-ful!*" Neil shouted at both of them. "Just to fuckin' *point* at that kind of joy, that kind of fun. Man!"

"Wasn't Bruno Ganz great?" asked Sheila, already laughing in anticipation.

"God, yeah!" Neil shouted, too loud for the lounge, then, too melodramatically soft, "standing on the chair with the fuckin' noose around his neck, your typical cheery Icelander, wracked with guilt! *God!*"

"And the look on his face at the end?" Frank blurted out, "when he's crooning away in the final scene?"

"Oh God, yeah!" Neil answered, hardly able to speak through his own contagious laughter, "that whole last scene . . . even including the little weasel that was ripping off the detective for the hotel!"

"That's right!" Sheila shouted, "I *knew* it was him. I *knew* it!"

"God!" said Neil.

"No kidding," said Frank.

"Jeez," said Sheila.

"I'd like to write something as funny as that," Neil sighed, the lounge abruptly quiet after all the laughter, "as political." Neil looked up at his two friends who were quiet now, too. "That's what I was trying to get at earlier," he said, "to be able to catch that kind of humour and play it back against everything else that makes us so serious, so anal, so competitive. It's crazy, isn't it? There are enough of these kinds of movies like *Bread And Tulips* — *The Full Monty, New Waterford Girl, Brassed Off, The Snapper, The Van, Waking Ned Devine, Like Water For Chocolate, Montenegro, Babette's Feast, Local Hero* and on and on — they're becoming a sub-genre, a *big* sub-genre. And they all tell the same, straightforward morality tale over and over again, a tale we only pay attention to in the theatre, then forget about. Over and over again, the same tale."

"It's true, man," said Frank, "too true. The loss of the spiritual, the move into possessions, success, the middle-class."

Neil stared into his empty beer glass. "The loss of intimacy," he said to the table-top, not looking up. "Why would we ever give that up?"

"Well, you two," said Sheila, sensing the moment, "I'm going to abandon you. I've got to leave early in the morning."

" . . . when it's the only fucking thing that matters in the long run," Neil said, looking up at her vaguely, but lost in another exchange the other two couldn't hear. "The only thing that matters, and, strangely, the one thing we believe is *not* political when it's the most valuable piece of currency any of us will ever fucking *have!*"

"Bye, guys. I'll e-mail ya!" Sheila said buoyantly, walking away.

"Bye for now," Frank said.

"Sure, sure, sure," Neil said, shaking a palsied finger at her, winking fondly. "Just leave, as *per usual*. Go ahead. *Leave!* This movie's over."

~~~

Shelley tucked her legs under her knees, settling in, "I'm not going anywhere," she said, staring directly at him," let's go."

"Let's go *where*?" Neil asked.

"Fuck *you*, you moron! You know *exactly* where."

"Okay, why *is* it always like this, Shelley?"

"Always like *what*?"

"Like I said earlier . . . "

"You mean about you never being able to be mad like everybody else?"

"Yeah, that."

"Well, first of all, I'm not sure it's even *remotely* true. You seem to me, looking back, to have been chronically angry for years. About all *sorts* of things."

"That's just me being whiny and sarcastic. That's different."

"Even so . . . and secondly, I guess you just have a terribly big dose of genetically programmed passive-aggressiveness from your old man. Who knows?"

"What do you mean?"

"You spend a lot of energy *pretending* you're happy, *pretending* to like everything and everybody, *pretending* not to be mad when secretly, beneath all that Irish charm you are *terminally* angry and sad. About a lot of things."

"But even knowing *this* much, then, how could you put me through this?"

"Because I have a life, too . . . we're not just talking about you . . . "

"I know that!"

"I'm not sure you do."

"Of *course* I do!"

"All right, all right."

"What's your answer then?"

Shelley looked at him with a tiredness he'd never sensed in her before. "You mean, why did I sleep with Colin?" she whispered.

"Yeah."

"I can't answer that."

"But I need an answer. I *deserve* an answer."

"Well, that may be, but I don't think I can give you one. It's too complicated."

"How?"

"God, Neil, you're the master of *that*! You shouldn't have to ask me *that*!"

"Just give me something . . . "

"Something to make you feel better?"

"I don't know . . . *something* . . . "

"What can I *say*, Neil? That it was purely physical, just sex?"

"Really?"

"No, Neil. Not really. I was just saying *what if* . . . "

"Was it just physical?"

"You're not listening . . . "

"If it was, I can at least take it in . . . I can make some sense of it . . . "

"I wish I could tell you it *was* just physical, Neil, because on one level, at least, it probably was. But I suspect it's bigger than that. It has to do with how far away from me you seem, how disconnected."

"That's ridiculous, Shelley!"

"Intimacy, Neil. You're scared to death of it."

"That's a load of psycho-babble *crap*!"

Shelley began to cry as she looked away from him and out into the street past the hedge. "I wish it was."

"For fuck's sake, Shelley! What do you *mean*? What's happening to us?"

~~~

Dave wasn't going to make it. Neil could tell. They'd started out all right, but they were too excited, too fast. Neil couldn't believe it. What's happening to me, he wondered, but couldn't take his eyes off the tableau. He kept watching anyway, hoping something would be revealed.

"Oh God!" Dave repeated, his eyes closed.

"It's all right, honey," Melissa whispered, taking a break and looking up at her husband, "this is what you wanted!"

What were these negotiations, Neil asked himself. What kind of politics?

"God! No! Shit!" Dave whispered one last time as he came over her hand. Melissa looked up at him dreamily, somewhere else. The camera stayed on her face for ten seconds before it faded to black.

When an image returned, Melissa was standing enfolded in the arms of a tall, muscular black man in his mid-twenties. Jack, Neil realised. It was Jack, finally. The camera followed Jack's hand as it took Melissa's tiny white hand and placed it on the largest penis Neil had ever seen. The elements in the scene were now *so* cliché, Neil

SO IT WON'T GO AWAY

laughed out loud at them, but they seemed real, too, and that made a difference. It wasn't just some cheesy male fantasy, or female fantasy for that matter. Melissa seemed astonished by the size of Jack's penis. She looked up into his face wonderingly, then glanced sideways, nervously, to find Dave's eyes located somewhere off camera.

~~~

Neil was walking back to the hotel down the main street of Penticton. He'd left Frank in the lounge, and looked forward to crawling into bed and forgetting everything. *Consummatum est.* He was tired and drunk. The tiredness went beyond the events of the day and the buzz of the booze was fading, as he knew it would. It always deserted him when he needed it most. The bastards, he thought, chuckling, thinking of his dad.

He wanted to forget everything that was happening to him and wake up in the morning to a new, innocent day, a safe day.

The main street bustled with young people roaming around in their hoods and baseball caps on backwards, slouching asymmetrically against benches and lampposts, hoping. Whatever it turned out to be, that old Saturday night fix still ran the world. Nothing had changed. Neil relaxed as he walked south into it. He'd always loved the night sounds and movement, the edginess of a street on a Saturday night.

He walked into a convenience store that shouldn't have been open but was, and bought a pack of smokes. One of the rows of magazines behind the East-Indian owner's head had a streak of porno mags standing on it, overlapping one another, and on the cover of one of them Neil saw Ted Smith's face smirking back at him.

Over the past year the citizens of Penticton had spent a load of money refurbishing the main street. Each of the valley's cities was trying to grab more tourist dollars. Here, they'd installed expensive black steel streetlamps and fire hydrants to give it that high-end, turn-of-the-century San Francisco look. They'd also peppered the branches of the sunburst locust trees they'd planted along the avenue with clusters of tiny white electric lights — they played a white lace to the shiny black of the steel benches and lampposts. With the young people walking in and around these new furnishings, the scene was an eerie mix of stately 'retro' and a kind of New Orleans sleaze, an accident typical of well-intentioned but square Valley planners, but great if you liked that kind of mix.

A fine late-night rain began to fall. Neil ducked onto a bench that was canopied. He sat back, looked around at all the activity rising and fading and falling like the rain, and opened the cigarette package. He was acutely aware of his hands, the skin of them, the molecules even, and what they were doing in a world of their own. There was nothing like getting the cellophane off — a sheer, invisible rectangle like glass that kept its shape until you decided to crumple it — then pushing the cardboard sleeve upwards, exposing the tinfoil wrap, discarding it, fondling the row of fresh smokes, extracting one, placing it between your lips, lighting it up with a slender match, taking that first long drag, then leaning back into the seat and letting everything else wash over you. Edward Hopper time. The forties. Aaaahhh! Man, there are some pleasures, Neil admitted. There are some. And what about Jane and Rick, he wondered. Jane had never smoked, but she'd drunk enough to have to quit. And Rick had not only quit drinking — though he'd been such an outrageous drunk even *Neil* was glad when he stopped — he'd also quit smoking, too. Christ, Neil thought. The drinking and smoking are the only things getting me *through* this. I couldn't do it without them and, just for a second, an image from the night before flashed through his head — a middle-aged man sitting in his sweats on the edge of a hotel room bed, chain smoking cigarettes, drinking rye from a bottle, eyeing a tacky porno flick on the TV — and he felt embarrassed, defeated. Fuck, he thought, why should I feel like that? *Life isn't easy.* I'm just taking a break on the sidelines for a second. It's not like I live like this all the time. Nobody works harder than me.

Neil was aware of the rhythm of the rain on the plexiglass above his head and he inhaled the crazy sweet smell of it and exhaust and wet cement and asphalt and cigarette smoke thick with memory. Somewhere in the back of his head a kaleidoscope of parallel nights tumbled by as he took another drag. An image of his father's face silhouetted against the window on the driver's side of their old car, their old Meteor, rushed in to supplant the others. An Export A rollie hung precariously from his father's lips while his large, veined hands held the driving wheel expertly, easily. The four of them were driving through Quebec through the night on their way to New Brunswick to meet up with their mother in Shediac. It was pitch black out there in those endless, dark trees. The highway was empty. Only the two diminishing triangles of yellow provided by the headlights and the small green glow of the radio shed light on anything. Rick and Jane were curled up in the back seat, sound asleep. "Pass me the bottle," his dad instructed him. "I'll just have another swig to get me through this next stretch." "Sure, Dad," he could hear his boyish self answer, "it's right here." All Neil remembered about the scene was his longing to *be* his dad someday, be drinking and smoking and driving his way through a future night, as confident as his dad appeared to him then. Well, Neil thought, flicking ash into the air, here I am. This is it, that magic place. He imagined a small boy looking at him from somewhere in the street, admiring him. He wanted to seize the boy and say, "Take it easy, kid. It isn't what you think. Not by a long shot."

"Jesus fucking Christ, it's Mr. Connelly!"

Neil almost swallowed the cigarette, the coincidence was so alarming. He turned around and saw Freddy Mowen standing there. His old student Freddy, *bold as brass* as Neil's mother would say, one arm around a pretty young woman's shoulder, the other waving a smoke dramatically.

"Well, hi there!" Neil said.

"What are *you* doing down *here*?" Freddy asked, grinning.

"I've been at a conference."

"Well, what are you doing *now*?"

"I'm on my way back to the hotel."

"Have you got another hour before you crash?"

"Well . . . "

"There's a great club just down the alley here. Me and Priscilla are just heading down there. There's no cover charge. You'll *love* it!"

"Well . . . "

"Come on, Neil! *Just one hour*. I promise."

~~~

There was nothing but silence between them now. Shelley was sitting, both feet on the floor, her forearms and hands resting on her knees. She was staring at the floor. When she looked up at Neil, her eyes were filled with tears and a tiredness Neil didn't want to see. "I just want to be by myself for a while, Neil. Sort things through. It'll be good for both of us."

"Whatever, Shelley."

"What does that mean, Neil?"

"It doesn't *mean* anything. Just do what you're going to do. You always have anyway . . . "

"That's so unfair."

"I don't know what it is, Shelley. I'm as tired of all this as you are. Maybe what you're doing will be good for both of us; maybe it won't. Neither of us knows. My feeling is that it won't, of course, but that's not going to stop you, is it?"

"I guess not."

"There you go, then. Whatever."

"I love you, Neil."

"Just quit it Shelley . . . "

" . . . I've always loved you . . . "

"Enough!"

"Why?"

"I don't want to be in that movie right now."

"What movie?"

"The one in your head, the one you're going to get the academy award for."

~~~

It wasn't what he expected. The three of them turned down a dark sidestreet, then walked into a pitch black alley. Neil could hardly see enough to walk.

Freddy had been one of Neil's most original students a few years back, but aside from being genuinely talented, he had a dark sense of humour that included the perverse, crazy landscapes of all-night 7-11s or sweaty adult movie arcades and a sense of irony that was uncanny and difficult to predict. Freddy could just as easily play some dark, twisted joke on you as show you a good time. Neil was ready for anything. Eventually, the three of them reached a purple door that was street level and above which shone a single, hooded light next to a small, hanging neon sign announcing "The Secret Garden Cafe".

They walked down a set of stairs. Neil could hear music playing, a soft female voice singing a hip-hop version of *My Romance,* and the low but steady rumble of whispered conversations, glasses clattering out of a dishwasher, espresso machines hissing. When they reached the bottom of the stairs, Freddy talked to a guy he knew and the three of them were escorted to a table tucked back in a dimly-lit corner of the place. They removed their coats and settled in, Freddy grinning triumphantly, and Neil, conceding finally, grinning back. "This is great, Freddy. Way to go."

"Yeah," was all Freddy could say, though he kept on grinning as he placed his arm around Priscilla's shoulder.

The place was like the old Yardbird Suite in Edmonton near the tracks just off Whyte. It had the same smoky, 'retro' feel, and a naturalness in its flamboyant mix of customers. As he took in the crowd, Neil sensed a wide spectrum of customers, young and old, people who had dropped in after their work shifts. Nobody was dressed up. There was no self-consciousness, no unnecessary flash to the place, just people relaxing. When a pretty young waitress came to take their order, Freddy ordered two pints of beer and tried to buy Neil a drink, but Neil stopped him and ordered an espresso. He was sober now, or on his way, and it felt fine. He didn't need any fuel.

This must be what Paris is like, he thought, remembering Rick and Jane's endless stories about their trips to Europe, sitting in small, intimate cafes late into the morning. The smug bastards, Neil snickered to himself as he recalled them describing crowds of people showing up off the sidestreets of St. Germain du Pre in the middle of the night and early morning. I've got them now.

It was good to see Freddy again. Neil asked him about his life and what he was doing with the writing, and Freddy filled him in, his voice animated, his arm around Priscilla's shoulder. Freddy was twenty-four and looked like Billy Bob Thornton in that movie with Bruce Willis: a kind of hip Fred MacMurray look that was, in fact, the other side of cool, the far side. Priscilla was in her early twenties, too, shy, pretty. She had a pale veneer about her, an Audrey Hepburn grace and angularity, and large brown eyes that never missed anything. She was a student at the Penticton campus, studying anthropology. The two of them had been together for three months and Neil could sense how happy they were in this first stretch. They reminded him how he and Shelley had lived at the start, how sweet it had been, how natural, and a bigness in him let it go and was pleased for them.

A small quartet — a singer, bass player, piano and drummer doing a lot of brush work — played in the far corner of the place, muted but sensual. To be this un-accommodated, but happy, Neil thought. To sit with your family or friends, yacking away, that kind of dressed-down, unapologetic life. Where dignity was not located in what you did or where you discovered yourself to be in the ascent or descent of the cheap hierarchy of North American life, but in the simple truth that you were who you were, and you were living with other people — in a wheel of day-to-day rituals and year-to-year rituals — and they knew all this about you and you knew it about them. It was the landscape Neil had grown up in on the Southside of Edmonton in the 50s and 60s with its Church bazaars and Whist nights, its Saturday evenings in The Legion, its gas stations and barber shops run by his father's friends, its refusal to pin people down much, its deep acceptance that the big decisions — all the flash and power and ascendancy of the wheels and clacking loud structures around them — were happening in another, more self-conscious way, on another stage somewhere, a stage you wanted to avoid if you could, a stage you'd sacrifice without hesitation for the kind of exchange occurring here. What has happened to my life, Neil wondered, between the jokes and laughter and coffee and beer? How has it managed to stray so far? And, for the first time since Shelley had slept with Colin, he had some small sense of who he was.

Then he heard them more clearly. The musicians had switched themselves around and were beginning a new song. What he saw was incredible. A sign, Neil thought. It has to be.

~~~~

Shelley walked across the deck to the gate, then took her time securing it. For years, they'd both fumbled with his makeshift lock, and every time they did Neil had announced, in a slightly martyrish tone, that he would install a new one the next weekend. Of course, he never had. She gave it one last tug, then walked over to the blue car she'd borrowed from her sister. He inhaled her long legs, her jeans, the soft earth-toned Scottish sweater beneath her long, rich auburn hair. She glanced back once, her face pinched in a nameless anxiety, looking for his face in the window but not finding it. He could hear the car backing up as he walked into the living room and clicked *Kind of Blue* on the stereo. As he stood in the front window and watched her disappear down the street, the opening notes of Davis' trumpet claimed the house, and Neil started to cry. It was for everything they'd had together and everything they hadn't seen in one another until now, the things they hadn't shared. He wondered, as he stood there, if she was right about intimacy, that he was scared to death of it. What if it's true, he thought, standing there, weeping shamelessly as Davis played the pain from another angle, what can I ever do about it? It all reminded him of something normal in his life that shouldn't *be* normal, something he needed to change on top of every other fucking thing that always needed to be changed.

~~~

It was a song his father had played for him over and over again on an old, cracked 78. He couldn't believe it. The middle-aged woman who'd been singing had switched places with the piano player. She lifted a bright, bulky, gleaming red and white accordion out of a case concealed behind the piano. She was sitting on the piano stool now, adjusting shiny green straps around her shoulders, smiling, then leaning down to pull a mic stand closer to the accordion. The man, meanwhile, a guy in his mid-to-late fifties who was dressed in a grey suit and whose grey-to-white hair had been greased back and combed to look respectable, was adjusting the singer's mic up to his level so he could sing into it without holding onto it. The crowd was cheering before they began to play. This must have been a ritual. Then the accordion, the bass and the soft brushes on the drummer's top-hat launched into the opening bars. *My heart is sad and lonely/I long for you/for you dear only/why haven't you noticed?/I'm all for you, body and soul* . . .

Neil walked back to the hotel. When he got into his room and lay down, his mind sped down a long, night-highway that went on forever into the trees, and, as usual when this happened, he couldn't sleep. It was 5:00 AM. The early light was beginning to pick off the streetlamps, the trees, the power poles in the back alley of the hotel, and he could hear the first birds through the screen in the aluminium windows. He stood up and drew the drapes back to let the sunrise in.

Whatever happened to other people had nothing to do with who he was. He didn't possess anyone else; no one possessed him. It was simple, obvious, but so fucking huge and terrifying and free he'd never seen it. He reached for the phone and dialled Shelley's new number. After eight rings he hung up. Of course she wasn't home. Instead of the nausea in his stomach, he just felt sorry he couldn't have told her. She'd have laughed if she'd heard him say it. He knew, even, what she'd have said back.

He slept like a boy.

~~~

"Dad! Quick! On the highway!"

"What the hell?"

His father must have nodded off and Neil hadn't noticed. He'd always monitored his dad when his dad been drinking and driving, but he'd screwed up this time. He hadn't wanted to scare his dad, but there was an elk standing in the middle of the highway a couple of hundred yards away and they were heading right for it. The elk just stood there, looking back at them.

Neil's father began to swing the car to the left and blow the horn, hoping the elk would take off in the right direction, but the elk moved with the car. Rick and Jane woke up, frightened, yelling things from the back seat. Finally, the elk just stood its ground, fixed, impassive, getting larger and larger as they approached. At the last possible second, the car swerved around the elk's huge velvet brown body and accelerated down the highway, straightening itself out into its own lane again.

Neil's father laughed sheepishly, nervously, "Cripes, that was a close call, eh?"

Neil's heart was exploding. He couldn't hear what anyone else was saying. He couldn't say anything back to his father, but just kept shaking his head. He didn't care what his father thought. It was the first time he'd ever felt that. He couldn't take his eyes off the road. He was never going to be caught off-guard like that again. He was never going to sleep.

A Day Of Rain

RAIN IS A LANDSCAPE ITSELF if it lasts more than a day. It makes another world, transforms the way we look out at things cleansed by it. We know it's good for everything — we like to get rain; we know we need it — but at the same time, like fire, it destroys things. I like rain because of a quiet, forgiving mood it creates in me, and because it makes where I am seem thick like how I see it in my head. Of course, I have to wonder, why would it take rain to make me feel the life around me is thick, but it *does* take something like it to make me pay attention. *Look!* There's a farmer up early in the field to the south. His pick-up rolls past those tall poplars, heading to Ellerslie, blue against green, behind the rain.

I'm stuck here, looking out my window. I've been up all night thinking of my brother, Rick, hoping he's okay. I have no reason to be worried. I just am. I'm his sister. It's the way things go sometimes.

~~~

Half-way through his ritual, Rick squinted through the window at the sun that bounced off the blistered grey of the back deck. It was a gorgeous May morning, just like the last four had been. A fat, squat robin thumped onto one of the lower branches of the pendulous Manitoba maple. A long, wriggling earthworm dangled from the robin's beak, but whenever it seemed the wet, wriggling worm might escape and tumble to the safety of the deck below, the robin would launch into a mechanical manoeuvre with its beak that wound the worm's full body around the beak the way you'd coil rope around a stick, but with a power-torque that accelerated the process. Rick thought of Donne's Holy Sonnets. *Donne's Holy Sonnets?* Yes, Rick admitted, being hauled up by a God, held fast in his relentless grip and, in time, annihilated: the glory of being hauled up, mangled and devoured by something ultimately more powerful than you. God! Just in time, the robin bolted off its perch on the branch and disappeared into the blue sky somewhere behind the shed, worm in tow, still resisting.

The kettle was boiling. He could finish making the coffee. He looked up and out the window suddenly as if expecting to see someone.

~~~

It is the same street again: the tall, hovering chestnut tree and the full, green Manitoba maple. Spring. May. Rain glistens off the objects on the deck: the wood of the deck itself, the cream enamel window frames, the flat blue paint of the house, the shiny black plastic of the barbecue cover, a screwdriver and orange extension cord left lying on the wooden shelf near the barbecue, the buckets of plants hanging from the lower limb of the maple, the half-empty blue dog dish sitting squat on the deck near the back door

It is early morning, the rain gauze. He approaches the window and peers into the kitchen. He can hear or sense movement, but isn't sure.

He sees a person who is himself walk from a dark hallway into the kitchen, switch the light on, open the fridge, take a gulp out of a two-litre container of milk, then approach the sink to look out into the rain.

He stands on the deck, peering in at his own face at the sink. There is something different about his face.

He watches his other self begin to put on a pot of coffee.

He reaches into a side pocket of a grey bomber jacket and retrieves a package of Players Medium. He lights up a smoke in the early rain, cupping his left hand around the tip of the cigarette to protect it from the rain, enhancing the glowing red ember there.

~·~·~

Sometimes, in his dreams, Rick dreamt he was dreaming, and when this happened it was as if he was standing outside himself twice: aware of a version of himself that was standing outside another version in the dream, watching. He could imagine compounding this situation endlessly with each new introduction of another version of the self being a legitimate, slightly superior addition because it knew one layer *more* — so the whole concept of self, eventually, was so huge and contradictory, so back-lit, that if you tried to find a core in it, you'd have to search a very long time. Rick didn't know how he felt about that, but it didn't feel good. It bothered him.

That's when he could imagine the texture of parallel lives, though. There's always an escape hatch. It was crazy, but he knew that each day he made decisions — big or small — that were irrevocable, but could have been different decisions, easily. With each choice, an unchangeable pattern began to emerge that became and defined your time and self. And you realised sometimes that *that* time and self could just as easily have become *this* or *that* different time or self if this decision here, or that one there, had been switched. The game you entered when you started thinking along these lines, of course, was an elaborate chess game with no end in sight, just endless configurations, plays, and futures. What fascinated Rick about it, though, was how fragile and vulnerable the machinery was in one way, and how arbitrary it was in another.

Lately, Rick had been dreaming that he'd visited another version of himself that had found safety and order, and that he was allowed to peer in on his world. He'd show up at a particular house on a particular street in the middle of the night, in the rain usually, and be there as his other self slept and woke up in the morning. He always arrived late at night; he usually left by noon.

This dream not only repeated itself and its features — a lot of reoccurring material — it acquired the momentum of a narrative that began to unfold a progression in the midst of an otherwise wacky dream logic. When Rick fell asleep sometimes now, he looked forward to returning to the story in the dream, finding out what was happening to this other version of himself: what kind of world was being told or built there.

He could never tell in advance whether he'd get back to this dream, but he suspected he'd be returning to it one way or another all his life. That's what it felt like, almost as if he were a mythical presence in the world of the dream itself, and they needed him there somehow.

~·~·~

Maybe I saw too many British films in the sixties. One of the reasons I like landscapes of rain has to do with mists, green fields in the distance, small British gravel roads winding through tall hedges, blustery skies closing in, all metal objects shining. And people quite sure of themselves, in scenes that accompany these landscapes. Snapping their umbrellas knowingly, walking brusquely into small, cream-coloured cottages with ivy clinging to wooden door frames. A murder has taken place near the village and these people will get to the bottom of it, soon. There is no doubt. Meanwhile, the landscape of rain is pulsing with something like hope, or a soft, vague safety. I wish I knew which.

It likely goes back to specific mornings and afternoons as a child. You're staying in an aunt's house for the weekend, but your aunt has gone out. She's left candies in blue ceramic bowls for you on various sidetables and all sorts of historical books and magazines lying around that you inhale as greedily as the candy. A small fire undulates in the ceramic fireplace across from the couch you've curled up on. The carpets beneath you have medieval patterning, repetitious heraldry. She has left an afghan quilt on the couch for you and you've pulled it up around your shoulders while you read her note again: "You just settle in to a good afternoon, Jane. I'll be back before five and we'll talk about supper then."

It's only two in the afternoon now. The stack of magazines and books is endless. The heat from the fire makes you drowsy. The rain is all around the house, drumming its tiny fingers against the window panes and — if you're really quiet and listen carefully — the roof is like another blanket, something blessed. You can just see the mythical roofs of Northland's horse barns across Ada Boulevard. Everything in North Edmonton is quiet today, muted by rain, waiting.

~~~

Rick poured the water over the coffee grounds and — the way rituals work in clusters sometimes — he could hear Wiley stir, then begin to bark behind the hall door down at the front of the house. Little yips, really. Wiley was only thirteen weeks old and didn't have much of a bark yet. She knew exactly where he was, though, that he was just about to pour the second load of water into the Melitta basket. It astonished him to think this little entity could become *so* sure *so* fast. When he finished with the water, for example, he would walk into the livingroom, draw the drapes onto the front yard, and then punch up CBC's morning show from Kelowna. He'd release Wiley from the front hall and they'd walk out onto the back deck together after a small ceremony during which Wiley'd roll over and offer her tummy to him and actually smile up at him when he nodded his exaggerated good mornings to her: *Hello, Wiley! That's a Good Little Doggie! It's so nice to see you!* Rick would grin back into her tiny face, then ask, *Do you want some breakfast? Should Wiley have something to eat to start the day?*

Early on, Rick had decided to say the same words, create a completely predictable ritual to see what would happen. What happened humbled him when he thought of his own life: it only took a few days to realise that Wiley believed his fiction unconditionally. Rick had created a world for his dog that provided complete safety and certainty. He could read the safety in the dog's eyes and in what Wiley revealed she didn't know. Rick knew it was the same with people and his heart wanted to break sometimes, thinking about that. He needed a new fiction. No wonder he'd watched that robin so carefully.

He wanted to be consumed.

He wanted to be consumed by a quiet in the midst of which his old restlessness eased off and disappeared. Either that, or he wanted a wonderful, long, slow smoke. Dancing girls to show up? Consumption.

"Shit," he whispered to no one. He was out on the deck now staring up into the early blue morning sky above the Manitoba maple. "It's going to be worse than I thought," he said to the dog, "not smoking."

~~~

Last week I was sitting somewhere in the rain, too. I was sitting in the Faculty Club having a coffee after my early afternoon class. I had selected a corner table near a window so I could peer out over the river valley. I was waiting for him. He was up from Winnipeg for a consultation and we'd agreed to meet again. I admit he's a crazy, eccentric man, but our backgrounds are so similar I can't resist the fun and excitement in him, and I know I can spend a night with him and my world won't fall apart afterwards. Pure sex? Maybe. I don't know. The truth is, I find him attractive and I don't mind letting that go wherever it needs to go for once.

We live in two different cities. It's a long-distance deal, no strings. That's fine with me. And he's attracted to me, too. I can sense it. "My god," he'd whispered to me on a tour bus in New Orleans, "I'm in a dream and I've found Natassja Kinski teaching at a university in Edmonton and

I get to fall in love with her!" Yeah, sure. As I sat staring out into the rain over the river valley, I understood how far I'd come, and, of course, I realised it was the excitement about Max that allowed me to see that. It's the way it works, isn't it? Not to see how far I'd come in a political sense — though the Edmonton I'd grown up in was a city sewn up in invisible economic lines that held people — but how far in a completely different sense. My mother, my father, my brothers Rick and Neil, our close, close dances together here in this landscape after the war. Dad's drinking and his early death. Oh, how we'd each of us scrambled into and through these landscapes full of rain and mists and hidden traps concealed everywhere in the dense, dark foliage clinging to the valley walls. Sitting in the Faculty Club, I could sense the shuffle, the weight, even, of my life so far, shudder through me as I faced the rain. It was physical. Me, poised to have a little fun in my life, rich in all the ups and downs that had produced me, alive! My body, pure flesh and rain. Me, peering out into the endless variations of green — close up on Saskatchewan Drive, but receding, receding into grey green, moist air, out over the valley, down into the valley, and up again, all over the riverbanks on the north side — all this green, this life, the juice of it spilling out over the earth, a wonder.

The waitress had come by and broken this trance, replenishing my coffee. I thanked her.

I loved the Faculty Club's coffee and the thick, porcelain cups and saucers they used. Coffee in the club had become a bit of a ritual for me.

I'd been trying to write about my brothers. I'm not sure why. Sitting in here with a coffee had become a place

I could do that in; it seemed the right place to be. Trying to get sight of them. Words. Of course, you always fail in these things, but that doesn't stop you trying.

It was happening again. I could feel it in the air that rustled by me as the waitress left and I brace myself as usual for some seam to tear the room sideways and there I am in Calgary. I know I'm in Calgary and I know it's twenty years ago, maybe thirty. I can tell by the clothes that whisk by me on 8th Avenue. That's where I am and the sound breaks through, too, and it's all cars and people. Everything is fast here and I've just picked up some smokes in a smoke shop down the street. I've just lighted one up and ah! It feels good to be smoking again and I go to a small park near a bookstore and sit on a bench to take it all in so strange to have almost two perspectives in this. Knowing what I know now, and knowing something, too, from then. How does that work, I wonder, and I see him, asleep near a tree over by the carpark machines. It's Rick. I know it. It's the middle of the day and he's drunk. He's passed out. But what's he doing in Calgary? He's never lived in Calgary. And he looks so small and defenceless lying there and the part in me that knows something from this time gets up and approaches him and he looks up and smiles, but the nearer I get the stranger the sounds become and the thicker the air is and as I reach towards his smile that's beaming right at me, and his mouth that's saying words right at me, I passed back into the quiet, sedate air of the Faculty Club, and caught my breath and reached out for my coffee cup that was lukewarm and here she was, abruptly, the waitress again, at my elbow with fresh coffee, even a fresh cup. The river was still shifting down there past the dark green of the trees outside the windows. And it was still raining.

~~~

Rick left Wiley out on the deck and took his coffee into the livingroom. He sat on the couch looking out across the roofs of Vernon, and downtown Vernon, to the soft, pastel orchards of Bella Vista in the distance to the west, and above their soft orchard grids and patterns, the dark, mottled blue mountains that cradled them. He and Jennifer had been so excited when they'd bought the house that it had taken them weeks before they realised they had this panoramic view of the valley through their living room window. Rick loved sitting there in the morning, listening to the CBC morning show from Kelowna, staring out the window. But it was like waking up hung over lately, and he certainly remembered *that* feeling. For two months he'd been waking up groggy, full of detailed, gloomy dreams stuffed with guilt and fear. All the goddamn Irish blood, he admitted. The Celtic head, wired for misery. He couldn't get around it. He'd walk into the living room, tired, before he was even starting out on his day. Not only tired, but full of sorrow. Some undertow was pulling him down into a depth he thought he knew but wished he didn't. It was all too familiar.

Maybe it's my age, he thought. Turning forty-seven. Maybe that's it.

Many of the dreams that fed these mornings were about death. One way or another. Not just his own, but many deaths. It wasn't simply his own mortality that intrigued him in all this but, instead, how the theme of death coloured everything that was full of vibrancy and life. His mind could acquire a cynicism Rick didn't know he could suffer, that had to do with undermining any pleasure or joy in his life because it was all going to vanish and crumble and decay quickly anyway. It was a childish morbidity that advanced like a virus and could only be stopped by sheer stubbornness. He'd sit on the couch, holding his coffee, staring out into the rain, and he'd laugh out loud at how silly and petulant his mind was. Most days, after a short struggle, he'd shake the thick, morbid dreams he'd woken up in and begin to see his day for what it really offered.

~~~

The Faculty Club was beginning to fill up, as it always did in the late afternoon, but I was being left alone mercifully, especially after what had happened to me about Rick and Calgary. As it turned out, Max wasn't going to show up that afternoon either, which was, in some ways, another mercy. The waitress had given me his note. He'd try me in the evening at home. So it was just me and my coffee, the rain on the window, and the dark greens of the river valley receding as far as I could see.

Rick and I had been through so much together with the booze: we'd both been almost consumed by it, like Dad had been. It had been a close call for each of us and we knew it; we understood the ironies, the paradoxes, and were grateful that we could lurch through it and out the other side.

But prices were paid anyway. All those stories, and their great fucking pilgrimages, martyrdoms.

There were days, thinking of Rick, when I became convinced that all these struggles actually take part in a larger, class struggle that will go on forever. It may sound facile to think along these lines, but when I consider our times, when I think of our family of five growing up on the Southside in the 50s and 60s, I can see it in two broad ways: from the larger perspective of twentieth century history, our family, and especially us children, were the beneficiaries of a huge struggle for market democracy and its so-called freedoms, but from a closer perspective, I could see each of us floundering in the vague but strong nets of a class system that granted and withheld privilege like a huge old rotten lung, wheezing its foul breath out over our childhoods. We were lucky; we were unlucky. We were privileged; we were not privileged. Two generations down the line, the grandchildren of the Salvadorian revolutionary will have to deal with the lower-middle-class introspection and sorrow and self-doubt I deal with now. This is not a trivial thing. Not at all. It's very real. It's my struggle, maybe even my most valuable inheritance in this strange evolution. So the revolutions are not clearly marked and none are necessarily superior to another. They're all necessary, all part of one big wheel that is, hopefully, rolling forward.

That's what it felt like, sitting in the middle of all that rain and green in the Faculty Club that afternoon: that we are part of a community of revolutions that hold us, define us and continually release us into next stages, even if we can't see them holding us in a green landscape wet with rain in May, consumed and consuming.

~~~

He'd been so lucky, he knew, so unbelievably lucky. He felt it in his bones. Life could have been so different. He'd worked hard to ensure it wouldn't be different, and he knew enough to recognise that.

Maybe the dreams and the guilt had to do with quitting smoking. Maybe some vast physical longing, buried away in there somewhere, was getting back at him for taking away his favourite pastime.

It was funny when he thought about it, but he remembered reading *The Confessions Of Zeno*, by Italo Svevo, when he'd been in his early twenties and working on Joyce and Lowry. Svevo had been Joyce's buddy in Trieste and had written this wonderful novel about having last cigarettes. Even in his twenties, already a heavy smoker, Rick had felt superior to anyone's wish to quit such a pleasure. Why would anyone want to do that?

He'd put it off successfully for ten years, but he'd run out of time now. In fact, even in the misery of his withdrawal, Rick knew he might have waited too long, but the quitting itself seemed something he had to do.

Of course, the actual quitting was made more difficult by all the do-gooders who'd come rolling up to announce breathlessly how happy they were for him, etc etc. Some of them — because they represented only too clearly a 90s kind of self-congratulation mixed with a desperateness about running, health clubs, and exercise, etc., etc. — almost convinced him to start smoking again, they were so offensive. He'd wanted to puke at their feet sometimes. He loved sin. He'd always loved sin. *If you're going to do it, do it completely; don't settle for half-way.* He'd never drunk half-way. He'd never smoked half-way. He'd loved both. He'd been consumed. There was something about that that had held him, comforted him even. Too hard to explain, but the bottom line was that he felt in his bones that he had a fairly good understanding of self-destruction. Not too many people could give him much advice on that one and what he couldn't understand was the mindlessly well-intentioned people who'd always lived cautious, reserved lives, now congratulating him on joining their fold. He hated that. He'd never be in their fold. He wasn't quitting to get there. He was quitting so he'd last a little longer, so he'd pass through a door he was fascinated by. Where would he be, he wondered, when he was standing in the world with no booze and no smokes? What would he see there? He had a sneaky feeling it was something big. He had a sneaky feeling he might be completely annihilated by it.

~~~

Jane kept thinking about what had happened in The Faculty Club as she drove down 111th Street towards the Whitemud Freeway and home.

Rick had never lived in Calgary, and neither had she. Neil had spent a stint there, about eight months back in the 80s.

And yet her experience had been as real, as textured as any of the others. This new twist to things was puzzling.

As she signalled and turned down the ramp to the freeway just after Southgate Mall, the rain began to come down even harder, like a monsoon now. Sometimes it rained like this in Edmonton in the spring, and when it did, you had to be especially wary of the freeways: they could fill up in spots so you were driving into a lake. People had had to be airlifted from their cars. Great, Jane thought, just great! Her windshield wiper blades could hardly bear the force of the rain and she gripped the steering wheel tensely and squinted through the silver wall of water. Fortunately, she was following a semi and its whole back end was covered with red lights. As long as she stuck with him, she'd be all right until she could pick off her exit ramp. She'd have to be careful, though. Her side mirrors were useless.

And she could imagine all of them so easily. Thousands of drivers like herself caught in this rainstorm on the freeway, unable to pull over, unable to signal, unable to stop. You had to keep moving right through it until something happened to change everything. And, she thought, almost laughing out loud, I could have stayed up on a street somewhere off the freeway. I could have pulled over. I could be having a donut, laughing with someone, safe from the storm, or I could be sitting in a booth by myself even, writing a story while the rain drummed down on the hoods of the cars in the parking lot outside the plate glass windows. Now, look at me.

She kept seeing faces through the grey sleet of the windshield: tiny faces along the side of the freeway, thousands of them, thousands of expressions. They were all trying to tell her something very important. Some were cheerful, some angry, some frightened . . . a wide spectrum, as infinitely numerous as the rain itself, as mysterious, as ridiculous in its force.

What is happening to me this time, she wondered, and she was sure she had struck something in the grey but she kept driving anyway; she kept her eyes on the red lights in front of her. Within seconds, the rain ceased, the window cleared; she could spot her exit ramp a half a mile ahead. She was going to be all right. Except for the cars and trucks all around her, there was nothing on the side of the freeway. There were no people out in this.

Jane signalled and turned up onto the ramp.

~~~

Last night Rick dreamt that the life he lived was only a pathetic dream of safety and order and success, dreamt by his real self who lived in Calgary, on unemployment insurance, and who smoked and drank and was single. This version of himself — the real version that lived in Calgary — had constructed an elaborate fantasy about living in the Okanagan, married to Jennifer, happy, house, car, job, dog — the whole package. This fantasy was so intricate the version of himself that lived in Calgary would visit it each night in his dreams, after he'd passed out from the rye. The Calgary version would show up at night in the rain standing on the deck behind the house, waiting for Rick to wake up so he could watch a self that knew safety and order, that had found a way to survive his dad's inheritance and not be destroyed by it. The self on the deck wanted to see these things but was shy and modest peering in on this privileged, happy world. The self on the deck was easily startled, didn't feel it deserved anything, and that's why it felt comfortable in the dark, in the rain, looking in, not hoping exactly, but observing with the kind of ludicrous pride a parent feels watching a son or daughter do something the parent could never do.

As the dreamer stood in his revolving self-destructions, consumed by them, watching, the other self he was watching was shedding them — the same pleasures, the same intensities — and in the shedding was becoming —

not dull and boring which was what Rick had always feared might happen — but hybrid, mutant.

Rick walked into the kitchen and poured himself another cup of coffee. He could hear Jennifer stirring down the hall in their bedroom at the back of the house. He could hear Wiley chasing an empty milk carton all over the back deck outside. He looked out the window.

~~~

Jane looked up from the clock. 5:00 AM. She'd been writing for a long time. Strange, Borges-like constructions of impossibly interlocking dreams. She couldn't get Rick out of her mind; no matter what, there he was, staring at her, reminding her of their lives together.

The sun was up. Jane walked down the stairs into her living room and pulled her drapes back so she could see south-east, into the sun. Her condominium looked out on farmland. She'd bought it in a new subdivision in the southeast part of Edmonton, not far from Ellerslie. The farms she could see would be developed sooner or later, she knew, but for now it was a comfort to look out, as she had as a child, into all the soft land and the smell of it in the morning, especially after the night rains in spring.

Jane loved being up early like this. Mulling things over, putting on a coffee, listening to the birds rise up, the wind glistening through the poplars that hovered and swayed near her dining room window. She'd sit on the couch and listen to the early CBC show on the radio, hold a porcelain cup of coffee in her hands, a ritual.

She couldn't get him out of her mind.

~~~

The rain is thicker tonight than it was last night. It's hard to smoke out here, but you can get away with it if you're careful. My jacket has a pull-out hood, so I'm okay. It was one of the reasons I bought it. I've got a mickey of rye in here, and every now and then I take a swig of it. It burns down into my stomach and rushes out into the blood.

I'm standing here in the rain, a bit bombed I admit, waiting for my self to get up and show me something. I feel so tender, so protective, it's stupid! Me, of all people, but I do! And if I have a few more slugs — which, let's face it, I'm going to do — I'll even get emotional, silly maudlin shit. But I'm weeping for everything when this happens. I'm weeping for all the things that could have been, not just for me, but for each one of us, my brother, my sister, you. I think how vulnerable and frightened each one of us is under all the bullshit we've manufactured to conceal ourselves, and I sense a wonder everywhere I look, and a good will — a love I'll even call it — and I don't know what to do in the face of it all but stare through this rain in the dark and hope to see myself eventually, then wake up knowing what to do.

Union

WHENEVER I STAY WITH JANE, hidden parts of her life fly up to ambush me. You know what I mean? You think, *she's my sister for Christ's sake, there are no secrets between us,* and you feel comfortable in her house *because* you know this person so well you won't be surprised. But that's not the case with my sister, Jane. She always surprises me. Over the years, I've gotten used to it, but this time, it was her obsession for miniatures that caught me off-guard.

I'd never noticed them before. That doesn't necessarily mean they weren't there. I admit I don't see things sometimes. Maybe the difference, the reason why I *did* notice them, was that I had a chance to discover them on my own. She wasn't around to distract me. I'd driven up from Vernon on a Tuesday and stayed overnight at an old friend's in Red Deer. I pulled into Jane's driveway in the morning, after she'd left for the university. She'd dropped a key off in the mailbox so I could let myself in and make myself at home.

The condominium development Jane lives in is in south Edmonton. When we were children this location was just sections of wheat fields. In fact, you can still look south from Jane's deck and see farms just across the way, to the southeast. That's how far south she is. You can see the Ellerslie Grain Elevators from her deck. They seem like they're just down the block. They *are* just down the block. When we were children, these grain elevators were miniature dots on the horizon that told us we were getting closer to Leduc. They were mythical then.

Jane bought herself a nice unit here four years ago after she'd returned from one of her trips to Europe. She said she liked the security of living in a housing development and even got a kick out of some of its social aspects. Though she probably paid ten-thousand too much for it, she'll never lose a dime. The unit she bought is a custom one, the old show home, and is finished off beautifully. All the trim work — the baseboards, door frames, staircases — are solid blonde oak. Very *very*. La dee da. Deluxe, for us. It's so strange that I'd use that phrase, *for us*.

I took my suitcase up the stairs and put it in the guest room, then came back downstairs and opened the drapes so I could look south over the fields. I turned on the CBC radio, Shelah Rogers and the usual suspects talking softly, under the hum of everything else. Two of the voices I knew, and the third sounded a lot like Peter Gzowski which would be great as I'd missed him. Jane had left a note on the kitchen counter to push a button for a fresh pot of coffee, and it was just after I'd done that, just as my finger pulled away from the white plastic, that I began to see all the miniature houses and animals and people everywhere I looked.

They were from all over the world: tiny statues of peasants from Austria, Hungary, Pakistan, Nepal, Iceland . . . each outfitted in bold, primary-coloured folk costumes from different periods. Jane had clustered these in small groups of threes. Three Russian children just left of the phone, three Belgian farmers on a shelf above the

sink. As I walked through the rooms, I noticed them everywhere, checking *me* out — that's what it felt like —
grouped on every available counter-space. She'd amassed a
vast collection. It *could* have appeared tacky — a variation
on the garden gnomes and trolls and Walt Disney squirrels
that pop up in back yards sometimes — but it wasn't tacky.
Not a bit of it. In fact, they seemed understated to me,
almost invisible unless you focused on them. I even
wondered vaguely how long they'd been there, how long
I'd failed to see them. Maybe I'd been drinking still when
she began to collect them. Maybe I'd been too busy doing
that. And it wasn't just three-dimensional, this field of
miniatures. She'd also collected many small, hand-painted
scenes — mostly of rural Europe — that represented the
same, eclectic range. She'd hung these in small wooden
frames or clear, unframed glass ones and displayed them
on her walls, high and low, so you were always bumping
into them. When I opened her cupboard to get a coffee
cup, I noticed her new set of plates were the Villeroy and
Boche 'Hansi' collection representing tiny Alsatian villages:
'Hansi' children chasing large geese through medieval
markets, that kind of sweet, highly designed pastoral
jumping with bold reds and blues and yellows.

Sometimes I'm appalled by a pettiness, a smallness in
me, something lost and vulnerable and either angry or
hurt, that sits way back, apprehensive, quick to judge, lash
out. This smallness is smack dab in the middle of what I
have to admit is a largesse in my life: how happy and
healthy I am compared to how I used to live when I was
buried in all my wonderful, wild, luxurious, and dark
addictions. I really *do* feel lucky now as opposed to before
when I drank so much and chain-smoked my ass off. An

interesting metaphor, but we'll let it go. The thing is, though, I am ambushed from time to time by this vicious smallness in me, this hurt, whatever its cause. It surprises me and I wish it would either go away or I could see it for whatever it is and root it out of my life. It's embarrassing. It surfaced this morning, in the middle of such quiet on Jane's couch as I sat listening to the CBC.

I was up in Edmonton for our reunion. Jane and I were going to have lunch, then drive out to the international airport to greet our mother Colette and our brother Neil who were flying in from Ireland, *from the auld country*, as my mother liked to say. They'd been over there for three weeks and it would be interesting to see how or if they'd survived one another in the process. We'd both received the usual, jaunty postcards from Neil — FAITH AND BEGORRAH WE'VE BEEN TO EVERY FRIGGIN CASTLE AND MONASTERY, HAVE KISSED THE BLARNEY STONE, AND THE HAIRY, FRIGHTENING ASS OF IRISH HISTORY EVERYWHERE WE'VE BEEN, AND MOM'S AS HAPPY AS A CLAM AND ME MY NORMAL, ASCETIC SELF — so we knew his sense of humour, at least, was still intact. And we also knew our mother would have taken nine-thousand photographs and collected every free brochure to be had. She'd be coming home armed. We'd have to be ready for that.

They're talking about alcoholism this morning, how it affects writers, and they're talking about smoking, too. And it's *good* they're talking about these things finally. We need to demythologise these addictions and no one knows that better than me. We need to understand what *causes* them, what holds people, such innocent people often, in such strong, fierce arms and won't let them go. I know that, too. It's just that I've been writing quite seriously about these things for fifteen years now and it's been almost impossible to get any editors or writers to pay attention, including the very three people I was listening to on the radio. You know how it goes. When celebrities finally discover these things, when someone famous is forced to wrestle with them, the book is out in two weeks and they're half-way through filming the mini-series. You know what I mean. And yet, it's such fragile territory, needs to be understood carefully. Thousands of lives are at stake when we talk about these things, and there is an almost infinitely recessive staircase of levels of denial, too, one of them being the early self-congratulatory tone of the new person in recovery. There are dangers everywhere. But it's still important to air the issue, no matter the venue, and I know that, and my normal, healthy self is grateful for it and impressed even. It *does* take courage to face these things, and more courage, even, to talk about them publicly. All that remains true. And the little, hurt person that sits way back in here, inside my head, and feels ignored and outraged, will simply have to stuff it. I wish I could get at that small voice somehow, though, could reach in and comfort it, grow it up, even. I keep trying to do that. That's something. It's great to hear a voice like Gzowski's again, like an old friend come back, still with us. And at the thought of him, of all the years I counted on him so much, my body eases itself out of the small darkness that had begun to grow, and relaxes once again into the morning, sitting back in my sister's couch, breathing in the fresh prairie air sifting in through the screen from the fields to the south.

Jane was busy tossing a salad in the kitchen, and I was placing two Hansi settings on the tablecloth in her dining-room. She was telling me about her trip with three friends to Newfoundland and the Maritimes. She'd just revealed that when they were in Halifax, she'd taken a day to herself, rented a car, and driven up to our father Charles' home town of Westville, a small coal town near Pictou on the east coast. She'd driven up to return our Uncle Fred's ashes to the cemetery where our grandmother and grand-father Connelly were buried. I imagined Jane driving those roads, Uncle Fred in an urn on the passenger seat beside her. Uncle Fred had apparently told our mother that when he died he wanted his ashes returned to his mother's grave; he wanted to be buried with her. Jane had decided to honour that wish, and had taken him home after all these years.

Though Uncle Fred was six years younger than our father, he died within two years of our dad's dying. Uncle Fred was only sixty-five when he died, but, like dad's, his whole adult life had been run by addictions. For years he'd been an especially flamboyant alcoholic who could have us laughing for days sometimes, then wanting to kill him the rest. Later, in his fifties, after he'd kicked the booze, he had to deal with its likely cause: a powerful manic depression. Though the medication for it helped, this depression allowed his eccentricities to refine themselves so that, in the end, for the last ten years of his life anyway, he lived like a hermit. We hardly ever saw him. In fact, the last time I'd seen Fred before he himself died was at my father's funeral. Fred was especially quiet and invisible there. After his own death, I felt guilty because when I was younger I was close to him. But I lived away from

Edmonton and I never saw him until it was too late. The way it goes sometimes.

Fred's drinking and my dad's drinking were so intertwined, so inseparable, it was easy, only later, to see why Uncle Fred played such a large role in our childhoods. He was an exaggerated version of Dad. Everything our father would do — his drunken sarcasm, his unpredictable temper, his outrageous sentimentality — Fred would enact on a grander scale. You'd find him sprawled out late at night in the kitchen, his arms splayed out over the kitchen table, his head flat down on the table top, pressed into it as if burrowing down into the texture of it for some magical forgiveness or unexpected empathy, sobbing wildly, incoherently, inconsolable. If you made the mistake of touching the cloth of his shirt, he could turn on you, fiercely, "Get the hell out of here you little fucked-up prick or I'll kill ya, ya bastard!" Or, just as easily, the opposite, "Aw fer god's sake, it's you and you're my brother's *son* by the jeez and I love ya, ya little godforsaken, fuckin' bastard, I tell ya!" Or you could get caught shopping with him on a Saturday when he'd been at it for a while, and he'd be ordering all the innocent clerks around in the Army and Navy Store on Whyte Avenue because he suspected they were patronising him, something no one in his or her right mind would ever think of *doing* to Fred. He was a crazy, mythical, cartoon version of our father, so much so he made dad look pretty *good* most of the time. You know how these things work.

In the middle of the ham sandwich she made for me, as I listened to Jane's recounting of her trip back to Westville to bury Fred, everything seemed strange to me and I don't know why. My senses had entered some impossible, impressionistic slow motion in which you register the atomistic parts of everything but never the whole. I was listening to her voice, but I was stumbling, too, through thousands of impossible images of my family, my life so far, images that could not acquire clarity, but just kept expanding into a breathless kind of complexity that was almost too much to bear.

"It was a funny morning, driving up from Halifax," Jane was saying, looking past me, out over the fields. "It felt disarming, private, moody. Just me and what was left of Fred in a box on the passenger seat. It was misty, low fog rolling over the highway all the way to New Glasgow. Every now and then you'd glimpse some bright trees, or a service station would pop up suddenly on your left or right and you'd go, oh! Right! Otherwise, it was like driving through a black and white early Hitchcock flick, the landscape complementing the situation perfectly. Do you want another coffee?"

Our father was Fred's hero, the older brother he needed to be near. It was simple. In his late teens, he'd followed dad into the war, then showed up all the way from Halifax one fall after we'd moved out west in 1952. Except for a short-lived, disastrous marriage, Fred remained single all his life, and tried to live close to us, to have Dad nearby. We were his family, the only family he had outside Nova Scotia. And we each of us loved Fred in our own, imperfect ways, and each of us dealt with his death with difficulty because of the inevitable guilt attending it. As far as we knew, he'd died quite friendless and alone. Among his few things, only a photograph of Dad taken during the war indicated any family. It wasn't easy. The other side of it, of course, was that Fred had put each one of us through the wringer many times over. He was a handful and we'd been pretty good to him, considering. Still, still . . .

"When I drove into Westville, down that tiny main street, past Nana's old place and out to the cemetery, I don't know, but suddenly, everything that had seemed so small, so disposable on the drive up — me and Fred included — seemed full of portent now, large, mythical even. Like some miraculous *return*, you know?"

"Yeah."

"I pulled the car up onto the gravel just outside the cemetery gates, got out, took Fred with me even though I knew I'd be handing him over to the mortuary people later on, and walked in. The earlier mist had turned into a fine, warm rain. All I could hear was the rain drumming on the corrugated metal roof of a machine shed over in the trees to my right and the sounds of my own feet walking along the red cinder path. A soft, but purposeful 'crunch.' And eventually there I was, with Fred, standing above Nana and Papa's graves . . . "

Jane's eyes had welled up suddenly and she covered them with her left hand.

"It's all right," I said. "I know."

"It was just so powerful. Nana, Papa, Fred, me, Dad, Mom, Neil, you. We were all there in different ways, caught in different struggles . . . even our drinking and how each of us got out of it . . . and I think it was the dignity of all that suddenly, the understanding of the hard parts of our lives, how much tap-dancing we'd all had to perform to simply get by . . . how sweet a child Fred must have been once . . . " Jane broke down at this point, looking at me urgently for something.

"All of us," I whispered, holding her hand, knowing full well the power of the word 'child' in Jane's life, the enormity of it. "You were right. We *were* all there, Jane. But you *led* us there. It was you. You were holding poor old Fred."

"He was such a child," she cried. "He was so helpless."

"I know, I know."

"He seemed so small."

"Yes."

"Small."

"It was a huge thing you did, that return. For all of us. For Dad especially."

"Especially for Dad."

Jane used a napkin to dab her eyes. "I was moved. Unexpectedly. I wanted to tell you sometime." Jane smiled up at me. "It was strong. I thought you'd want to know."

"Well, you were right, as usual. I'm glad you told me."

"It's funny," she said, smiling and shaking her head from side to side. "But I think I'd been prepared for it by something that had happened accidentally on the ferry coming over from Newfoundland to Halifax. On our way back."

Everything's crazy upstairs. Uncle Fred flew in this morning from Fort Chip and he and Dad have been going at it ever since. Drinking and smoking in the kitchen. Mom has been quiet. It's different this time. She's letting it happen.

They got the long distance call from Nova Scotia the day before yesterday. My grandfather died of a heart attack. He was sixty-eight years old. Of course, neither of them can go down home for the funeral. There's no money for that. All day yesterday Dad was quiet and kept to himself, but when he drove Uncle Fred home from the airport this morning, they returned with a couple of bottles. They're not in good shape, either of them, especially Uncle Fred. He's all over the place, crying one minute and mad at everybody the next. "Those bastards!" he shouts down the hallway to my dad who's just disappeared into the bathroom, "what the fuck did they ever know about what I was doing? Or care even? They didn't even think to phone, the fuckers."

"Now Fred . . . " my mom says.

"Don't 'now Fred' me, Colette!"

"It's the children, for pity's sake!"

"Don't 'now Fred' me by the jeez . . . those bastards . . . he was my pa . . . did they forget that even?"

"Oh Fred, for Christ's sake, Shut up!" my father says, back from the bathroom, "you sound like the village idiot." I can hear my father laughing now, cheering Fred up.

"You're my brother for Christ's sake," Fred sobs.

"It's all right now, Fred," my father whispers, his own voice breaking.

"Jeez, you're my brother, Charles. God!"

I'm downstairs in the basement near the furnace where it's quiet. Jane is upstairs in the living room, reading. Neil's out playing road hockey with Greg. I don't know what to do. I didn't know him, but I know he was my papa and I should feel sad. I don't feel anything. I keep thinking of shows on TV and what the good looking American boys in them would do in a scene like this, but I can't do whatever that might be. It's just not happening. If I go upstairs I'll start kidding Uncle Fred so he won't get mad. It's easy to do. I do pretty good impressions of John Diefenbaker. I can recite most of Shelley Berman's monologues by heart. I can imitate Uncle Fred back at him to make my dad laugh. But I'm tired and have nowhere to go. I could go over to St. Agnes Church, but it's Saturday and the confessions are on and there's nothing to do there either. I could try to rise up into the air above the house like people do in those stories of medieval Catholic saints, rise way up above the house so high I look down and see myself as this little dot sitting in the basement, and feel protected and indifferent, but I can't do that even. It doesn't work that way today. Hockey Night in Canada won't be on the TV for another hour, and I know that'll get them off it for a while. That'll settle them down maybe.

"What the hell is that?"

It's my father and he's found me. I didn't hear him coming down the stairs.

"It's nothing really," I say.

"For Christ's sake boy, what have you done?"

"A portrait of papa," I say, "from this photograph," and my heart is beating fast. I'm afraid because I don't know if this'll make Dad mad or not. I can't figure the situation out right. It's too hard. I'm twelve, but it's still tricky.

My father lifts the paper up close to his face and I see, for the first time ever, tears in his eyes. He whispers, "I'll be," to himself, then shouts up the stairs, over his shoulder, "Fred?"

"You're my brother by the jeez! Charles!"

"Fred?"

"Where the fuck are you?"

"Fred! Get down here. Rick wants to show you something!"

"The north end of a horse heading south?" we hear Fred shout, cackling maniacally to himself, then there's a loud crash as Fred either falls off his chair or knocks it over as he gets out of it. "Christ!" we hear him whisper to himself, and then we can hear him crying. Then laughing. My father

looks at me, holds one finger up to his lips to indicate we're going to be very quiet so Fred has to work to find us, then laughs and gives me a wink.

"The ferry back from Newfoundland was crowded," Jane said. "It's an overnight trip and we boarded in the afternoon. After I got settled, I strolled around, snooping for things, the way you do. Casual."

"Yeah?" I say.

"Well, I'd noticed this family in the line-up even before we'd boarded. There was this older man, two younger guys, and a small boy who must have been around ten. I figured the old man was the father of the younger men and the grandfather of the boy. Even before we boarded the ferry, I could see the boy was restless, hyper, but not in the demanding way you often see now. Not at all. He wasn't asking for things or complaining. It was the exact opposite. He was trying to make things better all the time. He was cracking jokes, making them all laugh, getting them coffees and smokes. He was always moving, jittery. And he had this big, freckled, generous face that was too old for its body.

The three men had gone directly from their car to the bar, taking the boy with them. I guess it's allowed on the ferry. Either officially or unofficially. There were other kids in there, too.

I knew instinctively the three men were all big drinkers. It was easy to see, especially in the old man, his face. And it's so deep in their culture there. Like it is in Nova Scotia, and how I imagine it is in Ireland and Scotland. You know.

I could see them getting completely loaded and as they did, the longer they went at it, the more guarded and quiet the boy became, the more trapped. His face would light up whenever any of them turned on him, but when they were lost in it amongst themselves, I could see him go somewhere else in his head. I could see this look on his face." Jane stopped her story and raised her hands to her face, covering her eyes, crying.

"It's all right," I said, placing my hand on her shoulder, "it's all right."

"I know, I know," she whispered, tired suddenly. Then she looked at me, "That look on his face," she said. "It was *you*."

I stood up and wrapped my arms around her while she cried.

"It was us," she said.

We joked all the way to the airport. I kept giving Jane a hard time about her little figurines and paintings. I asked her what had possessed her. I told her how they'd been tracking me mercilessly through the house as in some tacky, third-rate horror flick. Then I told her what Jennifer and I had seen in The Modern Art Gallery in Edinburgh two years back: an installation of Antony Gormley's *Field for the British Isles*.

Though we'd heard rumours about this show, we didn't know what to expect. All we knew was they were installing the exhibition the day we'd shown up, and he was going to deliver a talk we'd planned to attend later in the week.

When we arrived, we could tell the gallery attendants were in the middle of something momentous for the security guards were taking special pains to ensure people weren't entering this one, enormous white room on the first floor. They'd let you approach the room and stand in the doorway, but you weren't allowed to enter the room. There was a crowd clustered in the doorway when we first arrived so I told Jennifer I was going for a coffee in the cafeteria downstairs until the crowd died down. She stayed behind.

Eventually, Jennifer showed up and told me it was a good time to go up. "You won't believe it," was all she said.

When I got upstairs and approached it, I ended up being the only person standing in the doorway.

In the room, on the floor, were tens of thousands of small, red clay figures packed in so tightly they filled every inch of the floor space, from baseboard to baseboard, right up to your shoes standing in the doorway. These figures were six inches tall and vaguely human-like in shape. They each had a tiny head with eyes hollowed out, looking up at you standing there. It was incredible. Thousands of them. You couldn't stand there and not feel responsible to all these wee faces staring up at you, innocent, hopeful. That was the effect. I learned later that Gormley had had these figures made in Manchester or Liverpool. Thousands of schoolchildren, senior citizens, business people, artists, workers, and people from all walks of life had fashioned these figures according to a general template, but one by one, each figure being unique, individual. This knowledge only added to the sense that any observer would feel humbled by the weight of the expectations in the field before him or her. You couldn't stand there and retreat into some abstract theory or begin to analyse. You *could* do that, of course, but only later, only afterwards. In that first moment, you were simply humbled by an unending field of expectations aimed directly at you. And you had to take it on. You couldn't avoid it. From that moment on you had to begin to fulfil those expectations. There was no vertical. We were all there, smack dab in the middle of that field, and we were all standing there, too, looking at it.

The airport was its usual crazy self, stuffed with people arriving and departing. That's the thing about airports. Everyone has a buzz on one way or another. Excited. Expectant. Something big is always going to happen.

Jane and I made our way to the international arrivals section and watched the doors that released the arriving passengers out of Canada Customs. We joked about Neil and Mom getting busted, especially Mom, trying to smuggle in contraband from the 'auld sod.' There must have been several big flights arriving back-to-back for we found ourselves in a thick throng of people. It was so packed it was hard to move, and it felt sometimes as if the crowd had a life of its own, surging and retreating to an invisible heartbeat bigger than any one of ours. It was exhilarating and, sometimes, disturbing.

Then we could see the two of them, Mom waving excitedly to both of us and Neil mugging it up for us behind her, wearing a ridiculous Irish fedora, looking like some pathetic extra out of *Finian's Rainbow*. They both appeared tiny over the field of heads separating us from them and we lost track of them from time to time as they made their way through the crowd.

PORNOGRAPHY

The opposite of mystery is pornography.
— Leonard Michaels, *Time Out Of Mind*

SHOVE IT IN. STUFF IT UP. Wheeze, gasp, snort, dribble.
Inhale the whole fucking thing now. *Come on*! You can do
it! You've got enough air in those old lungs! Haul that
naked, pudgy, formless, toneless, overweight body of
yours out onto some specially designed field somewhere
under a noonday sun, haul it out there and scream up into
the sky as loudly as you can, *that is no country for old men*!
There you go! Now, stuff something up your ass or shit
something out and, while you fondle your own erection,
push at least five cigarettes into the hole of your mouth
and light them up, one by one, attempting to speak past
them, prattling on about some mysterious moment you
sense even, and stand there until you think you've used
everything up, hauled everything in, shit everything out,
ejaculated everything out of your system, gasp, snort,
wheeze, blubber, tremble, shake. Until you're done. Until
it's finished. *Consummatum est.* Then drag your emptied,
diminished body back in here and get down on your
fucking knees and promise the universe, one more time,
that you will accept this gift, celebrate it instead of

blowing it up. *There, there now.* It's all right. Everything's going to be all right again. You'll see.

If I could just have a smoke, I know everything would be okay. I'd be able to put up with anything. Really. *Anything.* Maybe that's what addictions are: nature's way of getting you *through* things, especially obnoxious people and/or ideas. Not bad, actually. *Not bad at all.* There's merit there, and I laugh out loud into the late night pressing up against the flat windowpane of my office. Fuck.

It's Friday night, 10:00 PM, and I'm typing in my office at home. This office was a veranda back in 1917 when the house was built. All the external siding is still in here. Somewhere along the line someone sealed it up, replaced the wire screens with plate glass, and insulated the floor against the cold. When we moved into the house ten years ago, she used this room as her painting studio, but three years back, when she discovered she needed more space, we fixed up the big bedroom at the back of the house for her and I moved in here. Though I never admitted it at the time, thus preserving a slight martyrdom to this day, I liked it immediately. When I sit, facing the computer screen, I'm surrounded on two sides by windows that overlook the lane to the south and, over the trees, housetops and buildings of downtown Vernon, all the orchards of Bella Vista to the west. If I move my eye from left to right — or, more precisely, from south to west — I survey a thick, pendulous chestnut tree, a yew tree that grows right against the corner of this room where the windows meet, a series of cedar bushes we keep trimmed to four feet so they won't block out the light, then two bridal wreath bushes that are burgundy, delicate and classy, and farthest to the right finally, a great old magnolia tree that coughs up its load of sensuous, heavy, tulip-shaped blossoms early every spring, then maintains a restrained, minty green over the rest of the summer and fall. I'm living in a garden and that's how I understand it. Though I do my own share of loading up wheelbarrows and moving dirt in and out in the spring, and mowing the lawn and trimming the front hedge throughout the summer and fall, I'll admit to anyone who cares to ask that it is her green thumb that keeps everything going, not anything I do. She's in charge. She understands the slowness of it, big and small, the intricate moisture of it all, the principles of water, the management of water. Left to my own devices, I doubt I could manage it. The whole thing would grow wild and close over the house like a caul within a year, me webbed inside, blinking out. But I enjoy it. I really do. There were times in my life, when I was young and hungry and angry, that I never could have enjoyed these gardens as I do now. They wouldn't have registered on my radar back then; I'd been so obsessed with other things. But now, here I am, sitting in this garden late on a winter night, three days before Christmas, writing away as naturally as the chestnut tree sleeps its dormant winter sleep, and sways in the moist feast of the black night air.

I'll tell you what's obscene, I write. *I'll give you obscene.*

~~~

Neil drove the car away from the pumps and parked it at the far end of the Chevron parking lot. He walked into the small convenience store and asked for a pack of Players Medium Regular. What he got back from her was a large pack of twenty-five and he knew, suddenly, he was in Alberta now, not BC. They didn't sell packs of twenty here, at least not often. Everything was bigger here. That was the idea. When he stepped back outside and walked across the pavement to his car, he couldn't believe the brightness of the air, the clarity of it. It was a brilliant, sunny morning in early November. There was still snow everywhere, but chinook conditions had created a false expectation of spring. Everything was melting and he could smell the moist soil. The clarity was not merely visual. The smells were intricate, too, subtle, discrete from one another: that crazy old mixture of gas, asphalt, earth under melting snow in a warm breeze, smoke and coffee. Sounds were distinct and easily separated, too, as if the earth's body, the entire landscape, was as alert as he was this morning, standing in a service station parking lot, gazing out over miles of snow and prairie fields to the east of Brooks, and into the sun.

He unwrapped the package, stuffed the awkward cellophane wrapper into his side pocket, took out a new smoke and held it between his lips. He flicked his tiny yellow Bic lighter up to light the smoke, then took a deep drag. The first long drag always made him feel hopeful, synthesised, as if everything fit together nicely and was going to be all right, under control. Ah . . . The fields stretched away to the eastern horizon in such solid patterns, such soft, but grounded surety, that his standing there in his old work boots and jeans, his grey jacket zipped against the slight, warm breeze, his new shirt he'd flicked out of his suitcase back at the hotel tucked trimly into the pants, his new winter socks soft in the boots, the new pack of smokes, his new life that was starting this morning — everything seemed the same thing suddenly: blessed, unfolding in sure, radiating lines connecting together like a mandala, a web of circles of light and smells and promises that was irresistible, and that made him feel, for the first time in a long time, unburdened. He thought of Shelley, but drove her out of his mind just as quickly. This was for him, this moment. This was something for himself.

"Take some time off," the chair of the department had said. They were sitting in her office at the campus in North Kelowna. "You're tired, Neil. Understandably. These things aren't easy."

It was strange to hear Elizabeth talking to him like this. They'd hadn't always gotten along; they were too different from one another. Elizabeth was socially awkward, artificially tweedy, abrupt when she should have been cautious, and cautious when she should have been abrupt: the old horsey thing only Brits or Brit wannabes have deep in their blood. Elizabeth was a bit anal about administering the department: fussy about all the wrong things and careless about things she might have been fussy about. Given all this, then, it amazed Neil to hear Elizabeth's voice now, comforting, solicitous, gracious in response to the trouble he was in. And Neil appreciated it and, as he listened to her, his affection and respect for her grew. He'd been wrong about Elizabeth.

"We've succeeded in securing you that half-sabbatical after Christmas," Elizabeth said, staring down at the pristine order of her desk. "And that'll be great for you. You'll get over to Europe again. You deserve it." Elizabeth swivelled in her chair to face Neil directly. She put her arms down on her knees, trying to be informal. Neil could sense the awkwardness of it and could imagine Elizabeth later as she described this sad scene to others in the department who'd relish it, who were likely exulting in Neil's fall from grace. And yet, in the moment now, Neil appreciated Elizabeth's struggle, and knew it was sincere. "All we need now," she continued, "is to get you through this semester."

"I'll take a week," Neil said, staring at his hands clasped in front of him.

"Good! Good!"

"As long as it's okay with the Dean . . . "

"It is! I assure you. Take a week. You've *never* taken sick days!"

"That'll help, for sure," Neil said. "It'll give me enough time to land on my feet. Then I'll finish off the semester just fine."

"It's merely a few classes," Elizabeth said. "Because you teach mostly night classes, it'll only be one class in each case."

"That's right," Neil said. "And it's not like they don't have a lot of work to do."

"Exactly," Elizabeth said. "That's what I want to hear." She turned back to her desk to retrieve the sick leave forms she'd already signed. Neil knew the interview was over. "Will you get away?" Elizabeth asked, smiling, relieved.

"Yes," Neil answered, standing now. "I'm going to drive down to Eastend, Saskatchewan, in fact."

"Saskatchewan!" Elizabeth shrieked louder than she intended. "Heavens! It's November. You really *are* a masochist."

Neil rescued her by responding quickly, "I have a good friend there who doesn't mind the company. That's where

JOHN LENT

I'll be. If you need anything, just call Rick. He'll know how to reach me."

"Wallace Stegner was from Eastend, wasn't he? *Wolfwillow*. Of course. And he wrote *The Angle of Repose*, too, didn't he?"

"It's one of my favourite novels," Neil said.

Neil finished his smoke, butted it out in the snow beneath his boots, and walked back to the car. If he was lucky, he'd get to Eastend by early afternoon, just in time to buy some groceries and give Tyree a call.

~~~

Yeah, obscene. Real pornography. I don't know anymore. These are strange times for sure. I get up to put a CD in the stereo. I select Miles Davis' *Kind Of Blue*. There's something about its rhythms that always get me. And the wonder of it, really, is how he managed to create any of it, considering. Talk about pornography on nine levels at once. But those rhythms, and his lean, simplified, strong bars over them, like air, like the night sky tonight. It's funny. I was reading the diaries of Leonard Michaels and at one point he talks about an idea he borrows from an art critic and it connects to what Davis is doing: "Style is the way an action continues to be *like* itself. It's an imitation of necessity. Max J. Friedlander, my favourite art historian, says, 'unconscious action leads to style. Conscious action to mannerism . . . the art form, insofar as it springs from the soul, is style, insofar as it issues from the mind is manner.'" Makes you wonder, doesn't it? Makes for some tricky passages if you're an artist. But it's good to think about these things, isn't it? I'm at an age now when thinking about them . . . really struggling with them . . . is wonderful because I do not have a lot of time to fool around anymore, and there is so much of that these days, so much foolishness, so much manner. Foolishness in the service of big, invisible, mammoth wheels of corporate steel that encircle us and enclose us, the real pornography of our time, its powerful rhetoric and our complicity, our innocence. I don't know, but these things keep me up sometimes, writing late into the night. Either that, or I turn the computer on and begin to surf the web, a pastime that reminds me of drinking and smoking, my old loves. Hard to say. I can e-mail long lost friends late at night; I can check up on people's careers, see what's happening in New York and London, snoop around the bookstores for new releases, stare at perfect, naked eighteen year old bodies. Or just think and write about these things, Eliot's Tiresias divining the future from the past. *Style. Manner. Spirit. Mind.* In all those classical, binary myths, it is never the mind that saves things, is it? What does that tell us about these times, then, the shape we're in? Where does that lead us? *Now that my ladder's gone . . .* I feel like a diminutive version of Falstaff, his grotesque bulbous old drinking nose shining in the dark, his awareness of his own limitations jangling in his head, trying to point the way. No, this path here. *This one.*

    I'll give you obscene.

~~~

The fields around the car shone like a plate under a bright light. Neil had forgotten about the width of sight out on the prairies, the endlessness of it, its power to humble anything. He'd lived in BC too long. It was a relief, suddenly, to be able to see this much. He flicked on John

Hammond's *Wicked Grin* and let the rhythms match what was happening around the car: the looseness of the creases in the hills, the way they folded over one another, the way the skin of the earth became more human the closer he got to Maple Creek. They must have had chinook conditions for a few days, he thought, for there was no snow on the crests of the hills and these larger undulations of the land against the sky appeared like naked bodies, smooth and tumescent skin against a bright blue. It really *was* rather erotic. You could get into it, he laughed. When he turned south to Maple Creek, he realised everything he'd heard about the Cypress Hills was true: he was entering a magical stretch of land where everything was obvious and concealed, where you were surrounded by skin and the promise of the warmth of that skin, and you were also completely alone, where there was nothing you could see and yet there was a wildness, of vegetation and animals, in every nook and cranny. It was like entering a sensual, benign labyrinth — benign because Neil didn't feel afraid or apprehensive, just compelled. He pulled into Maple Creek and picked up a bottle of Glenlivet for Tyree.

Of course, when the wheels had come off Neil's small train of self-indulgence and sorrow back in Kelowna, Tyree had phoned and invited him to come down to Eastend for a few days. It was just like Tyree to surface at exactly the right moment, old coyote that he was. He'd always had a seventh sense for Neil's ups and downs. It hadn't surprised Neil when he'd picked up the phone that morning and it had been Tyree, and his soft, chuckling Irish voice whispering the truth: "It's as bad as that, is it?"

They'd met years ago when Tyree's career as a writer was rising and Neil had just been starting out. They'd been at a conference in Banff and one night, when a crowd had ended up in a bar downtown, Tyree had grabbed Neil and whispered, "Let's get out of here. Let's go somewhere else." They'd stayed up all night, drinking and talking. It'd been so natural, so easy Neil remembered, knowing that the ease had been in Tyree's generosity, not his own. From that moment on they'd remained connected: by their writing, by something common in the spirit of things they both acknowledged, and by the kind of fun they could have. Tyree drew Neil's sense of humour out of him more than anyone he'd ever met. Tyree would sit, rolling his smokes, looking as droll and mysterious and enigmatic as possible — crazed Irish *makar* — and Neil would babble on, allowing himself to laugh more and more until they were both almost crying with it. The wonder of it was they rarely saw one another or even kept track of one another. Their paths simply crossed rhythmically when they needed to cross, and then, when they met in that inter-section, it was as if there'd been no time since they'd last seen one another.

And Tyree understood trouble, had had a surfeit of it himself. His whole life he'd been gipsying around, showing up on doorsteps in his tattered coat and irresistible smile looking for shelter, leaving a wake of puzzled women behind him, women who might never hear from him again. Coyote. He was often broke, always conning the system. And the tough fact was that a lot of his energy had to go *into* the con instead of into the writing, where his brilliance shone. Not a stranger to trouble, then, and not a stranger to the booze either. And yet, Neil confessed, though Tyree's eyes would water up at the sight of a fine bottle of Scotch — his large hands instantly proffering soon-to-be-filled glasses — Tyree didn't show any signs of being drawn into the dark *other* side of the booze as Neil himself had always felt drawn. That was not one of his troubles.

Their lives couldn't have been more different, either. Tyree was cagey, wary and mysterious. You never knew where he was, and he liked it like that. As a result, Neil knew very little about Tyree aside from his writing and his warm smile in the present, and their tenuous history as friends. In someone else, Neil might even have been afraid of what was hidden in Tyree — something primal, something truly Celtic, some dark force of nature — but for whatever reason he never was. The largest relief for Neil was that he felt relaxed with Tyree and that was rare for him with men. His instinctive shyness and guard-edness disappeared with Tyree.

Neil seldom thought about his own shyness. In fact, most of the time he saw himself as an outgoing, gregarious sort, even a loudmouth. But beneath all that, he knew, was his innate solitariness, a powerful sense of remove. He saw the same contradiction in both his brother Rick and his sister Jane, and he knew it had a lot to do with their father, Charles, and everything they'd been through. But he didn't stop to analyse it much, as he knew both Rick and Jane had. *Until now*, he admitted, reaching over to the passenger seat to retrieve a smoke from the package lying there. *Until now*. He was definitely thinking about it this morning.

Two years back he'd received a cryptic note from Tyree announcing he was living in Eastend. Neil had known

Tyree had gone there for a short stint to write. He'd heard about that through friends in Saskatoon. Later, through the same grapevine, he'd learned that Tyree had fallen in love with the place and stayed there. It made sense to Neil. Tyree had always been a loner. He'd lived in isolated places in Ireland, Greece, and Iceland; so it didn't surprise Neil at all. When he'd phoned Tyree finally, and asked him about it, Tyree had simply said there was something deep in the landscape he loved, and it was a place he could live in cheaply and write.

Until now. He was thinking about it this morning as he drove down the narrow asphalt highway, up all the bright flat ridges of hills in the sun, over the spine of the earth it seemed, and then down slicing, curved roads into the dark, moist folds of the hills where there was still a good deal of snow, but where the vegetation became thick, almost pendulous. *Until now.* He was thinking of this remove in himself, his distance from everything. It must have driven Shelley nuts. It must have. All those mixed signals . . . and what else, Neil wondered, what else? Come on now.

His own body. How removed it was from the sensuality he delighted in around himself . . . how denied it was, the intimacy of that mystery. That must have driven her nuts, too.

Though he knew it was ridiculous, even tacky, he'd become intrigued lately by pornography, what was *called* pornography, at least. And he wondered about being intrigued like that. Jealousy had drawn him there, masochistically, but he knew it wasn't just that. He even worried if he wasn't, secretly, a closet voyeur. But he knew that wasn't true, either.

Hard-core, commercial, triple-X pornography made him laugh. There was nothing erotic about it. It had no mystery. It was blunt, rough, and catered to such heavy-handed male fantasies of power and control that simply weren't his fantasies, ever. In fact, he didn't think they were the fantasies of anyone he knew. That kind of pornography never interested him. But he'd run across a vein of amateur pornography that did fascinate him in which couples or individuals had sex before cameras, were interviewed, and who even discussed their sexuality. There was, at least, the *illusion* of humanness in some of this material, a sense of fun or naturalness, even pride about sex, that he had never grown into himself. He'd always been too guarded. Aside from Shelley, most of his sexual encounters had involved loads of booze and he was lucky he could even recall some of them. But even with Shelley, he wondered how reserved he'd been and had a vast, sinking suspicion that he'd likely been too guarded and that that, too, had contributed to everything falling apart.

He knew this was what had caused him to collapse that night in Kelowna. There was something primal in him that couldn't accept Shelley being with another man. It was simple in one way. But there were other sides to Neil that weren't surprised at all, could handle it well, and somewhere in there, in the circle of these contradictions, Neil suspected Shelley merely longed for more naturalness in sexual intimacy, more fun in it. And, aside from losing Shelley now and having to accept it, the other great sorrow in Neil's life was his suspicion that he might never discover that kind of joy for himself. As he'd wrestled with Shelley's being with another man, as he'd tried to take it in, he found himself almost unbearably panicked by what he'd lost, what he'd squandered. But he didn't know what he might have done differently. That was the problem. He wasn't sure. That was why he'd rented those cheesy little videos and watched them: to help him find out. Many of them ran against the old, masculine insecurity about sex and territory, private property. If anything, they revealed a softer, more curious side to male sexuality, a side that understood monogamy was its own riddle, for both men and women, understood how interested in sharing pleasure men were. How could a woman sleep with another man just for fun? *It was easy.* Was that a kind of intimacy too? Had Neil brought too much self-consciousness and seriousness into that part of his life, too? It drove him crazy, these questions, because they were asked in the midst of a fear that he was allowing himself to miss out on part of the gift he'd been given, but didn't know what to do to change it. He was who he was. He was forty-four, after all. He *was* shy. He could hear some quack saying, "It's very simple, you know. It's called fear of intimacy! There! It's been said. It's on the table now. Fix it." But what *was* that fear? What *was* intimacy?

He was descending a steep hill and when he got to the bottom of it, he could see buildings tucked against the valley walls to his left. He crossed a set of tracks and came to a stop sign. He turned left and saw another sign immediately: *Welcome To Eastend*. It didn't take him long to find the house.

~~~

She's gone away for the weekend, with her sister. They've gone down to do last-minute Christmas shopping in

Kelowna where all the stores are. I have the house to myself. I can do anything I want. That's why I'm sitting in here so late, staring through the dark at all the soft lights of the city below, peering through the light snowfall down into the town.

It's quiet in here tonight. I have Coltrane's *Blue Train* on in the background now. I've turned up the volume and the whole, wide thing is rattling through the house, playing itself against the heat, the darkness and the soft snow falling through the dark. Sometimes you just get lucky, eh? You get these moments delivered on a platter. I am so lucky, sometimes even *I* can't believe it. But then, there's all those other times that make up for these, so I don't need to feel too guilty.

The thing is this: I desperately need to have a smoke, and I'm not going to let myself have one. I don't have any in the house. I'd have to get in the car. I'm not going to.

But fuck, this is awful.

So, I'm sitting here in paradise, thinking of leaving it. The old Malcolm Lowry vanishing act. What a great big pile of bullshit *that* is. What the hell's going on? What do I really need? And why do I always need it? Nuts. Revolting. Endless. And I'm in pretty good shape compared to most of the people I know. I'm doing all right. So, what's the deal? No art's going to redeem this, I tell ya. No sleight-of-hand here, no transcendence, epiphany, or any other *deus ex machina* is going to come to the rescue. Just me in my body and *it* just wants to get stuffed 'till it explodes or, simply, stops. Unreal. What *is* this? It's childish is what it *is*, but so what? What does *that* mean? What kind of comfort is *that*? Don't give me *that*.

Just a second. Three figures are approaching up the concrete path through the snow. I can hear them laughing from here. What the hell is *this*? "Ebenezer?" someone shouts on the other side of my front door. "Ebenezer?"

~~~

"Yah, you're fucked up, is all," Tyree said as his deep blue, wolf eyes focused on the cigarette he was rolling over a large, glass ashtray lying in the middle of a coffee table stacked with books and newspapers. "You've got to get out of yer head."

Tyree's house was like a hobbit house. It was tiny, low-ceilinged and stuffed to the gills with books and magazines and paintings and tins and pots and pans and one very expensive, state-of-the-art laptop computer that kept Tyree connected to the outside world. Everything was everywhere, but Tyree knew exactly where everything was. It was amazing to Neil, but Tyree moved about the place as if it had the space of a vast cathedral or castle. And Tyree was taller, bigger than Neil. Neil had expected him to be inching and crouching his way through the myriad of things he used and collected, but no, he glided through the place as if it were a vast medieval hall and he was its host wizard, which in many ways, he was. Neil had found the house easily, and he'd presented Tyree with the Glenlivet which they were both enjoying the first dram of. Neil leaned back into the big chair that sat across from the old, wide couch Tyree sat in the middle of, suspended above his ashtray.

"Yeah, I know," Neil said.

"I *know* you know," Tyree said, "but what the fuck are ya going to *do* about the knowing?"

"Now *that* I *don't* know.

"Well, you're going away after Christmas. You'll be getting out of here. That's something. That's a good start. Where're you going to go?"

"I'm going to spend some time in Ireland, near Cork. Maybe stay a few weeks in Cornwall. I might go to France. Both Rick and Jane have been there and have friends who might show me around, who I might mooch off of. I haven't worked it all out yet."

"Sounds good, very good. Just what the old doctor ordered. How about Shelley? How does she feel about all that?"

"Well, I don't really know, do I? She seems relieved in some ways. Of course, I don't know how I feel about *that*. But she seems happy for me." Neil laughed, then leaned forward so he could flick his cigarette ash into Tyree's ashtray, too. "Who knows what Shelley's thinking these days . . . it's very hard for me to tell . . . and it's *not* like I haven't given it a lot of thought. I tell ya! But I *do* know Shelley well enough to know she fears I'm on the road to ruin and that all this shit — our break-up — is just going to cast me farther and faster along that road, so I think the announcement that I'm going away, that I have these plans, I think all that has made her feel better, less guilty, more hopeful about me rescuing myself from disaster."

"And are you?"

"Am I what?"

"On the road to ruin?"

Neil laughed. He couldn't help it. Tyree looked so serious, so concerned, but was himself so eccentric, had lived so unconventionally, that for him to ask that question of Neil seemed, on one level at least, hilarious. Both Tyree and Neil *loved* ruin.

"Take me seriously. You know what I'm talking about here. I don't mean what Shelley means. I mean *are you on the road to ruin* the way *we* understand things."

Neil was disarmed. Someone had asked the right question. "I hope not," he said, "I really hope that's not the case. But I can't say I'm not a bit afraid of it sometimes . . . fuck."

"That's all you need."

"What's that?"

"The hope that you *won't* fuck it all up. It's all you need. Trust it."

Tyree jumped up from the couch, his cigarette balanced impossibly between his lips, and swept into the kitchen. He returned with the bottle of Glenlivet in his hands, holding it as if it were a grail, and placed it ceremoniously on the coffee table, next to the ashtray. "Now, we're going to have another dram of this, both of us. We're going to toast your imminent ascension into the heavens of things, then we're going to slam on our jackets and our gloves and scarves and go out for a walk. It's going to be perfect light on the hills in about an hour. We're going to place ourselves in the middle of it."

"Anything you say, boss. Anything you say."

~~~

I'm fumbling with the front door locks, my heart thumping. I expect to see Marley in rags on the other side of the door, railing against me — *bus-i-ness! They were your bus-i-ness!* — or even worse, Rick, Jane and Neil finally materialising before me to hold me to account for their lives, the final reckoning. But when I swing it open there's Callum, Alex and an attractive young woman named Amanda. I can smell them before they speak. They've been down in Checkers since mid-afternoon and are, as Callum might say in his thick Scottish brogue, "well-oiled."

"We've come to claim yer immartal soul, lad!" Callum yells, spraying all of us in the process.

"That's precisely correct," Alex mumbles, "we're going to take you down to Checkers!"

"Hi there," I say to Amanda, "nice to meet you."

"You too," she says, "Callum has told me . . . "

"Cut the pleasantries," Callum intones, "let's shoot the craw!"

"Did you walk all the way here from Checkers?"

"We did," says Alex.

"Why didn't you *phone* me for Christ's sake?"

"Because you would have refused to come," Callum replies, smirking, "Oh, you would have *said* you were coming, sure, sure, but you *wouldn't* have. So we thought we'd come and haul you down there."

"Fair enough," I say.

I've worked with Callum and Alex for ten years and we have our own rituals. Since Callum's marriage broke up a year ago, we've spent a lot of time together, great, long sessions in which we discuss the latest news in literature, all the hockey and football developments, and when we can't avoid it, the petty gossip and trivial viciousness that catapults around us where we work. Callum is a giant of a Scotsman, born in Falkirk, raised in Livingston, but the most international of all my friends because his dad was an engineer, and they lived everywhere. He's six foot five, often shaves his head, and has that presence that makes it tricky in bars late at night because belligerent males often want to pick fights with him because of his size. Sadly for them, he is skilled in the ancient Scottish art of the 'Glasgow kiss'. Callum has just turned forty, eight years younger than me. Alex is a mere pup, in his mid-thirties still, a good-looking man women are drawn to immediately, but who is happily married with two young children. There's mischievousness in him though; he loves pushing the edges of things; he loves the unconventional, too. The three of us are a good mix. I've never met the lovely Amanda before, but I'm sure to get the goods on her later tonight.

"Are ya goan' tae stand there a' fucking night in your jammies, or are ya comin' doon the pub?" Callum yells suddenly, waking me out of my trance.

"It'll just take me five minutes," I say. "Sit down in there. Grab yourselves a beer from the fridge. I think there are a few in there though, as you know, it's tricky. I can never tell with her. It's just the way it is."

I can hear them laughing as I disappear down the hall to get dressed.

~~~

Everywhere he looked on the walk out of town — even in this seemingly isolated part of an isolated province — Neil saw evidence of larger wheels whirling around people like him and Tyree more and more in the past ten years since Mulroney had initiated the great corporate, global giveaway. Companies like Cargill had insinuated themselves into the grain industry, and even the business of ranching, which was what most of the farmers around

JOHN LENT

Eastend did, was falling under the whims and wishes of international cartels and invisible agreements and arrangements. As they walked up the hill out of town and into the setting sun, Neil was hit by the vertigo of walking over two planets simultaneously, as if he was walking over the simple, rich earth that he and everyone like him inhabited and explored and inhaled and exhaled, but sensing, above his head, another, steel-like construction, a world that whirled mostly invisible, and that had another sense of itself and was dedicated to using everything up in such vast acts of ignoring the human, ignoring resources, ignoring the sensual complexity of all that was alive and nurturing itself on the planet beneath it, that it was hard to think about. It was hard to think about because the steel world, the invisible mesh of it, was constructed of such sure, brutal, distances of will and such a patronising sense of the smaller world that moved capriciously beneath it, that there was no awareness of that smaller world. Sure, Neil thought, people down there might complain or raise issues, even whole countries might seem concerned or alarmed, but by the time anything they raised was dealt with, such smooth acts of deception had taken place, such breathtakingly adroit manoeuvres of diplomacy had done their work to conceal things, that it was always too late.

The other world always won. The handlers of the political machinery in that higher, suspended, steel world, had become so cunning that by the time ordinary people noticed something was wrong, the corporate powers who might have committed the wrong seemed also to be on the same side as them, struggling to solve things too, suddenly concerned with solutions when, in fact, they'd counted on these delays of perception all along.

There were moments when a door like this one opened in Neil's head and he could smell the visceral stench of this pornography, this fuck of everything in the name of the short-term, the fast-cash, and the mean-spiritedness of these times, but then the door closed shut again and shorter, smaller versions of it seemed like paranoia, or left-wing Cassandra-like hysteria. But what he saw when the door opened like this was, he knew, real and frightening. It had opened this time because Tyree had warned him as they'd climbed over a rancher's fence, to keep his ears peeled for hunters from the States, up for their annual kill.

"They fly them up into Swift Current," he said. "They get loaded and show up in black four-by-fours for a week, two weeks, roam the hill with weapons, looking for something to take back."

"Aren't there laws against that sort of thing?"

Tyree stared back at him, balefully.

"Is there nothing you can do?"

Tyree held the same doleful look, then muttered, "Read John Ralston Saul?"

"I know, I know," Neil whispered back. "I know."

"Here we go," Tyree announced, turning left up a small trail lined with slender, low poplars, and which led to a mysterious perch Tyree had already hinted at, concealed in the trees somewhere.

~~~

We're packed, impossibly, into my little Tercel, driving down the main street on our way to Checkers. We're an encapsulated Babel, something that always happens when we're out having fun. I'm speaking in my shamelessly fake Scottish accent. Callum is trying to sound like a tweedy, upper-class English twit. Alex is speaking some kind of broken Russian, and Amanda is attempting a southern drawl. Voices. Go figure.

Downtown is deserted. This would have been unusual on a Friday night ten years ago, but is standard now. Something is happening to this small city that is happening everywhere else, too. All the franchise, box stores have set themselves up out on the highway, past the city limits so they can pay cheap taxes, and have constructed malls where people go to look for things, even restaurants and bars. Downtowns have been emptied, and the sad truth is that these shifts have been welcomed in the name of progress and prosperity. Except, of course, that things are getting worse, not better. A new kind of feudalism is settling in and, on some level at least, we all know it, participate in it, and, to a certain degree, help it along. It's crazy, but it's happening. "You're either with us, or you're terrorists." Variations on a large theme.

I pull into a Chevron because they have a Royal Bank ATM and it strikes me, of course, that it's a self-serve place in every sense. If I want gas, I do it myself; if I want money, I do it myself. What strokes of bloody genius, I think. Earlier this week, in a more frightening improvisation upon the same theme, Don Mazinkowski released a new set of recommendations for restructuring health care in Ralph Klein's Alberta. The most talked-about item had to do with issuing patient cards that would work like Interac cards. You'd be in charge of your own annual health care allotment. *We want to make it easier for people*

to keep track of these things; we want to help them. Brilliant.
It was like the gas companies and the banks ten years ago.
How can we cut back on our expenses, get the customers
to do all the work and take on all the responsibility, then
charge them more for doing the work themselves and
increase our profits wildly? How can we get rid of all the
service bays, mechanics, tellers, service people? *I know. I
know exactly what we can do.* We'll make everything self-
serve and charge for the service, then raise the prices, too.
We'll close down all the service bays, fire all the
mechanics, open up little convenience stores that sell
everything at the highest prices the market will bear, and
hire sixteen year old high school dropouts to run the
places and be mugged late at night. We'll close half our
branches down, cut back on our hours, fire a passle of
tellers, install ATMs everywhere, get the customers to do
all their banking electronically, and charge them for all
these changes and efficiencies. Perfect. Brilliant.

And it's working.

Sure, something in me knows it isn't quite this simple,
but there's something going on that is ushering in a new
kind of, seemingly benign serfdom. I don't know, but it
sure feels like it. I'm looking at the three of them laughing
and talking as I approach the car, and I see all of us,
suddenly, caught in these larger wheels I'm imagining,
and I register some strange sense of us being at the mercy
of things and our laughter as some hollow gesture back,
some inept defiance. I don't know. This is compounded in
me, I know, because I *didn't* buy a pack of smokes in the
store, even though I *almost* did, and instead of feeling
triumphant, this longing for a smoke, on top of my being
so mad at how helpless I am, makes me want to puke I feel

so fucked. Maybe it's just me, I think, as I round the corner of the car to the driver's side. Maybe it's just me that's causing all this to seem real. Maybe I'm just floundering, as usual, and things aren't as bad as they seem. Things'll get better. But somehow, I don't believe it *is* just me, and somehow I *don't* believe things'll get better. They're just hard to see. I wish I could *see* things more clearly.

"I've got the money now, lads and lassies! I'll be okay now for sure," I say as I buckle up.

"That's lovely, old chap," Callum mutters. "Let's repair to the pub where all manner of human release awaits and promises."

"In Canada, you do such things?"

"Ah yes, old bean. We have the luxury of such things here. We have cultivated our own culture, after all."

"Oh boy, oh boy, oh boy!"

"Ah shut yer gobs, the lot of you!"

"Mercy, you gentlemen are a strange gathering!"

"That we are, miss. That we are."

~~~

"You better let the booze go."

"You think?"

"I do."

"Why?"

"'Cause you're not having any fun. It's just dragging you down."

"I wanted to be the one member of my family that could live with it," I say.

"Well, you're *not*, though."

"But what will my life be like?"

"Without it you mean?"

"Yes."

"I don't know, but I suspect you'll feel better." Tyree looked away, across the valley, and pointed his hand to the far horizon. "See that?"

Neil stared over the hills, trying to see what Tyree was looking at. They were sitting in a small clearing at the top of a cliff that overlooked the small valley that held Eastend. In the centre of it, beginning to twinkle with electricity in the dusk, was the town itself. And surrounding it, on all sides, were bare, leathered hills, creasing and folding upwards, to another prairie table and more undulating ridges in those further distances. The hills were brown and mauve in the late fall, spotted with creases of snow and clusters of bare poplar trees, and, in the deeper folds, spruce copses, thick and dark. There was an overwhelming silence, a vast acoustic broken by small, random sounds: birds, coyotes, the odd truck gearing down for the descent into the town, an occasional door slamming in the dusk. Otherwise, there was a limitless quiet, thick with its own soft sound. Finally, Neil did see what Tyree was pointing at: on the far side of the valley, an eagle circled above a copse of spruce trees, looking for supper. Neil wasn't sure. He didn't know much about eagles. And though he loved landscape, though he loved situations like this, a long, quiet sadness engulfed him as he realised he didn't know much about anything physical. He didn't even know the names of things. He wondered how he could have paid so much attention to some things in his life, and so little to others. He thought again of Shelley, of what she might be doing at this moment, and he imagined her as another landscape he hadn't seen, hadn't paid attention to, receding from his life forever. It was hard to bear. Maybe Tyree was right about the booze.

Neil looked at his hands in amazement. They were *his* hands. This was *his* body, after all. *Hoc est enim corpus meum.* He looked sideways at Tyree. Tyree grinned back.

"Watcha thinking about," Tyree asked.

"I don't know," Neil answered him. "but it's great to be sitting here with you." Neil forced a grin onto his face, then meant it.

"To descend into the body is a magical thing," Tyree said cryptically. Typical.

"Really?

"Oh yes! It's so easy to forget about. As easy as not noticing this." Tyree gestured his large hand from left to right across the landscape, indicating everything before them. "We only have this time here, in this place. All the rest of it . . . " Tyree stopped suddenly, then sighed, shaking his head sadly, "Ah I don't know . . . I'd *love* to think I did, but I don't."

"What do you mean?"

"Just how it all works. I live in my head, too."

"But you're way healthier than I am," Neil laughed, "way healthier."

"Sometimes, maybe," Tyree said. "Other times, no."

"It's the spirit, isn't it?" Neil asked.

"It's the spirit as body, though," Tyree said, "and it's funny and mysterious and contradictory, boy. It's never easy. You're not the only one who feels such sorrow. Or anger." Tyree fumbled in his side pocket and produced two cigarettes he'd rolled earlier. "Here, have one of these." He slipped one over into Neil's hand, "Let's have a smoke, at least."

Neil took the smoke, put it up to his lips, and leaned forward and sideways to get a light off the match Tyree had struck against a stone. He saw Tyree's face shine suddenly, illuminated by the fierce light of the match, his face twinkling, playful, mysterious. They both lay back smoking, staring up into a vast sky shifting blocks of darkness above their heads like renaissance clockwork. Neil could hear birds in the distance. A car rolled over a cattle gate. Then silence.

~~~

Checkers is wild tonight. It's packed with people so you have to shout to be heard. It's the usual Friday night mix of workers celebrating the weekend, and students on the prowl, time-honoured traditions in these small, interior cities. Once I get used to it, though, it works just fine.

It's strange for me to sit in a place like this on a Friday or Saturday night sometimes. In the old days, when I used to drink, I'd be half-way there by now, calculating where I'd be in another few hours. I don't even think of that now, and never imagined I'd ever feel like that. I thought I'd miss the buzz too much. I don't miss it at all. Doesn't even cross my mind. Don't get me wrong. For the first few years, I thought about it all the time, but I never imagined I'd reach this stage. I'm taking heart in it tonight because someday, farther on down the line maybe, I'll feel the same way about the smoking. I sure hope so. I'm sitting here now, talking to Amanda. Callum and Alex are outside on the patio having a smoke which is where I'd like to be, too, but am refusing to go. Christ!

As it turns out, Amanda is Alex's cousin from Ottawa. She's here visiting Alex and his wife Naomi. She's just completed a Master's Degree in journalism at Carleton, and she's taking a few months to drive across the country, reward herself before entering the PhD program in the fall.

"Yeah, conventional wisdom is that his handlers, especially Collins, are simply attempting to duplicate the New Zealand strategy. Make all the major cuts quickly; do all the damage at the start, in the first two years, then start to kiss ass in preparation to get elected again, get another majority," Amanda says.

We're talking about the cuts to Social Services that are scheduled here in British Columbia next week. Gordon Campbell and the boys are riding high, forgetting we've witnessed this scenario at least twice in the last twelve years — first Klein, then Harris — three times if her connection to New Zealand is accurate, and I know it is. "The big difference," I say, "is that Klein had a charisma — a perverted charm and folksiness — to pull a lot of it off, and Harris had the will, the mean-spirited will to withstand the criticism. Campbell has neither. He hasn't shown his face more than two or three times since he was elected. He's completely inept. He can't articulate himself without a script. He's wooden, graceless and defensive. He'll never manage the heat he's going to get. Gary Collins might, not Campbell."

"It'll be interesting to see," Amanda says. "He was given such a majority. But even when you get that, you have to remember the popular vote and they appear to have ignored it."

"I don't know," I say. "It's just sad that we have to have this constant pendulum. Left, right. Right, left. Left, right. We can't sustain any middle ground. Before the left has a chance to rejuvenate itself, he'll have given half the province away. We'll be strip malls with Casinos and Wal-Marts. We'll be pumping every ounce of water we have down to California. And we'll have people, many more people than we have now, sleeping in the streets, disen-franchised. It'll be a big fucking mess. And then, if we're lucky, the pendulum will swing back the other way, to the left, but by the time the left is thrown out one more time, they won't have managed to do much but reverse a small portion of what these guys will achieve. It's a mess. It's going to get ugly."

"You think so?" she asks.

"Yeah, I do," I say. "And it doesn't make me feel good to say it. I wish it weren't going to be the case. It just feels like it. Everything is pointing in that direction."

"And what direction might *that* be, son?" Callum asks, looming suddenly at my side, casting his big grin down onto the table like a thrown dice.

"Ah, fuck off then, ya big poofter."

I know what's coming. I can feel it in advance. He's reached that stage now. Callum leans down and gives my bald pate a big, sloppy, perfectly aimed kiss. "I luv ya, ya auld eejit."

I roll my eyes at Amanda and we're all off again.

~~~

Tyree must have dozed off. Neil was sitting up, holding his knees in the circle of his forearms, staring out into the darkness of the valley. He'd just watched the sun descend into the hills to the east flinging shards of light out over streaks of the landscape so Neil could see the spectrum of colour in the very hills that had seemed so drab earlier. Everything had taken on more colour and texture. He could feel a thick wheel of things whirling around him, making him almost dizzy in the dark. But he couldn't take his eyes off the landscape. There were too many things happening in it. Some he could see. Some he could hear. Others he could only sense vaguely through smell, or the taste of different kinds of moisture in the air.

His own body felt heavy with moisture, too, all its fluids, as it sat there pressing itself into the fine gravel of the spot he was sitting in. And as his eyes took in the landscape in front of him, flickering from hill to road, from tree to branch, his mind raced towards clarity, trying to cast a net of order over the chaos it had created. Neil felt buoyant when his mind raced like this — it was a physical buzz — for it was always in the strong hope that such a net could be found. *Here it is right here. Go ahead. Everything's going to be all right. You'll see.* He always felt he was just on the verge of solving everything, making everything all right. But this afternoon, in the thin, late-afternoon dusk, with Tyree dozing off right next to him, though he felt the usual exhilaration, he didn't have the sense of order that usually accompanied it. If anything, it was the opposite, as if everything were moving surely but inexorably outward, unresolved, unrestrained, and that it was, for some strange reason, all right. The only order in this maelstrom was the distinct sense of his own body, sitting squarely upon the ground, a weight that was real, expectant, vigilant and which had powers that were unconscious, automatic. He held his fingers out before his eyes and marvelled at them. His heart beat on its own. His lungs breathed in, then out, on their own. If a stone fell from the sky, his head would move out of the way instinctively. It knew what to do. And even his mind, the thing he was most suspicious of, even his mind seemed to know what to do as long as it hauled the rest of his body with it.

And that is what I've missed out on for so long, he thought. *That's it.* He had considered his spirit to be something disconnected from the rest of this weight, or at least capable of being disconnected. He began to see how dangerous that separation was. How had this happened? If this was how he imagined himself in his body, how could he not also feel the same way about the world around it? Or the people trying to connect with him in that world? *Think now. Don't lose it.* But it isn't something you *lose*, he chided the voice in his head. I've had enough of that striving. It isn't something you think about. It's something you *feel*. There's a huge difference. Even I suspect that, he thought. Across the valley, half way up the hill in the distance, a plume of burgundy smoke rose up out of a red ochre chimney and began to ascend into the mixed darknesses above it, twisting, sinewy.

What's wrong? he heard a voice wailing up into the same air. *What have I done to make me so stubborn and afraid?*

And while another rational part of him wondered *what the hell was that?* his body settled into a wide field of possible and impossible replies. Neil felt his arms sway outwards at his sides and found himself standing suddenly, his feet wide apart, his head arching up into the night sky, looking into the first stars and the rest of the ever-increasing darkness. And while that other part of his mind began to mutter things about finally losing it this time, Neil decided to go with his body, see where it would take him.

He was suspended in mid-air, on a forward angle, high above the landscape. He was looking up into the sky, but when he stopped and gazed down he could see he had risen at least several hundred feet above the spot he'd been sitting in. He was in the air, but not moving in the air. He was hanging above the landscape. *What's wrong?* He yelled up into the sky this time, at the top of his lungs, *what have I done to make me so stubborn and afraid?*

There was nothing but a thick, dark silence around him and he heard himself begin to weep. And, suddenly, he knew what he was weeping for: the loss of Shelley, but then, behind that, he sensed his father's face smiling at him, then shaking his head regretfully, mouthing words Neil couldn't hear, and then, unbelievably, he saw the other face. It was a face completely forgotten from his childhood, completely erased. It was the face of a much older boy in the neighbourhood, a boy who was in his late-teens when Neil was nine. He had Neil cornered in a basement somewhere. He could smell all the old papers. Rick was nowhere to be seen. Neil was alone in this and the boy had him cornered against a shelf somewhere in the midst of all these old potato smells in the moist dark and the boy had turned him around and was whispering things to Neil as his hands moved over Neil's jeans and his voice sounded so reasonable, so old, so relaxed, so urgent, and Neil didn't know what to do, what *do* you do? And the boy was telling him he just wanted to rub against him in the dark, that he wouldn't mind, that no one would ever know, and it was so easy, like *this* the boy whispered, and

Neil could feel his pants being pulled down in the dark and there was nowhere to go; he was struggling against the boy but he was so big and Neil's voice couldn't get out of his body couldn't get out of his body couldn't get out of his body and there was no-one around to help him and what do you do and how do you get out of this and his mind kept panicking trying to figure out some way of loosening the grips on his back and sides and not being able to move because he was being held so powerfully not being able to move not being able to move being held like this and what was moving up and down in the crack of his bum and getting wet and slick until suddenly the older boy sighed and grunted and fell against him his stinky breath against Neil's neck and everything was over in the dark everything was finished and Neil could feel a cloth on his bum suddenly and the boy's voice whispering about secrets and parents and trouble trailing off into a whimper as Neil broke free finally, pulling his pants up as he raced up the basement stairs and, instead of running home, sprinting down the lane in the opposite direction and not stopping until he was walking, exhausted, on Whyte Avenue, near Chick's Shoe Store in the dark, miles away, his secret something he'd never tell a soul he was so mad, to be held like that so you couldn't move, you couldn't move, to be trapped in your body like that, and Neil was crying still as the scene on Whyte Avenue faded and he saw his father again, his father Charles, rowing away from him on a lake somewhere, rowing into a permanent distance at the far end of the lake where the water lipped the sky, and where he could see Shelley, too, also disappearing, everything fading away on him, everything leaving him alone it's just the way things are, and he was pleading for Shelley to come back, for his father to come back, but then realised the distance was *his* distance, not theirs, and he was fading away from *them*, fading away from them, fading away from them, mumbling it's just the way things are, it's just the way things are, it's just the way things are . . . "It's just the way things are. You're going to be all right." It was Tyree, next to him suddenly, whispering, holding onto him. When Neil opened his eyes, he was kneeling in the same spot they'd been sitting. He looked sideways at Tyree's face full of worry and confusion.

"What the hell?" Neil whispered to him. "What the hell was *that* all about?

Tyree smiled his old smile, his face creased by years of smiling like that. "I don't know, but you gave me a start. You woke me up! Are you all right?"

"Of course I am," Neil said, suddenly furtive. "You bet.

"But what happened?"

"I'm not quite sure."

"And you're sure you're okay?"

"Yeah, I'm okay now."

"We'd better walk back to town. It's getting cold up here."

"Sure. Let's do that."

~⁓⁓

Alex and Amanda left twenty minutes ago, and Callum and I are ready to leave. He's downing his last pint. We've had a good night. It's been fun to sit and gab away. We have jobs that are so serious most of the time, it's great to sit around and be silly. People need to do this. We'd go bonkers otherwise.

We pause outside the gigantic front doors of the hotel so Callum can have a last smoke before we get into my car. I watch him wrestle the smoke out of the package, plant it between his lips, light it up, then suck back that first, sweet drag. Christ! My eyes must be bugging out of my head with longing, but I maintain my composure. I can do this. I *have* to do it. For *me*. Otherwise, I know what'll happen. The typical deal. On the day I receive my first early retirement pension check, I'll get the news from the doctor that I have three months to get my things in order. You know how it goes. I still want to have a bit of fun. There are places I want to see. People I want to talk to. I also don't want to let those big, invisible wheels win *everything*. I don't want to think I spent *all* my adult life anaesthetised, Auden's "Good Citizen" incarnate, pathetic. I *do* want to tell them they can kiss my ass, and I don't want to follow that up by asking, feebly, "By the way, you wouldn't by any chance have a *smoke* I could bum off you, would you?" You know how it goes. I love sin, fun, flesh as much as the next soul, but there are wheels within wheels, and you have to start somewhere, and, if that's the case, it might as well be with me, right here, right now.

There was a Junior Hockey game tonight at the Arena and many of the young men and women in Checkers have either been at the game, or, even, players in it. Whenever that happens, things get a bit frisky. There are usually a couple of fights in the parking lot, or, later on, accidents on the highway. The usual deal. As Callum and I stand there, making small talk while he finishes his smoke, a car pulls up to a stall to receive four teenagers who've been drinking inside. They're loud and loaded, two guys and two girls, but the guy driving is in the worst shape. He has a look on his face you only get when you're so looped you stare but you're not focusing. We take this in for a few minutes while they joke and tease one another, then I can't stand it and approach them. I reach into my back pocket, pull out my wallet, and produce a twenty dollar bill I wave at the driver. He's looking up at me in his own way.

"Here," I say.

"What's your problem, old man?" he asks.

Another guy in the back seat yells, "Yeah, what's the deal you old fuck?" and a young woman in the back with him laughs hysterically, urging him on. He leans forward over the back seat now so his head is close to the driver's head.

"Take a cab," I say. "It's on me."

"What the fuck, man. Fuck off, "the driver mumbles.

"You're too smashed," I say. "Here. Take it. It's no big deal."

"I'm okay," the kid says.

"Yeah," the kid in the back seat says.

"Yeah," the girl in the back seat laughs.

"No you're not," I say. "You'll get busted. For sure. You don't want to do that."

"I'm not going to get busted," the driver says, smirking, trying to focus.

"Yeah, you are unfortunately," I say. "It's simple. Here's the cab fare. Take it."

"*Take the cab fare,*" Callum intones in his most imperious voice. He has appeared as a gigantic shadow behind me. "*We're trying to help you.*"

There is a split second when things could go wrong. I see it in the face of the driver, but more in the face of the kid in the backseat who has his girl with him. Miraculously, the driver gives in. He looks up at me and Callum. I look over my shoulder and Callum is smiling at the driver. "I'll phone for the cab," Callum says gently, and walks back into the hotel lobby.

"We have to stick together," I say to them as they get out of the car and stand, shuffling around in the dark, not quite knowing what to say now, wondering if they've won or lost. The driver extends his hand to me. "I know I'm a bit shit-faced tonight, man," he says, "but thanks."

"It's okay. I just don't want to see you busted or hurt."

The kids stay, standing around the car, talking to one another. A cab pulls up and takes them away. Callum and I watch them disappear.

"All right, lad," I say finally. "We've done our good deed for the night. Let's head up the hill."

We pass two police blockades on the way up to Callum's house, and one bad accident just off Pleasant Valley Road. Some young buck in a new Honda Civic has miscalculated the turn onto 39th Avenue and has wrapped his car around a pole. The ambulance pulls away from the scene, its lights flashing and its siren screeching, just as we pull up. Two cop cars flank a clutch of people standing around the twisted car, and the blinding strobe of the red and blue flashing lights flicker through the tableau like a nightmare, a warning.

When I get back to the house, I put a Ry Cooder CD on, an old one called *Jazz*, and I stand in the dark looking out my front window as the music fills the house. It's funny after what I've just seen to have this old music playing. The juxtaposition is eerie. Cooder's music suggests the simpler, less-complicated life of turn of the century North America one-hundred years ago, the same era of the house I'm standing in, built in 1917. It's the exact world Ronnie Reagan used to evoke every time he was in trouble and needed support. All those Norman Rockwell images of east-coast towns with barber poles and fourth of July picnics, little guys with freckles and open, smiling white faces pulling the pig-tails of smaller, equally innocent blonde girls. It's the same ideal world routinely evoked by any interest seeking power over people on this continent, and it works every time. "You're either for us, or you're terrorists." I can hear the sirens through the plate-glass of my front window, competing with those wonderful, dangerous old tunes. The tunes are insidious dreams really, of an order that never existed but still has the power to convince us, hold us so tightly we cannot move, but are trapped against its weight while it works away, while it whispers softly in the dark, then slides itself into us, stealing our dignity, using it up.

So It Won't Go Away

For Mike Lent and Jay Ruzesky

AND IT SEEMED THIS WAS MY LAST CHANCE TO SPEAK, even though that had never occurred to me before. My life had shuffled forward on principles of logic and modesty that hadn't seduced me into thinking my work had to be voiced in another, more strident way. The sudden urgency felt odd, until I accepted it as easily as I have, for years, accepted its opposite: being quiet, learning things.

I'm talking of games, of course: playing them, resisting them, acknowledging how they always play a role in the world of art, of painting, of writing, the whole field. And the games are understandable, forgivable even, if they do not interfere with the real work going on underneath them.

All my life I had criticised how mediocrity inevitably announced its own success and power before anything else could. How to put this right? It seemed rare, in work, in politics, in art, that people, who were genuinely talented, conscientious, or well-read, advanced into any situation in which their strengths were acknowledged or celebrated even. Instead, it was the people whose "art" it was to lust for that kind of acknowledgement and power who ended up in those situations. And that always seemed okay to me, though I whined about its relentless energy, as long as it didn't prevent other things from happening. As long as it didn't hold up the real work too much. The arduous work. The ardour. The love.

Now, for whatever reason, I did want to speak. Maybe it's just that I'd arrived at my own intense moment of mediocrity. Maybe not.

~~~

Look through the window! There! Have you ever seen anything like it?

It's May here in Vernon and a sheen of bright green velvet has overtaken everything: the distant hills that will become bleached by July, all the elms and birches and aspens and Chinese maples that line the side streets and hover above the bright-coloured clapboard houses here on the East Hill, the long lawns and backyards full of domesticity and the careful attention of flower beds and rockeries and hedges dripping with dew. This sheen wraps itself around the most cynical of observers; you can't resist it, and soon, in spite of yourself maybe, you, too, are stumbling down the cement sidewalks early in the morning, the meadowlarks and chickadees whispering through the leaves and power lines above your head, your heart moving itself outward, into the world, as green as your heart was when you were a small boy and you got up early in the morning and threw on your jacket to go serve Mass at St. Agnes Church. You whisked by the poplars back then, smelling them, lost in fragrances you couldn't even name but were grateful for because they made you feel buoyant, hopeful, alive. Just like that small boy now, you find yourself lost in the green of spring again, covered by it, a landscape yourself. Ahh! I tell ya! There's nothing like it. Everything else pales in comparison.

~~~

My old friend Brian had written to me after Christmas and told me he was going to the Leighton Artists' Colony at The Banff Centre for three weeks in May. Did I want to meet up there for a stretch? I thought about it and decided *why not*? I was always drained in the spring and maybe a week in Banff would be just the thing I needed. Against all odds, I applied on time and received a letter back in April saying I could have the Henriquez Studio. Of the eight studios designed by Canadian architects for the Colony, the Henriquez Studio is a bit bizarre because he took a real, ancient fishing boat called "Elsie," that he'd found down on the Fraser in the lower mainland, and installed it in the Colony in Banff by building a wooden cradle for it and suspending it from a beautiful, but simply designed wooden and plexiglass structure. You can imagine all the landlubber jokes that get told about anyone using this studio. It was full of metaphors before you got going even, just the thought of sailing those woods, casting out on your own sea in the pine and cedar fragrances of all that solitude.

I have to tell you at the outset that I'm a bit anxious about a kind of weary darkness in me that's just beyond my reach but seems to be getting closer with each word I write. It surprises me because, generally, I'd be the last person to be described as weary and dark. No matter what my other faults might be, I'm quite energetic and positive. But I think it's because I can sense that what I want to talk about is like saying the unsayable, and I guess I feel the sadness of that in advance. And it's not just sadness. It's the risk — not just the risk of exposing me for the petty, needy, vulnerable little soul that I am, but the even greater risk of exploring the obvious. Speaking about it.

Every artist who has ever lived knows what I'm talking about here, but nobody ever calls it in public. People are either too nice, or too embarrassed, to write about it or say it. Sure, we'll all whine and gossip about it late at night, laughing our heads off in the process, but we won't sit down, like I'm doing, and make a complete fool of ourselves by actually announcing these things. I'm an idiot, but I can't help it. I see a lot of young writers and I want them to know about love. I don't want them entering some slick game played on the sidelines of art. I want them right there, smack dab in the middle of it.

So I drove in from Vernon, through the snow and hail on the Roger's Pass, pulled into Banff and, sure enough, I couldn't believe it: the Kingdom of Being Spoiled. There was a room in residence waiting for me — even a TV so I could watch the Stanley Cup Finals — and Brian smiling away — a great old friend I hadn't seen for years — and a grand new dining hall full of terrific food, linen table-cloths, sterling silverware, and even a new lounge that hadn't been there the last time I lived there, plus this isolated boat of a cabin to work in out under those swaying, cracking pines. I'd forgotten how beautiful it was, how accommodating. I'd joked about it being the only place in the country you didn't need to apologise for being an artist in, but I had really forgotten. And it all came flooding back, and I wept for the calmness of it, the break it represented from everything else that was going on in my life.

The first night, after calling home and feeling quite guilty after I'd itemised all the wonderful things about the place to her, I fell asleep to the sounds of the jazz musicians rehearsing late into the night, the pianos and saxophones twisting up into the mountains like reverse snow. When I woke in the morning and opened the drapes, the sun was up, glistening off the wet surfaces of everything, and, in the distance, the mountains stately and dignified, encumbered by a heavy fall of snow through the night. I felt humbled and alive. I felt like a child.

But I'd forgotten about the elks. For anyone who has not visited Banff in the spring, the elks are protected, and they come down from the higher ranges to eat and calve. The result is they overrun Banff. You'll see them sauntering down side streets, nestling into neighbourhood gardens. And there's nothing you can do, really, but ignore them and try not to startle them. They can become quite aggressive and, over the years, of course, there are stories about people almost being killed, ending up in the hospital, all sorts of real and mythical tragedies. The female elks are especially aggressive if they have calved. You have to be particularly careful around them. They'll charge you for simply walking past them, and many people have been hurt because they didn't know about the calves. You get so used to walking past these creatures you can forget the dangers.

On the first morning, after I'd had a quiet breakfast by myself down in the dining room, I collected all my stuff — my backpack full of notes and files, my supplies of coffee and cream, my small notepad computer — and headed out to board my boat. Just before I reached the Colony, I saw a bright yellow sign in the middle of the path: WARNING: AGGRESSIVE ELKS. I assumed these signs were everywhere and just part of the spring drill until I reached the entrance path only to find a second sign: WARNING: AREA CLOSED: AGGRESSIVE ELK AND CALF SPOTTED IN VICINITY.

I stood at the entrance to the path, staring at the sign, all my stuff either on my back or suspended from both arms, ready for work. The trees above the path were fifty foot pines and they canopied me so I imagined myself a diminutive figure in some illustration for a Grimm's fairy tale, peering into the opening of my own *selva oscura*. I didn't know what to do. I felt like an idiot. If I went back to my room I'd feel silly. If I ventured into the colony and got chased by an elk, I'd feel sillier still. I had a hilarious image suddenly of my body crumpled onto the path, a huge elk footprint branded into my crushed forehead. Neat. I really couldn't decide. I walked twenty yards, my ears alive for every sound, and stood on the old stone bridge that takes you into the colony. On the crest of the bridge, I paused and faltered. I heard something rustling. I walked quickly back to the entrance where the sign was, my legs trembling from trying to walk slowly, with some dignity. You know how it is. It's like all those stories about grizzly bears and sharks. *Just pretend you're dead. Keep perfectly still.* Yeah, sure. I heard a tractor just up the hill, above the colony, and I flagged down the guy running it. He hopped out. He was a young guy and I could tell instinctively, a nice guy. I told him my problem and he said he'd come in with me. We headed in. I noticed, with some satisfaction, that his eyes were as alive for elk as mine. Suddenly, we heard a sound breaking the stillness behind us. We both stopped, alarmed. It was Brian, grinning sheepishly, and drawing up to us rapidly, grateful for the company, same as me. Now, with the three of us, we were almost cocky until another loud sound stopped us. We all thought it was a bleating calf — *Great!* — and we laughed and were somewhat embarrassed when we realised it was only a tall tree creaking in the wind. We arrived at our studios in a burgeoning ecstasy of confidence and goodwill.

Ten minutes later, my phone rang. It was Brian. "Look out your window," he said. When I did I saw this gigantic elk standing, staring into the floor-to-ceiling window of Brian's cabin. "Christ," I said. The funny thing about this was that as we'd arrived at our studios earlier, Brian had commented, almost expansively I thought — he being the veteran and I the rookie — that if I found the boat too claustrophobic he was sure I could switch to a studio that was airier and more full of glass windows like his studio was. At the time, I thought, well, maybe I will. Maybe the boat is too suffocating, and some stingy little asshole part of me wondered why I got the boat and Brian got the deluxe, floor-to-ceiling window unit with five times the space. Now, of course, I was in the inaccessible boat, strung up beyond the elk, completely safe. I told Brian I'd keep an eye on things and for him to phone me if things got worse.

What happened was this elk started stalking Brian. If Brian moved to the kitchen, there was the elk, huge velvet head and brown eyes staring back at him. If he went to the bathroom, same thing. It got most ridiculous when Brian finally sat down to write. His desk was situated before a ten-foot wide, floor to ceiling window, and the elk nestled down right in front of the window and began to watch

Brian as he stared back. In desperation, Brian closed the venetian blinds, but the elk was not discouraged. She just sat there, mesmerised, devoted; her big brown eyes batting coyly back at Brian whenever he peered through a slat in the blinds to see if she'd gone. "She only has eyes for you," I whispered to him an hour later on the phone, "No, seriously, Brian! I think she has a crush on you! Lucky bastard."

In the end, the elk jilted Brian and wandered off looking for something else, something better, and we both settled in to work for the day, images of elks ruining any chance of being serious.

I arranged all my stuff in the boat and got comfortable. I wanted to write a story that alternated between cynicism and wonder. I wanted to write about what it felt like to be constantly suspended between those two fields of perspective and emotion. I wanted to write about how necessary it was, sometimes, to allow voice to speak somewhere beyond, but out of those two fields, the way Kundera sometimes could, or Berger. What it felt like to speak or play your music somewhere beyond technique, somewhere out in an un-accommodated space, antici- pated by discipline maybe, but beyond discipline, closer to love.

In the lounge the night before, Brian and I had talked about these things quietly, whispering our feelings about them beneath the roar of the hockey game. I admitted that I was thrilled that jazz musicians were here at the same time because I felt jazz musicians faced precisely this same problem. To me, the history of jazz was the history of the shift from temporal to spatial forms, and it was the parallel shift in writing that always grabbed me and drove me. And in that shift in forms there was, innately, the paradox of control and improvisation, and somewhere at the heart of that paradox I sensed a door through which a person had to go to get beyond technique to voice, to love. I knew in advance that it could be a terrifying door to pass through. "Show, don't tell," they advised, over and over again. I didn't care anymore. I'd just tell it. If it didn't work, so be it.

~~~

As I said, there's nothing like it, this street early in the morning, these green smells, the smell of the wet sidewalks, all the early evidence of spring in the yards and flower beds, all the anticipation in the warm, wafting air, the scent of it, shining. And you do feel like a kid. You can't help it. And you know that's a good thing, the best thing, maybe. You trust yourself when you're a kid. You don't play those triple-thinking games with yourself, those mournful tunes. A big fat robin sits squarely on the sidewalk just down from you, near the corner of 28th Avenue, where St. James Catholic Church sits squat and grail-like in the morning sounds. It flutters away as you approach and you watch it flicker into the leafing elm tree hovering over the green-roofed house across from the church. A semi rolls past on 27th. The thick hop smell of the brewery trundles up from down below the tracks. It's early in the morning before everybody's up and it's spring again.

I remember a wonder in me when I was a boy, before I became, like everyone I suppose, self-conscious about it, and started to conceal it for the trouble it would get me into with other people. And it's that wonder that intrigues me right now, Boy, so much farther on down the road, approaching my fifty-first birthday in a month. It's that wonder in you that I want. And I think about it, the origin of it in all of us, and what happens to it when we begin to hide it. I have a sneaky feeling that a good part of my voice comes from it, in fact, from you, Boy, still turning around on those early morning streets in Edmonton, your nose in the air for smells, your heart stuffed with God, fresh from early morning Mass.

It's funny. The other day, in my Popular Culture class, students presented two sides of a debate entitled, *The history of popular music is the history of the co-option of the authentic.* And as they struggled and talked and questioned one another, I drifted off on a private tangent. I remembered reading Thomas Wolfe's *Look Homeward, Angel* when I was the same age as these students. I remembered, still, the sadness in one particular part of his vision: that old class paradox that Joyce and Lawrence struggled with, too: that the very authenticity that gave you voice was also the thing that sealed you off from your origins in the long run. You can't go home again. Can't get back to where you once belonged. You can never escape your origins in your art because that's where the key to your voice is, but you can never live out your origins again because of your art. The weight of that line drawn in the air. The solidity of it.

I couldn't help thinking of all those garage bands, the original visions in them, the lack of sophistication played against the crazy sincerity of the vision, then ironically, after success maybe, a futile attempt to recapture the sincerity while the sounds became more and more sophisticated. Almost as if you couldn't have both things; you had to choose. Strange. And I thought of how that pain of

SO IT WON'T GO AWAY

choosing was redeemed through visual imagery. If you abandoned the original sincerity, you could still be marketed, visually, as having it; hence all the hip, cool, ironic, and playfully rebellious imagery connected to selling music. The desperate game of authenticity, of irony. And I wondered who was responsible for this virus and I knew in my bones that I blamed Sartre for it. I remembered stumbling across a tome of Adorno's in which he railed against Sartre, and I knew Adorno was right. The corruption inherent in the virus of authenticity, as innocent as it was initially, or as disconnected from real ideas, or as misrepresented as it became in time.

No, I'm heading down to the Bean Scene on the main street of Vernon, out for my morning walk and a coffee. I'm fifty years old and my head is a fragile piece of cotton fabric, shifting haplessly in the soft spring air. And I want to sing this innocence right back into itself, into the traffic stopping now for the lights at 27th Street, into those faces staring ahead down the asphalt or behind into rear-view mirrors, into the starlings swooshing in large chattering clusters from tree to tree, into the eyes of that man across the intersection there, the man in the beige suit, clutching his briefcase, striding purposefully down into the town, to his office likely, a smile on his face, too. Into everything around me, not an ironic bone in my body.

~~~

The Jazz Police. The Jazz Nazis. I'd never heard these terms before I came to Banff. I listen to a lot of jazz because I find that if I have John Coltrane, Miles Davis or Pat Metheny on in the background while I'm working, a soft undertow of parallel forms pulls at me while I write, draws me under into rhythms I know but cannot talk about. They help my rhythms, those rhythms. I do not know much about the history of jazz, just the superficial shifts that everyone knows. So when I bumped into a young musician named Gerard in Props Lounge on the second night, and he started talking about these things, I was hooked.

Gerard was a bass player who'd been successful as a stand-up jazz bassist, but who supported his wife and five children by playing bass for a series of high-profile pop singers, and by producing music in a variety of genres. As it turned out, he'd been hired by The Banff Centre music program as the resident bassist, on staff for the duration of the jazz program, which was quite varied: from jazz vocalists working mostly in traditional be-bop to outside jazz musicians working in free, non-traditional forms. I could tell Gerard was excited and wired. He confessed that his work the week before, with the jazz vocalists, had been gruelling, twelve-to-thirteen hour days, and that he'd approached this week with some trepidation that the schedule would be just as demanding. As it turned out, though, the new person in charge of the jazz program was a pianist-teacher from New York, Kenny Werner, and his approach to jazz was very different and, for Gerard, a gift from the skies. Werner's emphasis was on the spirituality in each of the players, how they had to draw a joy out of themselves and into the music, how they had to transcend the pettier issues of egos and competitiveness that Werner felt could hold musicians back rather than make them better. In this approach, Gerard said, Werner was outrageous because so much of the history of jazz had been driven by a fierce, ruthless competitiveness. And that's when I heard about the cutting sessions and the Jazz Police or Jazz Nazis.

"In the early days of bee-bop," Gerard said, "the performances weren't really jam sessions. A jam session is open and encouraging. They were called cutting sessions."

"Why that word," I asked. "Why 'cutting' sessions?"

"Because if you couldn't cut it, you were thrown off the stage," he laughed. "Seriously! That's how bad it was. In the days of Parker and Coltrane and those boys, that's how it went up there. They'd try to blow each other off the stage. That was the whole point of it. And that's what made it so edgy, so competitive. That's what Miles Davis was so pissed off about in the early days. When he showed up, playing all those smooth, slow, lean phrases, the be-boppers booed him off the stage. He couldn't cut it. It was ruthless."

"And that's where the Jazz Police come in?"

"Not exactly, but it's where the seeds of the Jazz Police were sown. The tradition of criticising players in this brutal, competitive way, sure."

Gerard went on to explain how a purist tradition developed in jazz during and after the bee-bop era and took over so certain aspects of playing became fixed and inflexible. People refined superior notions of the purpose and function of jazz, and many of the players themselves could not mix genres or do standards because many genres and older traditions simply didn't work anymore, were considered lowly and beneath most players. Or they didn't know how to do it, another issue entirely, but an important one to Gerard, who could move sideways through genres with ease and respect. Gerard, of course, was excited by Werner's obvious mission to work against these notions, to open up jazz instead of closing it down, to free younger musicians from these arbitrary notions and encourage them to play more out of themselves, to incorporate other genres into jazz, pay more attention to both the world around them and to themselves, what's inside, as voice for their playing. Humility was one of Werner's themes, and Gerard couldn't believe it because for a young musician like him, a musician whose chops extended through many genres, it was a great freedom to hear someone announcing humility was a good thing. Werner felt the new, younger jazz musicians of the next millennium would be hybrids, mutants, listening to the world around them and the world within for new voices, new sounds.

It was draining but exhilarating to listen to Gerard talk himself through these ideas, and when I walked back up the hill to the residence, I felt tired but excited. I looked up into the deep blue cowl of the night sky over Banff, and I couldn't help extending his ideas sideways into the history of writing, especially into the surges of contradictory energy in contemporary writing.

We had our own hierarchies and feuds. The games I mentioned at the outset. All the aggression and competitiveness that marks our genres, too. Some of it healthy enough, some not. We had writers who made a living off writing mostly by gearing their work towards larger audiences. We had writers who were also teachers of writing, like me, and whose work surfaced slowly and was pitched to smaller audiences. We had, in the past thirty years, set up more and more writing programmes so that young writers could learn their chops just as musicians and artists always had. That was a good thing because until the early seventies, it had been difficult to take any instruction in writing. The bad aspect of it, though, was the danger of institutionalising the writing, especially with recent advances in post-structuralist theory in literature, philosophy, history and anthropology. So even the writing programs were struggling, walking fine lines that reminded me of the Jazz Police. For example, depending upon where they were in this hierarchy of contradictions, instructors could sway students to despise realist narratives, or, on the other side, students could get an instructor who only believed in writers like Cormac McCarthy, Richard Ford, Alice Munro, or Carver, and who despised writers like Julian Barnes or Salman Rushdie, and be swayed back to psychological realist forms. There could be much aggression in these struggles, and a good deal of counter-productive competitiveness that had little to do with voice, real voice and vision. If Harold Bloom was right in *Anxiety of Influence* — and I'd never found his arguments convincing — good writing only came out of a constant attempt to dethrone the powerful voices that had preceded you. Cutting sessions. That aggression and paranoia again. The elks, for God's sake! And it was out of this chaos of contradictory approaches that young writers were surfacing, good or bad.

There must be another way to pursue this art, a way that acknowledged both the joy that had anticipated your voice in the voices of other writers, and the mysterious and inarticulate joy you had to unearth in your own vision, your own voice. There had to be a way to resist the arbitrary games and move more into the openness of the craft itself. Beyond technique.

I thought, of course, of Ken Kesey's theory about adult art: voice that had surfaced out of someone who had

grown up, someone who had recognised and surrendered
to the barriers of ego and dependency and addiction and
ambition, who had moved beyond these adolescent
barriers into pure, unattended voice. Kesey's argument
was brutally simple in one way and incredibly complex in
another. How could you create mature art if you yourself
hadn't grown up, if you didn't know who you were, if you
didn't have the strength of humility? And it seemed funny
to me, the way the games we'd set up to run our art form
ran against Kesey's straightforward view. Games that
resisted the obvious right down the line. The veneer of
success, imagery, the marketing of the intellect, even,
which was especially funny. You couldn't *be* an intellectual
writer in this country. People despised you for it. You were
written off as an academic writer. Your work was too
precious and self-indulgent. You had degrees for chrissakes! And yet, these same readers would sail the seas and
come to the holy city of academics if the intellectuals were
from France, Italy, Czechoslovakia, South America, or
Mexico. It was hilarious: Milan Kundera, John Berger,
Carlos Fuentes, Umberto Eco, Peter Ackroyd. But you'd
never mention their names in a poem or a short story!
Never. If you were a jazz musician, you could allude
constantly to the tradition you were blowing out of; in
writing, you couldn't. Ridiculous. But human.

I'd had a big night. My head was full of ironies in the
darkness of my simple room in residence. I heard a
saxophone wailing up into those stars outside and I
dreamed paranoid, bitter and envious dreams all night
long, dreams of the Jazz Police, the Jazz Nazis, taking over
the world.

~~~

The holiness of being in this body in this early light, the luck of it! Sparrows flicking in and out of my vision, leading me on into the downtown of this small mountain city full of brightness and colour, and the natural smiles and openness of morning. Nothing like it. For whatever reason, all the dependencies and greed and desire that's in you, all those small and pathetic needs that beg stuffing through whatever orifice, literal or figurative, all that machinery that can interfere with this light, is often subdued in the early morning. I'm not distracted by it or pulled into any darknesses or half-shades because of it. I can walk out into the world more free than I sometimes am, and that also makes me more open, more receptive to the textures and voices and small vulnerabilities around me. And I think the cats and dogs and birds and people know I'm more receptive, too. I think they can sniff it on me, this smell, this spirit. And, I'm not kidding, sometimes I just want to sit down and weep for the pure light in it, these double landscapes I wake up into sometimes, when both worlds collide and mesh. I tell ya!

There's The Bean Scene now! Look at this little place! A turn of the century, two-story brick building, refurbished as a small coffee place. Its wee green and glass wrought-iron tables and chairs clustered outside on the sidewalk in the sun, its green enamelled windows with the ancient lettering and indistinct images of people behind the large sweeps of plate glass. And through the door, past the chimes that hang above it, into the old, polished oily smell of dark wood furnishings and hardwood floors, all the stainless steel coffee urns and espresso machines hissing and burpling against the far wall, the scones and muffins cooling off beneath the glass buffet to the right of the till, the vibrant grins of the young workers saying hi to an old regular lining up with three or four people to get a mug of coffee, exchanging small but big glances and stories, taking the mug outside and sitting in the sun, holding the porcelain in two hands before raising it to their lips. *Matins. Hoc est enim corpus meum.* And you know, some mornings at least, you know you are alive, and you are in your body, of your body, and you didn't know that, you'd forgotten, and that's all there is and it is more than enough, this blessing of the world and of you, too. You, in the world. Both. The pulse of it, the heart. You and me, boy!

"How's it goin, eh?"

"Just fine. Not bad."

"See ya later."

"You betcha!"

~~~

After an especially difficult day of writing, elk-free, up in my boat, sailing those woods again, stopping occasionally to have a coffee with Brian, I asked him if he wanted to slip over to The Club later in the evening to hear the new jazz students play. We seized a table right up front so we could get a sense of the dynamics on stage. It was a great distraction, after the day I'd had, to watch these young cats get up and do their stuff. The first ensemble was a quartet that included young players from Texas, Montreal, Toronto, and Chicago. They improvised upon a composition written by the young sax player who was from Chicago. It was essentially abstract, free form, from the outset, but eventually an old dance tune, some ancient wedding waltz, the bare bones of it, was introduced as a

SO IT WON'T GO AWAY

weave in the structure, and this helped me follow the shifts and tangents. Three different times the four musicians swelled out into an almost impossible width of sound, so wide it threatened to collapse entirely, but didn't. The journey of it was intense, though, and when they wound it back to its origins in the last thirty-two bars, I was relieved. The tension in it, the tightness of it, and the chaos it was attempting to seize, reminded me too much of where I'd been sailing that day on the boat, and I whispered to Brian that I likely wasn't going to stay much longer. I was bone tired. Then Werner himself came up and invited three young musicians to play with him.

Coincidentally, he launched into one of my favourite old standards, *Body and Soul*. I relaxed into my chair as he started to build up the song. At the beginning, his approach was completely traditional. So traditional, it was almost shocking after what we'd just heard. He had a wonderfully light touch, bubbly stretches of glissando like a canopy over the structure of the melody. It was beautiful in that refreshingly traditional way, especially after the intensity of the tune before him, and he was doing it on purpose, just to create a backwash. Then he began to smirk and shift keys diabolically, seeing if the students could keep up with him or anticipate him. Instead of looking anxious or forsaken, the students began to grin back, especially when they screwed up, and he just smiled more widely at those moments. Soon, he began to shift the tempo too, even more diabolically, and it was great to watch the drummer's eyes glued to Werner's body gestures and hands, looking desperately for signals. The old song swelled out, in time, to a crazy improvisation of its essential shape, then back again, and finally, in the end, to its solid, soft opening notes played only by piano and bass.

I stared into Werner's face while he played, into the fun he was having, the generosity of it. He was a world-class jazz pianist, and he was leading these students somewhere, and you could see it in his eyes and mouth, in the way his body almost rose up out of the chair sometimes, floating above the keys like some image from Chagall. It was an incredible experience for me, a teacher as well as writer, to see the whole, magic thing unfold right in front of me, an arm's length away. When they were finished, I left the club. But instead of going up to my room, I decided to go back up into the boat, into that darkness, to write. I had an idea now. A hunch.

The darkness in the woods was so thick, it was like another element. And I did think about the elks, but there was an energy in me stronger than my fear, and it pushed me onto my boat. When I got inside, I turned on the small lights. Because there was so much mahogany in the panelling and fixtures, the boat took on a warm, buttery glow. And it really did feel, suddenly, like a boat. I was adrift out there, sailing my voice out into the darkness, the thickness of it only broken by the small lights of the cabin and the powerful scents of pine and cedar everywhere on that ocean. I sat down and fell forward into all the humiliating smallnesses in my head and heart, all my grudges, dependencies and addictions, all the darkness in them, the feeble, pathetic grunts for fixes that defined me so often and ate me up even, and especially when I didn't want them to.

I imagined sailing through all these things, the thick, dark swell of them, sailing over and through them, the violence and anger of them, home to the light I knew was there somewhere. I also knew, though, that this thick dark was a constant somehow and that all the little angers and pettinesses in me were a part of another, hard world in me that would always be there, maybe, waiting in the dark. So it won't go away, I thought, so what? Maybe it'll take me somewhere, or maybe it's a map of some mysterious return to something else. I wasn't sure, so I set a course for the night, in that darkness, and eased away from its shore.

~~~

It's like an ocean I'm arriving on, Boy, all this texture the weight of its sacredness I tell ya you just can't tell boy it's loose it's tight it's shimmering it's spring it's me it's you out here and these waves of traffic the roar of coffee makers this whole undulating sea of people so fragile so deep so vulnerable these waters rising and falling and rising these waters of morning this light glistening off the water now off the surface only concealing the depth of us rolling here now you and me boy like *Treasure Island* like *Island Of Adventure* good old Enid Blyton like Joyce's Captain Leopold coming home finally to that weaving she is and Geoffrey Firmin falling and falling and falling all these arrivals in the soft green thin thick scented lilac air old possum finding his endings and his beginnings in small harbours approaching New England shores and his beginnings always arriving at endings always like pilgrims here in the soft swell of it like Williams' *Paterson* where are we now dad how far is it to the next town the next ocean the swell of them boy I tell ya just like that out on this water here of molecules combining and separating all one bubble of life colliding with itself out there on this water this street in this tiny town I love where home is and we're waltzing Matilda *avast ye mateys* all the crazy streets past those stores and people and movies to rewind and pop to buy and scones and milk and bread and you could get you hair done matey out here on these waters boy look at that old church thrusting its steeple out of these waters like Dali like William Stafford's well in spring or Heaney's fields all open and rising and falling here like music on the water and women in rowboats thinking of kingdoms thinking of love like that bus rolling in from Calgary right over there returning we're all falling into the returning from everywhere from now from this moment and these molecules here from Dante Cervantes Sterne De Quincey Proust James Richardson Joyce Aiken Lowry Miller Celine nobody gets out alive Celine Faulkner Dos Passos Burroughs Pynchon Vonnegut my waters different waters maybe all returning these molecules all returning there's the house where she'll be waiting boy waiting for me my smile my oldest smile her smile the porcelain touch of her moist nakedness an offering on shore on the vast undulant shore we know as home that land those feet this earth and I will for now until the darkness presses this light out of me into the light there shining even in the rich garden next to her standing on the shore waving a welcome to me in this morning light and I'll fall forward into all the selves I've ever been light and dark these bodies of water always returning in this soft strong light always and I'll return always to this moment these moments and sear them into this sailing head my boat and promise to stay this wide and rolling an empty vessel for this light and love and light to fill so it won't go away.

ONE MORNING IN ANNECY

For Mary Ellen Holland

From childhood on, Barbara Hepworth had possessed a strong sense of rhythm — especially the rhythm of the human body. Her sister, Elizabeth, felt strongly attracted to dancing and trained for the ballet, despite her family's disapproval. She found a home with the young Skeaping family in London and as a result Barbara became familiar with the world of ballet [...] The sculptor's awareness of the spatial by way of movement, is undoubtedly an all-important factor in determining the nature of the form she creates. Would it be closed or open? [...] It was then [1931] that she made a sculpture in pink alabaster (destroyed during the war). It was an irrational, inorganic piercing of the closed form — a significant invention, which was to become one of the main elements in all her further work [...] We may, therefore, accept it as fact that in England the hole, introduced by Barbara Hepworth in 1931, followed by Moore in 1932, was her invention [...] this piercing of a shaped mass, this abolition of the closed form, placed volume in a different category overnight.[...] a three-dimensional rhythmic feeling for the spatial . . .

— A.M. Hammacher, *Barbara Hepworth*,
London: Thames & Hudson, 1968.

HE'D DRIVEN DOWN IN CHRISTIANE'S PEUGOT from Strasbourg. They insisted he make the trip. There were no *ifs, ands* or *buts*, as his mother would say. At first, because he was alone in the car, Neil felt nervous on the highway, especially the *autobahn* through Germany south to Switzerland. He couldn't wait to get off it. There was no speed limit; you could drive from Amsterdam to Italy in excess of 200. The problem was that the Peugot was not the car to do that in; it was great at 120, but anything over that and it would begin to shimmy. Mercedes and Audis appeared out of nowhere in your rear view mirror, and it was terrifying, how fast they approached. He'd had a close call when he'd shifted into the left lane so he could pass a car in the centre lane, then discovered the flashing lights of a car that had pulled up behind him, right on his ass, travelling twice his speed. So he stayed in the middle lane, never ventured left again, and in time got used to the other small differences and relaxed. By the late morning of the first day, just as he was crossing into Switzerland, he felt he could have been driving anywhere, anywhere in North America really. Just him, a closed car and the road: long, soft sessions like wind over land. He was a prairie boy, after all, a coyote. He was driving south of Maple Creek, maybe. Anywhere.

Two nights before, they'd been gobbling down slabs of *tarte flambé* in a restaurant on the highway north of Robertsau, ten minutes out of Strasbourg. Christiane, her sister Marie, Simone and Malcolm and Pierre had all been as generous as Rick had promised they'd be. What a crew to be adopted by, Neil admitted. They'd made him promise to meet Rick and Jane in Annecy, not Aix-en-Provence where they were staying, waiting for him. Annecy. So he'd phoned Jane and insisted. Of course, he blamed the change of plans on Pierre and Christiane, but stuck to his guns anyway. Annecy it was.

And now, Switzerland, for God's sake! He was in fucking Switzerland, driving down the highway through this incarnation of Heidi-land to meet up with his brother and sister in the French Alps, in a medieval village called Annecy. He was as un-accommodated, as open as the car window to the spring air, the fragrances of flowers and trees blossoming above the tar and gasoline. That open. That reduced. That simple — so simple he thought sometimes he'd become everything, and having experienced that clarity he might cease to exist. Hard to tell. Neil smiled, his hands tapping out a blues beat on the plastic steering wheel.

~~~

Nicolas Bouvier, the Swiss poet, wrote a poem which I translated from the French. It's called "*La Derniere Douane*" — in English, "The Last Custom's Gate" — and it ends in this moment of light:

Mais par ou commencer
depuis que le midi du pre
refuse de dire pourquoi
nous ne comprenons la simplicite
que quand le coeur se brise

I still have a photograph tucked away somewhere of that evening back in 1988 in Paris. The dark, hushed auditorium in the Centre Georges-Pompidou. Sitting with Lola Lemire-Tostevin. Getting up to read with Nicolas Bouvier and Gerald Godin. I remember I was thinking of my mother that night. I was reading about her, my words returning to Europe after all they'd been through to become those words. North America, the great experiment, after all. And after everything I'd been through, too, to be standing there, returning. And the graciousness of the two men standing with me, their voices, like mine, out of joint with the cast and crew of the conference we were all part of, the camaraderie in that, how good it felt. But why now, after all these years, why would I remember this? Where is all this going? How will I ever end it? *Until the heart breaks*. No kidding.

As Thomas DeQuincey used to say, *be patient, dear reader. I* don't even know. I've got Barbara Hepworth, Nicolas Bouvier, Pat Metheny and Charlie Haden winnowing out at once into this tiny room.

~~~

Man In Car, Wondering What To Do On A Spring Day in Switzerland . . . The solidity of the whole situation from one angle, Neil thought: him sitting there in his new jeans, the freshly washed T-shirt, his decent running shoes, the new woollen socks in them, the Nepalese silver bracelet on his left wrist, the jangling weight of it, his hands on the wheel, the surface of the pressed, plastic, moulded dashboard with all its usual bells and whistles, all the small, textured details of the car's design. Then, the larger abstraction — but so funnily *real* if he thought about it — of the weight of the whole moveable feast itself: the steel-blue Peugot and him in it hurtling across space, tumbling through these Swiss valleys bisected by late-twentieth century charcoal highways and overpasses and garish highway signs and other hurtling vehicles like his. And, chafing against these images like the usual tease of history, a bucolic landscape rife with clusters of heavy-laden, slow-moving cows, tractors inching their grid-like paths in slow motion heat hazes across fields opening up into rich, dark loam — the labia of earth as Don Gayton would write — and stretches of green so green you could only become a child looking at them. No matter what else you'd ever done in your life, you'd be transformed for a few seconds into such innocence you could barely stand it. Neil felt a surge of gratefulness he didn't know he'd ever experience again it was that simple, so far beyond any absolutes in his life, any orthodox sense in him of assessing anything, so close to nature itself he could hardly feel the usual distance: the fragile membrane that separated one from the other. Unreal. Real. Magic. But real magic. Magic of the real. Who knew?

Abruptly, the car was in deep shadow. Neil had driven under a heavy, concrete overpass. As he, too, became invisible in the dark, he remembered something his eye had caught just before it had lost the sun: a green sign announcing the turn-off, in two kilometres, into Bern. As he re-emerged into the bright, pink and red childhood dream of the Swiss landscape, he thought of Bern and Klee, the largest collection of the artist's work there. *Of course!* He signalled right and took the exit ramp into Bern. He'd forgotten all about the connection. He could afford to spend a few hours in Bern. He had nothing else to do. He was as free as he'd ever been.

~~~

Jane ate her modest continental breakfast in a tiny room of four tables just off the lobby of the dark hotel she and Rick had found the night before. A large oak table held the usual array of fresh croissants, baguettes, milk, juice, and large, steaming bowls of coffee. When she'd descended the baroque, polished mahogany staircase fresh from her shower, she'd hoped Rick would have been there waiting for her, but, typical of him, he'd gotten up earlier than she had and was out on the main street of Aix-en-Provence somewhere, installed in an outdoor cafe for the morning, reading. He'd left her a note with the *concierge*. Busy, busy, busy. Industry, industry. Purpose. They all suffered it, each of the three of them she knew. She knew, too, that it was much larger than them. It was *so* Canadian, a vestige of the rich, contradictory Puritanism that had settled the west she'd grown up in anyway. Busy, busy, busy. *Idle hands . . .* she could hear her father scoffing. *Idle hands make . . .*

She ate the last section of the croissant she'd buttered and smothered in strawberry jam, and took another sip of coffee. The trip had been great so far, all parts of it — flying in with Rick from Edmonton to London, staying at The Tavistock in Bedford Square again, renting a car and driving out to see the Barbara Hepworth gallery in St. Ives. Then they'd taken the train from London south to Arles, in Provence, where they rented another car and drove to Aix-en-Provence to meet up with Neil. They'd had some great laughs. She'd forgotten how much fun they'd had as children, the games they'd make out of the most ordinary things. Colours on the highway. Road signs. The intimacy of brothers and a sister at play. It was a gift if she thought about it, hard to come by, too. Being this close to Rick, of course, had allowed Jane to breathe him in more carefully, watch him, register all parts of him in the rhythm of his days. He was healthy right now. He looked strong. He'd lost the weight he'd put on after he'd quit smoking, and had that lean look again that had always suited him, had made him irresistible when he'd been in his twenties. Of course, they'd all grown out of that stage now and had entered what Jane called the battlefield of middle age where you kept running into the ruins of your former self everywhere, every day, and where you tried to resurrect a modicum of dignity *from* those ruins. Rick had grown into his late forties and early fifties easily. His looks hadn't changed as much as Neil's had, but Rick hadn't abused himself as much as Neil had in his forties. He'd cleaned things up earlier than Neil. Neil was still in the first stages of the clean-up, in fact, and it showed in his tiredness, in the slight pall of greyness caused by the smoking and whatever else Neil thought he was getting away with. But he was, she knew, getting there and nobody was more proud of the new Neil than Jane and Rick. It was partly in celebration of him that they'd set up this impulsive trip to France. Neil had been over in Ireland and England, then France for three months now, and the chance for the three of them to meet up in such exotic territory had been irresistible. They were already having more fun than she'd anticipated considering how she'd felt herself the few weeks before leaving. But she *did* look at Rick sometimes and wish she had a magic key which, if turned just the right amount in the right direction, could slow the whole, industrious machine of Rick down.

She worried, too, about Rick and Jennifer. It hadn't been easy for them to oversee the break-up. The four of them had been close for such a long time, and Jane knew the protracted disintegration of Neil's marriage had made a lot of demands of Rick and Jennifer. So this trip was a good thing for the two of them. It gave Jennifer a chance to get away from the Connellys and all their stuff, the claustrophobia of it. The only problem was that, without Jennifer to draw it out of him, Rick had to be working all the time. When he wasn't driving or eating or joking, he

was working. Will we ever shake these patterns, Jane
wondered, forgiving herself and her brothers everything
that haunted them still, all the sub-conscious energy that
pushed each one of them, knowing full well that none of
them would ever completely escape these drives, would
ever rest or play. From that point of view Rick was merely
doing what came naturally, and the good side of it was it
wasn't self-destructive. Still, Jane thought, still . . .

She'd go up to her room, grab a sweater, then head out
into Aix to find him. They'd pack the car for Annecy, and
Neil would be there, waiting for them. He'd booked them
into a small hotel in the old district. They'd love it, he'd
said. Jane smiled to herself. Neil was always so damn
optimistic about everything, exaggerating most things
shamelessly. As if I don't, she laughed to herself. As if I
don't.

~~~

Who would have thought such an insignificant thing as
Hepworth's sculptural 'hole' could be so interesting and
influential? But if you think of the self-consciousness it
introduces when you imagine three-dimensional sculptural form — the destroyed relationship, abruptly,
between the solidity of the formerly closed sculpture and
its landscape, the supposed objectivity of its representation, and the now obvious interplay between both, all
illusions of representation having been destroyed by introducing the hole — you can imagine a parallel shift to the
spatial in the literary arts, too. What then, is the equiva-
lence, in literature — in fiction — of Hepworth's discovery
of the 'hole' in sculpture? What is it, what is it? Speedily,

some of the work of early metafictionalists like Flannery O'Connor, Durrell, Heller, Vonnegut come to mind in the early to mid-fifties. Borges. Cortázar. But the struggle, too, in fiction at least, to steer a precarious course through Scylla — the seduction of the representational as solid, linear narrative — and Charybdis — the temptation to move into pure abstraction — is something we sense in Burroughs, in Pynchon sometimes, in Gass, and it's not an easy course at all. The manipulation of narrative, the blowing up of linear and realist narrative especially, is tricky business. There is something in its spiralling openness, though, that intrigues me and makes me suspect that it might open up onto an area of human territory being *represented* for the first time.

~~~

Everything Faustian is alien to me. I place myself at a remote starting point of creation, whence I state a priori formulas for men, beasts, plants, stones and the elements, and for all the whirling forces. A thousand questions subside as if they had been solved. Neither orthodoxies nor heresies exist there. The possibilities are too endless, and the belief in them is all that lives creatively in me. [...] Do I radiate warmth? Coolness?? There is no talk of such things when you have got beyond white heat.

— Paul Klee, March, 1916.
The Diaries Of Paul Klee (1898-1918),
Berkeley: University Of California Press, 1964.

Neil was standing in front of *Composition (1932)*. The bold African colour, the primitive simplicity of geometrical line and dot, the echo of Egyptian hieroglyph . . . but more than any of these, the sheer, child-like glee of the piece. How it made Neil feel. Over and over, in painting after painting, Neil was astonished by an intricate and bold fun in Klee's work, how his canvases kept catching something about being human that was inarticulate most of the time, difficult to catch *because* of its complexity, *because* of its emotions, even. Not as specific or cerebral as Joyce's *ineluctable modality of the visible,* but more visceral and political, even, than intellectualising about it could ever reach. It was humbling, radiant, and mysterious. As it should be, he thought, just as it fucking should be because what it was trying to *represent* was. *A priori.*

After an hour, he left the gallery and walked out into the central square in Bern. There were many restaurants and the owners had set thousands of tables and chairs out so the whole street was alive with people eating and drinking and laughing and smoking and adjusting sunglasses to protect themselves from the glare of the early spring noon sun. After checking out several fast-food restaurants, Neil bought a hamburger and fries even though it cost twenty dollars, and disappeared into the crowd. He sat at a small metal table near a green fire hydrant in front of an ancient stone cathedral and ate his lunch. He watched the dogs sniffing from table to table, and listened to the huge, soft sound of thousands of people talking and whispering and laughing, and the gulls circling and cawing overhead and pigeons clucking and cooing their way to crumbs on the cobblestones below the gulls. What we must look like to the gulls flying highest: this erratic, rocking cradle of colour and movement, eating and drinking, celebrating spring.

Neil had never missed Shelley more than he did in those moments in the square: how much she would have loved this scene, these elements of wonder. She deserved such a moment herself. He wanted it for her. As he approached the car on the sidestreet where he'd parked it, he knew his love for Shelley was still there if he wanted to allow it to rise up and engulf him again. It was still there; it *had* to be. As he drove through the downtown streets and back onto the freeway to France, he regained the width of the play of the landscape and saw Shelley's undulant body as the luminous skin of the landscape itself, her eyes its squinting sun. It was all so simple sometimes.

~~~

Rick shoved the postcard aside and took another sip of coffee. He'd promised Jennifer he'd send her a postcard from every city he stayed in, and so far, so good. Of course, it was his old, wise-cracking, ironic self being stupid over and over again. Ah well. The funny thing was — and they both knew it — many of these cards would only arrive at their house in Vernon after he himself had returned. "Oh, here's another card from that Rick fella," he imagined himself shouting as he walked onto the deck to give it to her. "You're going to have to tell him it's *over* soon, you know." Yes, well . . .

He'd also written two letters this morning. That was the difference between him and Neil at this point. Not only was Neil on a half-year sabbatical — the first he'd ever had from the teaching — and as a result removed from departmental intrigues, but Neil taught Creative Writing, not Literature as both Rick and Jane did, and teaching Creative Writing removed you in another, more fundamental way. Neil had always avoided the politics of the institution. Creative Writing was considered a hybrid discipline and still under suspicion, and this suspicion made it easy for Neil to remove himself. He never sat on committees, never came to meetings, only surfaced if a crisis over Creative Writing occurred. Then his highly engaging, burly, and martyrish King-Lear-on-the-Heath self would show up. Most of the time, though, he seemed invisible, so much so students didn't suspect they were brothers, but simply imagined a coincidence in the last names. This separation suited them. They liked the confusion of their roles at work, and so did their colleagues, it seemed, though what their colleagues *didn't* know was how often the two brothers sat and howled at the pathetic spectacle of the meagre office intrigues, the eccentric staff, and the predictably insane academic life that fuelled all these things. In these sessions, they were united in a gleeful common purpose and would be as dark and cynical and awful as they needed to be to get themselves through whatever was being exorcised at that point. Rick looked down to make sure he'd stamped the two letters. He had.

No, Neil would not be writing such letters this morning. He'd be driving like the crazy dumb shit he was down the wide, jammed freeways from Strasbourg to Annecy, just avoiding major collisions, picking up suicidal hitch-hikers, getting into trouble. He always had. All his life. It was how he went about things. The fact that he'd quit drinking finally — and there was even a chance he'd quit smoking, their mother had told them in the airport in Edmonton — wouldn't affect his style. It would alter an *edge* to it maybe, but it wouldn't remove it. In fact, Rick thought, quitting the booze and the smokes might actually have made Neil more *dangerous* than he used to be. It was hard to say. It would be interesting to see. Rick was more worried about Jane than Neil. Neil seemed to be doing all right. Some deep-rooted acceptance of his separation from Shelley must have flowered over here in Europe and freed him into being himself more easily. All his letters pointed to that anyway. And his turning away from the booze seemed to be the first *result* of that acceptance, not the *cause,* and that was a good sign, Rick knew. No, it was Jane he was worried about this time.

He knew she was having fun. He could see it. They'd had a great time in St. Ives, in Cornwall. They'd stayed in a small, white-washed B&B on a raised side-street overlooking the harbour. The family running the place were characters, each one of them, down to earth, welcoming, full of jokes and directions. They'd ended up in the family's pub, just down the street the first night, eating and partying until late in the evening, singing old English ballads, listening to endless jokes about innocent American and Canadian tourists. Rick had never seen Jane laugh so hard. They'd spent most of the second day in the Barbara Hepworth gallery on another sidestreet, where they'd become lost in that complex, early-modernist world with all its experiments and names and personalities and astonishing achievements. They'd sat out in Hepworth's back garden for hours examining the pieces installed there. It had been lucky and privileged, their whole time there. On the last night they'd gone for a walk along the damp seawall and talked about their lives, what was happening in them, how far they'd come from that house on 61st Avenue on the Southside of Edmonton, and how they'd never left it. How it was still there like the harbour Rick and Jane were strolling past, still there shimmering.

There was something else going on with Jane, though, and Rick wasn't sure what it was. There was an essential solitariness in her and it was connected to the fact that, for the most part, Jane lived alone and it appeared she always would. This solitariness created its own conditions of detachment, a remove that had, built into it, a limit to what Jane might reveal about herself, a line she was unwilling to cross. Rick wasn't sure. He also wasn't sure it needed to be tampered with. It was what it was. It existed as a shield against other things, maybe even to protect a vulnerability that might otherwise be intolerable if it were allowed to float freely.

Over the past ten years Jane had had a series of affairs. Rick was aware of most of them. She was still very attractive, and had always had a powerful sensuality men found haunting and irresistible. But the men who had drifted in, then out of Jane's life were, like her, people who taught at universities in other cities, and whose lives were rooted in independent rituals and textures not easily converted into long-term relationships. These affairs lasted a few months, then burned out, sacrificed to the practicalities of other rituals. It made sense, and the affairs themselves, the duration of them even, created a counter-cadence in her otherwise fairly consistent rhythm of teaching and living in Edmonton, of keeping a close eye on their mother, and of participating, too, in the ups and downs of the lives of her two brothers living in the Okanagan. Jane had created a rich, complex life. Rick just worried about a chronic distance he registered in her, a distance he'd be happy to close if he felt it was something she wanted. It was hard to tell at this point, and he wondered if this trip might close it somewhat or, at least, reveal its cause.

He raised his head from the notebook he was writing in, swivelled around in the morning air, set his pen aside and sat back to look around. No matter what else had happened to him over the years — all the ups and downs in his life, the surges of excitement and the drifts of inactivity, all his highs and lows, all the earnest struggling against himself even — he'd always preserved part of himself just *for* himself. Ever since he'd been a kid walking down Whyte Avenue to the Southside Public Library on a Saturday afternoon, he'd instinctively set up situations where he'd be alone, away from everything but in the midst of everything at exactly the same time. He loved sitting in cafes with his notebook, wondering about things, letting himself be by himself or, simply, *with* himself. It was hard to say which. But right smack dab in the middle of crowds was where he found the most intense quiet and where he found, too, the best kind of anonymity: a privacy cradled in a rush of connectedness. It was a buzz to have it both ways like this. Whenever his life got so busy or filled with people that he couldn't experience this, he'd get restless, cranky, overwhelmed. It was something he had to do no matter where he was.

Here in Aix-en-Provence, the wide, broad boulevard of the main street had to be one of the most beautiful places for this Rick had ever found. He'd spotted its potential the night before, when they'd driven in. The street drifted for a mile, south to north, and on its western side there were endless cafes, bistros and bars, all with outside seating in all seasons. Though it was spring now and they were unnecessary, Rick had noticed a network of gas-powered heaters installed above the patios to provide heat in the winter months. You could sit outside like this all year round no matter the weather. Running parallel to the patios of chairs and tables was an unbroken line of Linden trees and these trees had just recently leafed and had that first, fragrant lace of green that added a veil of sensuousness to the skin of the street. Playing themselves against all this solidity were thousands of people, all ages, in bright-coloured clothes, wandering back and forth, back and forth. Rick felt like Telemachus, afloat on a sea of everything, undulating, loving the rising and falling, the surprises and certainties of all the movement and voices stranded terminally on an ocean of everything, overpowered by a strong sense of always returning to something and, still, even now, ten years after his father's death, he had the sense that somewhere, in the rise and fall of these waves of everything, somewhere in their liquid creases and folds and tumbling, somewhere in the vortex of all this shifting, rolling movement, his father was making his slow way towards him, seeking him out, in disguise maybe, willing to transfer magical powers from father to son in the crisp, bright morning air of a small city in Provence. Rick grinned into the morning and ordered another café grande.

"I knew I'd find you sooner or later!"

"Ah fuck! Just what I need now like a hole in the head. *You!*"

"You brought me with you, you bastard, and now you're going to have to put up with me."

Jane sat down beside him, tucked her purse under her chair, stretched her long legs out away from the chair toward the street, and leaned back facing the crowds, mimicking him. "This is the life," she sighed.

"It sure is!"

~~~

The thirteenth and final cut on Charlie Haden and Pat Metheny's *Beyond the Missouri Sky*, is an eight minute number called "Spiritual." You can tell the roots of the melody are buried in old hymns and lullabies. The piece opens with such solidity in its understructure, a classical solidity, like Pacobel's *Canon*, a steadily descending, but returning procession of musical elements repeating themselves in an endless rondo, always coming back to the starting point eventually, then beginning to descend again, shuffling downwards and outwards, filled with variations, sure, but variations that do not stray far from the solidity. Stretched over and above this descending, however, Metheny hangs a simple, repeated high note that pulses in the background while the rest of the piece tumbles forward through a variety of moods and tones, heavily laden with shifting emotions. It's the effect created by that high, repeated, and pulsing note that provides a tension the other material has difficulty competing with. The note is so simple; it pulses by itself while the rest of the material builds and fades. In the end it is this single note that stays in your mind and you realise it is the spiritual centre of the piece: this one thing that is being played beneath, above, behind all the other movement, all the other stories, and it is something singular that embodies all the other stories, draws them into itself. It changes everything else that is happening.

~~~~

They were sure right about Annecy, Neil admitted. The drive into the city presented the usual jumble of commerce — endless billboards and ads, small strip malls and gas stations, the brazen evidence of the influence of disposable, postmodern American architecture — but once he'd passed over a small bridge and entered the ancient heart of the city, he felt he'd ended up in a movie set for some medieval Arthurian tale. Here the buildings collapsed into two or three-storied ancient structures, cobbled together at strange angles to the street, giving the impression that they were almost leaning, one against the other, for support. He'd seen much the same effect in Strasbourg — around the Cathedral and throughout the old district named Petite France — but here, in this smaller city, the buildings were less restored, more haphazard, more genuine. "You *must* see the old town of Annecy," Pierre had shouted at him back in Robertsau, "there is simply no *question* about that, *certainement!*" All the soft rose stone, the bright, wet flowers set against the enamelled, boldly painted Tudor frames and beams, the moist cobblestone streets, and the muscled, bright, chaotic human traffic that redefined the streets as other entities, beautiful!

For anyone, like Neil, who had spent hours as a child devouring ancient novels set in medieval Europe, Annecy was the incarnation of all the imaginary landscapes ignited by those novels, and because of that, because it *was* the word made flesh, there was a rush of *return* built into sighting it for the first time. Neil couldn't believe it; part of his head felt completely pried open, child-like. It was the boy reading about Roland in the back of the old bookmobile that pulled up to St. Agnes School once a month when he was a child. And through some strange, magical process, here was that child suddenly, deposited in the very landscape it had once fleshed out in the dimly-lit bus on a late winter afternoon in Edmonton, the pitch black sky crouching outside the bus like primal chaos while the young head had flown to Europe, a silken bird on a spring wind.

After he'd checked into the hotel and left a note for Jane and Rick, he walked out into the city, ambling down its endlessly circular cobblestone streets, past small cremeries and patisseries and restaurants, past cafes and bars and bistros and all their colour and movement, through the ancient palace grounds elevated above the other roofs, then down to a quay that fed a series of small stone bridges over a network of canals, and out onto the wider quays that fed the beach and the lake and the mountains beyond. While he'd been exploring the downtown area, he'd forgotten that Annecy was in the French Alps, that it was a mountain city. When he surfaced out onto the broad lawns and quays that lipped the lake, he walked into a familiarity that surprised him. He could have been standing on the promenade at Lake Louise, or the boardwalk at Harrison Hot Springs, or, even, on a smaller scale, the quays circling The Grand Hotel in downtown Kelowna. When this occurred to him, the whole experience acquired a vertigo, a double return, a return within a return. He stood at a railing just off the park. A Romanesque cathedral slouched down in its cream-coloured stone and whispered behind him, and Neil had the sense, for a moment, that he was inhabiting a multitude of times and spaces simultaneously. That crease again, strange, breathtaking. Once more, he thought of Shelley, but this time of her heart, not her body. He realised his love for her *was* real, *wasn't* just a selfish abstraction, or something *he* needed in order to exist. There was something in him that was thinking about someone else.

Every now and then he'd pull out a short passage by a writer and read it to his students, hoping to confound them. When he was feeling particularly brutal — trying to steer them away from sentimentality or a forgivable tendency not to see enough in human relationships — he'd unearth these two sentences from Richard Ford's *Wildlife* just to see if they could handle them: *And what there is to learn from almost any human experience is that your own interests usually do not come first where other people are concerned — even the people who love you — and that is all right. It can be lived with.*

~~~

"Do you ever think about it?" Rick asked her, a heavy Brinks-like truck nudging its way past them in the other lane. There were driving a two-lane highway north out of Provence and into the mountains. It was a wild, clear spring afternoon, and the landscape was jumping in a communal sense of renewal, that hilariously overdone exhaustion of metaphors even, that the arrival of spring can *be*. They'd been on the road for an hour and they'd arrive in Annecy in the mid-afternoon, the late afternoon if the traffic got heavier.

"Think about what?"

"The drinking."

"Not much, actually, "Jane replied, squinting into the sun, "not for a year or so."

"Yeah, same here."

"You're never tempted, like now, away from Jennifer and where no one knows you?"

"In the old days, yes," Rick answered. "I *would* be struggling with it in a situation like this. It would be very tempting, in fact. To lose myself. Completely."

"But not now?"

"No. Not for several years."

"Why did that temptation stop do you think?"

"I'm not sure. I know *when* it stopped, but I've never been exactly sure *why*."

"It's pretty fascinating to me. Pretty hybrid."

"Yeah," Rick said, "I know."

Jane leaned forward, both hands circling her cup of take-out coffee, her eyes staring at some spot on the dashboard, but focused elsewhere. "Do you ever worry you might simply *replace* one way of losing yourself with another?"

"Hah!" Rick laughed, looking over at her hair, then away into the rear view mirror. "All the time."

"So you *do* worry about it."

"Of *course* I do. It's waiting for each of us, all the time. The whole thing is deeper than drinking. The addiction is more subtle than the booze. *You* know that."

"Yes, I think so. We've never talked about it much, though."

"True."

"You're always working, for example."

"And you're often somewhere else."

"Really?"

"Do you actually want to *have* this conversation? It might spoil things."

"Yes I *do* want to have it, and, *no*, I *don't* think it will spoil things. Not at all."

"Okay. You asked for it. Yeah, a bit distant, removed. I don't know, but it worries me sometimes."

"Maybe I'm simply afraid," Jane said, flatly.

"Maybe . . . "

"*You* know how it goes, eh? When I drank, I knew all those contradictory emotions in me — all the mixed up love and anger and general suspicion of things — would come out like breathing the more loaded I got. Just like Dad, for heaven's sake. No surprise. But when I quit, it was as if I were thrown into this hard world of emotions with no protection. The way my head worked it was too intense, too raw. So you look for ways to keep a lid on that sometimes. Otherwise, you might be walking around sobbing at the almost intolerably sad things . . . not just in your own life, but in everybody's . . . in the world's life. Like walking into a propeller blade every morning. I don't know, but things just seemed so immediate — even the positive things like the texture of objects or the life of the senses — everything just seemed so *real* and *unavoidable*, you know?"

"I think so . . . "

"So, I don't know, but it's possible I drew some cowl over myself as protection, as a retreat from the power of all that. I mean, I *want* to live in the day-to-day. I *want* to be in the midst of everything."

"Without being overwhelmed? Without falling apart?"

"Exactly."

"Yeah, I know."

"So, if there's a distance, I don't know . . . I don't know if it's necessary or not . . . or how great it is, even."

"I don't know those things either. It's just something that has come up from time to time, when I'm with you, or when I'm thinking of you, and I'm not sure if it's anything I should bring up, or try to *do* anything about. You know how it goes when you don't know. You worry. Sometimes I confuse the distance for a . . . sadness . . . maybe even a chronic sadness . . . and that makes *me* worry . . . *you* know. I'm your brother fer chrissakes, as Uncle Fred would say . . . "

"Aw Rick, honestly," and Jane smiled at him directly, took his right hand off the stick shift and held it in both of hers, "I'm *glad* you brought it up. It *is* something I need to gnaw on. *Really.*"

"Well . . . you know how it is . . . I don't want to make you self-conscious or anything . . . god!"

"Forget it. I'm glad."

"Really?"

"You bet."

"Good."

"And now for *my* question," she said.

"And that would be . . . " Rick tried to mock her.

"Now watch out. I listened to *you*!"

"Yes, you did. Fair enough."

"All right."

"Shoot."

"Well, it's just about the obsessive working. Work, work, work. As if you thought if you weren't producing something, you wouldn't exist."

"Is it that bad?"

"I see it a lot in you. I worry."

"It's a pleasure."

"So is my distance."

"They could be *good* things."

"Yes, you're right. They could be."

"But neither of us believes that."

"We both worry."

"Yeah, we do."

"I don't know about you," Jane said, "but I don't want to go from one way of filling that old hole to another way . . . even if it's healthier. Sometimes I have the feeling that the need to fill the hole itself is just an ancient, primal impulse, like breathing, something which we might have outgrown even . . . but which we fall back on out of a lack of attention . . . "

"Me too, me too."

"You said earlier that you knew when you had ceased to be tempted by the booze. What happened?"

"Remember that spring you took a short stress leave? You were having a tough time?"

"Of *course* I do. You came to visit the day I finally phoned Personnel to set up the leave. You drove in from Saskatchewan. I was scared stiff."

"Well it was that day."

"You mean the day you arrived at my place?"

"Exactly."

"What happened?"

"I hadn't been drinking for a few years then. But I had taken a trip to Saskatoon to see everybody about the book. Things went okay in Saskatoon, but I was feeling the old jitters, and feeling, well . . . you know . . . a few drinks would be a harmless thing really . . . who'd know or care, etc. etc."

"So?"

"On my way out of Saskatoon, in the usual I'm-not-really-doing-this-trance, I pulled into a liquor store and bought a mickey of rye, my old favourite, Canadian Club."

"Okay."

"I knew it'd take me five hours to drive to your place and I guess I was thinking I could pull over into a suburb on the north side when I got to Edmonton, have a few blasts before I got to your place, tuck it away in my pack, and get a hit from it from time to time."

"But you were as straight as an arrow at my place. I was in a mess. I never needed you more than I did that afternoon. I was desperate."

"I know that now; I didn't know it then."

"So what happened on the highway? What happened to the bottle?"

"I pulled over into one of those highway rest stops with the big garbage dumpsters just outside of Lloydminster — the turnoff to Kitscoty and Marwayne — and I tossed the bottle away, unopened."

"Why?"

"It's hard to explain. I was thinking about Dad and it occurred to me that part of the reason I drank was because I had the strong feeling he'd abandoned me for most of my childhood. No matter how much I loved him, laughed with him, no matter how much, even, I *knew* that on some level he loved *me* even, the brutal truth was that I felt he had deserted me a lot, especially when I needed him."

"Okay. And?"

"Well, this is the hard part my dear and our humour isn't going to carry me through this."

"That's okay."

"I was thinking of *you* as I was driving. I knew from our talks on the phone that you were having a tough time. *I knew it.* And I guess I stumbled onto the obvious. You were the eldest of the three of us. More than me or Neil, you carried the can for Dad's drinking. You juggled it more face-to-face than either of us ever had to do. You'd dealt with it longer. You were a woman. You were his daughter, not his son. But I realised in a blinding flash . . . as cliché as it actually was, in fact . . . I realised that if I showed up with a buzz on at your place, I'd be re-enacting something that had *always* happened to you. I'd be abandoning you just when I might be able to help you."

"You have no idea," Jane said.

"What?"

"You have no idea how great it was that you were straight. I *was* frightened that day. I did *need* you."

"Well, that's what happened. But the thing is . . . "

"Yes?"

"Well the thing is, the act was like a bridge. Once I'd crossed it, it felt permanent. I had seen, in myself . . . almost cruelly . . . the fundamental selfishness of being addicted . . . and once you've crossed that bridge, you never quite go back. It's a new territory suddenly."

"That bridge might kick into my distance or your working, eh?"

"Absolutely."

"Well, let's hold that thought my dear old brother."

"All right then. Let's pull over into the next small village, pick up some food, and have some lunch."

"Good."

"These things will never be over, will they?"

"I'm afraid not, I'm afraid not."

"But what the hell, eh? We're doing all right?"

"We are."

~~~

For some reason I have just replaced *Beyond the Missouri Sky* with Glenn Gould's *Goldberg Variations,* the later version. And I'm wondering why I did that. *It must be nice,* you're thinking, *to live in such a fucking small, trivial, self-reflexive world that you can not only insert various obscure CDs in your fucking stereo, but can sit around wondering why afterwards. Great!* Wait a minute, wait a minute. I know, I know. As Letterman shouts out some nights, "Put down the remote!" I know what it must seem like from a distance. But just bear with me. You've hung in this far. You might as well keep going. Trust me. I'm onto something. Imagine I'm a computer geek and I'm just about to discover a new leap in technology that will change the history of software forever . . . or I'm an astrophysicist and I've just stumbled onto something about chaos theory that will explain the physical world and the interpenetrating mysteries of time and space in an *entirely* new way . . . there *is* something about listening to Bach bubbling up into the room, crackling like Christmas wrapping paper, and listening, too, to this crazy, random voice appear suddenly behind or beneath them, the sense of Gould's physical body, the sounds of his breathing and sighing, and, occasionally, his even singing along with the music. At first, it seems *insane*, doesn't it? You don't expect it. But then, in some perverse way, it starts to *get* to you, doesn't it? You start to look *forward* to hearing this other *thing* happening. Finally, you're even unsure whether you could ever *like* this music again *without* Gould's voice, what it means and what it is saying about itself, and about you, too. I'm sure I'm onto something. Something about intimacy. It's not as if intimacy isn't *important* or anything.

~~~

Neil turned away from the lake and retraced his route to the hotel. He was exhausted. As he was walking through the lobby to get his room key from the concierge, someone grabbed his shoulders from behind. "We've finally tracked you down, you fucking *fraud!*" Rick and Jane were standing there, smirking at him, then the three of them were hugging and shuffling around, shy, two brothers and a sister dancing the ancient waltz of hello on a patterned floor, still children, still bound by blood.

~~~

The reason I'm reminded of it is that it's the same time of year, late November. The day I'm remembering was one of those warm late fall days in Edinburgh and we were bored by our work and decided to take a hike instead, or, a hillwalk, as they call it there. We packed a lunch, hopped into the Volvo, and drove south of the city, skirting the

Pentlands, to a small spot on the way to the Borders, called Nine Mile Burn. The hiking book Laurie had loaned us had marked a hike there. We'd tried other hikes — one up in Crieff, north of Perth, another along the Tweed just outside of Peebles, and another through the marron grass along the coast east of Edinburgh — but we could tell this one was longer, more demanding. We parked the car alongside the road, found the wooden gate that marked the path, then started ascending up the bare, blonde hills. In the distance, we could see small trees that had assumed flyaway forms created by years of wind, as if a plant could be fossilised by wind. The closer we got to the top of the second hill, the fewer people we met along the way, and the more snow we encountered. We were both in pretty good shape, though, and the sun wasn't a factor that day. When we reached the top of the second hill, we realised we'd climbed close to three miles and were now standing on the spine of a hill that was going to lead us back down to a village close to the car. Standing on the crest of this hill looking south, we could see miles and miles of the Borders stretching out as they fell away towards England. We knew in advance, from Laurie's book, that this trail had once been named the Monk's Trail and had been a fast walking route in the medieval period from Edinburgh to Newcastle. As we began to descend, we were flooded by the most hilarious of pathetic fallacies: we were filled with the buoyancy and brightness of the land itself as it began to fall away, down into smaller valleys where tiny, mixed farms announced themselves, and where, in time, there was richer vegetation and warmth in the soil. You know that crazy feeling where you and the landscape seem, unaccountably suddenly, the same thing, the same body,

the same spirit. Neither of us had felt that rush all the time
we'd been in Scotland, but it washed over us that morning
as we descended the stubbled Monk's Trail down into the
buttery sun and green of the valley below. We were just
two people in love, a vast, contradictory landscape blessed
by elements.

~~~

"Oh Neil, you look so *good!*" Jane smiled at him across the
small outside table. It was late in the evening, the sun
setting somewhere off in the mountains around them.
They were sitting beneath a burgundy umbrella adver-
tising Cinzano, and the warm night air encircled them,
wafted against their skin as darkness overtook the old
town of Annecy and all the night sounds began to rise and
fade and rise again like another kind of music beneath the
late forties Django Rinehart jazz playing in the
background.

"Well *good* for me!" Neil laughed, "I'm glad *you* think
so."

"Yeah, you do," Rick said.

"God," Neil laughed, looking away from them, secretly
pleased, and out into the crowds milling about in the
square, "It almost makes me nervous to hear you saying
that. I mean, how *bad* did I look before I *left* for Christ's
sake?"

"Well, lad . . . " Rick chuckled.

"Not as bad as you think," Jane said.

"That bad, eh?"

They sat quietly for a moment, no one speaking. The
night lay ahead of them. They had no plans. They'd had a
feast of a supper and were sitting out on the patio now,

sipping strong coffee, getting used to the idea that the three of them had pulled this reunion off without a hitch. Each of them was excited, tired, buzzed. Wary.

"I really can't believe we're here, the three of us," Rick said finally.

"It's hard to fathom," Jane said.

"The three Connellys, having fun. I don't know," Neil said, shaking his head. "There's something wrong about this, something obscene."

It must be like this in all families, Jane thought, squinting into the last of the sun flickering off a plate glass window down the street. You know so much that each thing you say echoes back and forth, back and forth. You could rarely say something that wasn't multi-layered. Their own family's humour, its bottomless pit of sarcasm and irony and self-deprecation, simply compounded those layers in an endless teasing, a different kind of affection full of relief but complicated in other ways, too.

She was so aware of these two men she'd been thrown together with for a lifetime. Her brothers, always there, always looking out for her. It was nice, what they thought they knew about her, she admitted. What they thought they knew, and what they *did* know. Nice. She recalled that afternoon in North Dakota, in the corn field with their father that summer driving home from Nova Scotia. The three of them had played hide and seek with him in the bright green stalks, getting lost and found again and again, his eyes like the summer sun above them, full of a kind of awareness of them they'd never experience in quite the same way again. She thought of her father suddenly, of his retreat into the darkness of his drinking, away from them after that point, what that must have felt like for him, how happy he'd have been to imagine them all sitting here tonight, in another country, still connected, still rustling beneath his gaze, still playing hide and seek in more elaborate ways maybe. They were all older now than he'd been in that memory, and that seemed surprising, too, for he seemed suddenly so much younger than she'd envisioned him before, and she had to shake her head at the vertigo it caused, a sense of humility about judging others from the wrong angle. He'd been so young and *he'd had so much on his plate* as their mother would say. Squinting at him from this distance, in the wonderful soft quiet of their connectedness in Annecy, she could see that he *had* done well, in fact. That was the summer he'd tried quite seriously — probably for the last time — to quit drinking. It hadn't worked out, but for a short period of grace, they'd seen a sustained version of their father that was not usually easy to see: a side to him that was quiet and tender. Jane sensed a metaphysical aperture, a kaleidoscopic opening she felt she could drop and disappear into, but then, instead of remaining empty as it often did, she could feel its sides and walls filling up, flooded by longing and an element that became the volume of that longing and satisfied it, unspeakable, immeasurable. A gift.

"So we'll give the old girl a call when we get back to the hotel tonight?" Rick asked.

"Yeah . . . it'll be morning there," Jane said.

"It'll be great to surprise her," Neil said. "She'll be pleased."

Rick sat back and watched Neil as he began to tease Jane about the size of her sunglasses. He was acutely aware of what each of them was doing and of his own two hands cupped around the heated cup he was holding. It was a moment that came and vanished quickly. He'd learned not to try to hold onto them or force them or try to arrest them into any permanence, but let them rise and fall in the swell and ebb of everything else that was also happening. The three of them were sitting out on this patio tonight as full of love and hurt and anger as everyone else on the planet, he thought. The trick was to be as open to these elements as you were to the weather, as supple in their midst, allow them to wash over you instead of resisting them, fighting them tooth and nail, always full of surprise and a kind of resentment at the surprise. In the old days, he knew, in the old times, organised religion had always blown in as a way of allowing these elements to have their unpredictability, had erected architectures that could hold them, make sense out of them, use them to create dignity and modesty. The trick now, in these secular fields, was to allow a wind like that to blow in again, a new kind of wind, more natural, less accommo- dating — not some artificial, mechanical transcendence that allowed people to rise and fall within a life — but some kind of immanence, a spirituality as natural and as dignified and as modest as breathing. To grow a head that could take the always restless, always rising and falling of these ups and downs, these elations and sorrows, this love and anger, and know they'd always be there, in different mixes and intensities. They'd always be there and you had to be aware of them, responsible for them, willing to accept the swirl as a condition of existence instead of always expecting something else, something easier, something passive. All right. Let it go, Rick sighed, as he heard Jane's laughter ring out and up into the night air.

"You really *are* a miserable, perverted maniac," Jane said to Neil, laughing.

"I know," he said back, "I know. It's what makes me so *interesting though!*"

"It does not!"

"Sure it does!"

~~~

I did sit out in the old town of Annecy one night in 1995, in the restaurant I'm describing. I walked those quays and stood in front of that ancient Romanesque church for an hour, just looking at it. And the next morning there . . . the next morning in the sun . . . in the fragrances . . . the selves I was, all the possibilities, returning now, into this room, here.

We've just received our first real load of snow through the night. If I look out the window all I can see is this perfect, lace, embroidered version of my own world, looking back.

~~~

Neil wasn't sure what time it was, but he suspected it was between five and six in the morning. He'd hardly slept through the night. They'd had such a great visit and they'd slopped down a lot of coffee and rich desserts over the course of four hours. Each one of them had been tired in the first place, and, for Neil sometimes, when he became overtired — as he often did when he was marking student papers — he couldn't get to sleep.

When they'd returned to the hotel, they'd gone into Jane's room and phoned their mother. The call had its own secondary and hilarious drama to it — a play within a play — because while whoever was on the line attempted to be straight and answer their mother's questions, the other two would be mugging it up, making obscene noises, pretending to be barfing in a corner or having an attack of diarrhoea right next to the phone. They were cackling and sobbing all the way through the call, alternating endlessly between the two. Fortunately, their mother was used to it.

When he'd returned to his own room and got everything ready for the morning, he sat on the edge of the bed and decided to phone Shelley. He wasn't sure if phoning her wasn't just a predictable perversion in him — take the wonderful night they'd just had and ruin it by introducing a regret that could do nothing *but* ruin it — or a good idea considering how he'd been feeling about Shelley all day. When she answered the phone, he was panicked for something to say. "It's me. Neil," he said.

"Well for heaven's sake! Hi!"

"Hi!"

"Well, where *are* you for God's sake?"

"In a medieval town in the French Alps called Annecy," he said. "Look it up on the map when we're though."

"Aw, for heaven's sake. Isn't that wonderful, Neil. Just wonderful."

"And Rick and Jane arrived today, too. They're here, too."

"I knew they were meeting up with you, but I thought it was going to be in Aix-en-Provence?"

"Well, it *was* supposed to be there. But we changed plans. You'd love this city, Shelley. Just love it. It was *made* for you. I saw Klee's permanent collection earlier today in Bern, in Switzerland!"

"Holy shit! You're on a roll."

"I guess I am."

Neil could sense in the pause that followed that Shelley was trying not to cry. He knew her too well. "I have to tell you," he said.

"Yes?"

"I never missed you more than today."

"Oh Neil . . . "

"No. Listen. I just mean that I flat out wanted something *for* you. That's all. Not for me, even. I just wanted you to see what I was seeing because I knew what it'd mean to *you*."

"I've missed you, too."

"Even if I *am* an old, fucked-up pile of crap?"

"Yeah, even if . . . "

They talked for a while, just to hear one another's voices, then Neil let her go.

Now, four hours of tossing and turning later, he was getting dressed in the dark. He could hear the birds through the shutters, and see the pitch black of the sky beginning to bleach into a luminescent mauve. The sun was on its way. *Will it be you, then?* he wondered as he turned the door handle. *Will it be you out there?*

JOHN LENT lives in Vernon, British Columbia, where he has taught Creative Writing and Literature Courses for New Okanagan College for twenty-six years. *So It Won't Go Away* is his seventh book and is a sequel to his 1996 work of fiction, *Monet's Garden* (Thistledown, 1996) in its third printing. Other books by Lent include *The Face in the Garden* (Thistledown, 1990) and *Black Horses, Cobalt Suns* (Greenboathouse Books, 2000). Lent has read from his work in many cities in Canada, the USA, France and England. He was a founding member of Kalamalka Press, the Kalamalka Institute for Working Writers, and the annual Mackie Lecture and Reading Series at New Okanagan College in Vernon. Lent is also a singer/songwriter and plays in a roots/jazz trio.